Slowly, Slowly Catch a Frenchman

First Printed in United Kingdom 2017

ISBN – 978-1-9996559-1-4

Transcription Editor – Sarah Skinner

Social Media Editor – Tammy - Abigail

Email - info@slowlyslowlycatchafrenchman.com

Website - www.slowlyslowlycatchafrenchman.com

Author – Publisher

David Lenderyou

'Slowly, Slowly Catch a Frenchman'

The Initial Planned Exit

In the year 1705 during the reign of our good Queen Anne, the two masted Galleon with cannon loaded and ready to fire, lay as close as the Captain dared in the foreign inlet. The anchors were straining to hold the ship at bay while the wind and rain howled and ravaged around her. It was two o'clock in the morning and the sky was dark as the sea was deep. The three people in the little rowing boat having struggled through the rough sea from the shore eventually attached itself to its side. Henry Hosking went up the awaiting ladder first to hold it steady for Jeanne, and then John to follow last. "Quickly, the boson shouted, quickly hurry up."

Whoosh! A canon had opened up from an unidentified ship coming round the rock point. Missed; Whoosh! The small rowing boat went up in the air. Henry looked down mortified. The Captain immediately shouted the order to hack away the anchor ropes. Within an instant the Galleon drew the wind as it turned on its axis flowing freely away out to sea and the wrath of the incoming cannon balls. Henry, leaning over the top of the ladder, couldn't see John but saw Jeanne bobbing up and down as the ship passed her by. He heard her shouting something over and over but with all the commotion, he didn't quite hear it properly. Then she went down he thought it sounded something like Ante...

Chapter 1a

Joshua, living and working in Bristol, got the vacancy through his ability to think straight and analyse things from different angles. His military career of ten years in the marines also helped. However, sitting in the pub drinking yet another tankard of ale he felt lonely. Yes, people were around him laughing and joking but Joshua liked to sit on his own and think life through. At thirty-five years of age he was considering where it all went wrong, why was he alone once more. Even when he was married to his beautiful wife he still felt alone.

Maybe it was the brutality of his service in the army or navy, he never quite knew, as being a marine you served both. Either way front line fighting in wars cannot be normal in a civilised world.

A man approached him and asked if he was ready. Joshua picked up his tankard and in one long slurp finished his ale, wiped his mouth with his sleeve and said, "I am."

Joshua had a really soft side, he knew it. When his wife was pregnant with their first child she could wrap him around her little finger. He chuckled to himself at the thought. But that was a woman, they are delicate and lovely.

However, the person standing in front of him now was a man who thinks he owns the place. They are alone in the stinking outhouse where people urinate and loosen their bowels.

The man has been spouting off that he rules the Munitions factory yard in Bristol Docks and all the men in it. Joshua doesn't say anything, he keeps quiet, waiting. He wants this man to make his move. Sometimes Joshua will attack first but this time the inner feeling is to wait.

The man acts first and moves quickly forward. Joshua standing six feet away instantly raises his inner tenses to breaking point like a praying mantis ready to jump. Joshua waits a further split second then tacks forward, slightly off centre, and in one flowing movement drops to the floor with his feet stretching forward whipping both legs from underneath this heathen of a man. Brutal as it is there is, only one person going to walk out, it's the rules.

Being taken completely by surprise and off balance the man crashes to the ground. Joshua needs no further introduction as what to do next, he immediately goes for the head. When it's done, it's done, Joshua backs off.

Opening the door, the pub is silent, Joshua walks to the bar picks up the money and without saying a word walks out heading for his two-bedroom terraced house alone.

With brandy bottle in hand in front of the fire Joshua feels nothing but shame. Why does he do it, there must be something out there better than this or is this it. He misses his wife and his lovely Mum and the warmth of the Cornish family. His Father is working away and hasn't contacted. Joshua tells himself again that there is only one person who can change the situation and that is you my friend. You have a good brain and a good heart.

Fumbling his way to the bedroom after polishing off the brandy Joshua finds his bed and falls on it. Trying to undress proves impossible as he cannot coordinate mind with body so gives up and lays outstretched half clothed and quickly finds rest through sleep.

The morning appears and Joshua is awoken by a continual knocking on the front door. Thinking it a reprisal from last night he starts to make plans of escape but then quietly moves over to the window and looks out onto the street and sees a well suited young man looking up. Joshua acknowledges him and walks down to open the door.

"Mr Pendragon?" "Yes, that is I," Joshua replies. "My master has asked me to ask you if you could come to our offices this morning as he would like to talk with you." "And who are you?" "Oh sorry my name is Clive and my master is Mr Bray of Bray and Butler Solicitors in the high street." "Is it about last night?" "I don't know sir only to give you the message." "Fine, tell him I will be there within the hour."

Joshua didn't know whether he should go or not. If he did it could be trap and if he didn't he would never know what it was all about. He decided to freshen up and go to this Solicitor but with a fully loaded pistol as support.

Being a Saturday morning the streets seemed to be a little emptier which Joshua appreciated. He wasn't feeling great but was sprite enough to be curious as to what these people wanted with him. On arrival he was ushered into Mr Bray's office where a middle aged man got up and said, "Mr Pendragon thank you for coming please take a seat." "Is this about last night?" Joshua asked. "I don't think so, why what happened last night?" "Sorry, I think I have my lines crossed, may I ask what you want of me?"

"Please, I have been told to inform you that your Father has died whilst away abroad and that Mr Trevean at Trevean and Trevean Solicitors in Helston have asked that you visit them this Wednesday morn to go over his last will and testament.

Everything has been arranged for your carriage from the Queens Head this early Monday morn including overnight accommodation and, all has been paid in advanced. I am also to give you a purse of ten shillings today."

Joshua looked in disbelief and was quietly letting the thoughts of his Father subside before he said anything. "Yes of course I will go as requested." With matters concluded Joshua slowly walked home in deep thought. His Mother, his wife, his still born daughter and now his Father, how life goes on and still the world turns. He will get himself ready.

Joshua didn't venture out after the news of his Father. He stayed by the fire with brandy and pipe reminiscing over his family and the laughs and love he got from them all. He also made himself some hot food, tidied the house and washed some clothes, something he hadn't done in ages. Sunday and Monday he shaved. Although money doesn't do it for Joshua, having the ten shillings gave him the confidence to forget about work for a while and stop trying to make ends meet whilst saving a little on a weekly basis.

He was to stay in Exeter the first night, then the Blue Anchor in Helston the following night, ready for the meeting Wednesday morning. Joshua felt good about going home to Cornwall.

The Wednesday came all too slowly but never the less he arrived in Helston on time at the said Solicitors.

"Joshua, thank you for coming and please let me say how sorry we are to hear of your Father passing away, he was a good man." "Thank you," Joshua replied. "Well, let's get down to things shall we, I have your Fathers Last Will & Testament." "Before you start, where is my Father?" "We do not know exactly but understand he drowned somewhere abroad in Spain and his body lost. A memorial service is being held in the Church at Gunwalloe this Sunday coming." Joshua never really knew what his Father did and so the drowning and loss of his body didn't surprise him at all. Mr Trevean went on to discuss the will and testament.

"Joshua, your late Father John, his last will and testament is very specific, everything is to be passed to you including his cottage at Gunwalloe. There is one proviso, that you should live there directly and receive a small stipend type pension of twenty pounds paid out of his Pension fund every month by the executor solicitors Trevean & Trevean in Helston."

Joshua was quiet throughout and listened intently. "And what if I decide not to live in the cottage?" "Then the will is not completed as your Father wished and you get nothing." "Where will the cottage go?" "It will go to our good Queens Estate." Joshua loved the Queen, that much is true, but not that much. "And I receive Twenty pounds per month also for doing nothing"? "Correct." "Where's the catch?" "Mr Pendragon, your Father was a good man and worked hard, there are no catches. Now please could you answer whether you accept or not?"

Joshua looked up to the ceiling trying to find some kind of help from his Father. He looked back at Mr Trevean and realised that this is the opening for a better life and why not take up his Father's wishes. It just felt strange that he need not have to toil for money anymore.

He would also have to leave Bristol where memories of his wife and daughter lay and that would be hard. Leaving the Munitions Factory would be a joy. Joshua silently thanked his

Father and with calm said, "You are right Mr Trevean and I feel lucky that I had a Father as you described."

With that Mr Trevean asked Joshua to sign in several places. "By the way Joshua, there is a small footnote at the end of the Testament which I have been asked to read to you." "Please do." "It reads, should you my Son meet a person who asks you to help a colleague, trust them."

Chapter 1b

"The peas are beautiful Rebecca, well done." She looked up across the table and smiled politely but said nothing. However, inside she wanted to say "the pea's, the bloody pea's, forget the bloody pea's, the bloody peas are pea's." She wanted to throw a saucepan at him, she wanted to jump on the table, take her skirt off and wiggle her bottom at him. She just wanted to scream.

Three years she had lived with Simon a respectable clerk at Samuels Ship Builders in Plymouth. Three years and they hadn't had sex for two of them. She looked across the table at him while he was in full focus of cutting a roast potato on his plate to the exact size before entering it to his mouth. Rebecca started to drift her thoughts back. Simon was a really nice man in his late fifties when they met. Rebecca was twenty-eight. She had been hurt badly from her previous relationship that suddenly went astray and so decided to be on her own. After two years and numerous no thanks from many different men she decided to hitch up with Simon who seemed exceedingly decent and see how they get on.

She didn't love him as she had loved her previous man Cuthbert. Simon really just wanted company and someone who could cook. Rebecca could do both and agreed to move into his small cottage. She knew Simon had been married for twenty years and that his wife had passed away. She also knew that he had loved his wife very much. However, in this relationship there was no love, just living and eating under the same roof. They had tried sex but Simon preferred not to and so Rebecca obliges every night by saying "Good night Simon." And the response comes back, "Good night Dear."

Cuthbert, on the other hand, would have had none of this and would have kissed Rebecca to death, but Cuthbert was rebellious and liked his drink. They had been together for four years in which time she had miscarried twice. She shouldn't really think about him as it upsets her but one thing she knows, she cannot stay here and waste her life away in the kitchen of a man she doesn't love, just for the sake of it. She was only thirty-one years old, shapely and full of spirit, surely there must be more out there. However, one thing about Rebecca is honesty and not letting people down. She knew that if she did indeed leave him, he would be alright and she would be sure he would understand.

"Are you alright my Dear?" Rebecca realised she was day dreaming and hadn't eating hardly anything. "Yes thank you just thinking," she replied. She then continued, "I think tomorrow I will get up early and go into town to buy a new bonnet." "You know I have a lie in on Saturdays my Dear," Simon replied. "Yes I know, I will not disturb your required sleep and will go on my own. I think I need some fresh air around me and it will also give Lilly some needed exercise. I will put some breakfast out for you."

After dinner and the washing up, Rebecca went outside to the little side yard to see her lovely horse Lilly and brushed her down while talking to her as if she were another human being.

Rebecca spoke about her missing her Father who died when she was young and also of her Mother, Jeanne, who she had not seen for many years and was working abroad somewhere.

Rebecca was already up and getting herself dressed for the run into town when she heard a continual knocking on the front door. Not wanting the noise to wake Simon she quickly rushed down the stairs and opened the door.

"Ms Pendarve?" "Yes, that is I," she replies. "My master has asked me to ask you if you could come to our offices this morning as he would like to talk with you." "And who are you?" "Oh sorry, my name is Benjamin and my master is Mr Johnson of Johnsons Solicitors in the Kings Street." "What is it about?" "I don't know my lady, only to give you the message." "Fine, tell him I will be there within the hour." Rebecca closed the door and quickened her pace to get herself ready. She decided she would not tell Simon.

On arrival she was ushered into Mr Johnson's office where a middle aged man got up and said, "Ms Pendarve, thank you for coming please take a seat." "Excuse me," she replied, "before I do anything please tell me what you want of me?" "Please, I'm sorry, I have been told to inform you that your Mother, Jeanne, has died whilst abroad and that Mr Trevean at Trevean and Trevean Solicitors in Helston have asked that you visit them this Tuesday morn to go over her last will and testament. Everything has been arranged for your carriage from the Kings Arms this early Monday morn including overnight accommodation and, all has been paid in advanced. I am also to give you a purse of ten shillings today." Rebecca looked in disbelief and was quietly letting the thoughts of her Mother subside before she said anything. "Yes of course I will go as requested." With matters concluded, Rebecca went out to Lilly and slowly walked home in deep thought of her Father, and now Mother gone. She must be strong and get herself ready.

"Where is your new bonnet?" Simon asked. "Oh, I couldn't find the right one," she replied and quietly let herself out to be with Lilly. Something inside her would not let her inform Simon on anything about the Solicitors visit and what had been discussed. Rebecca remained mostly silent over most of the weekend, often in deep thought reminiscing over her family and the laughs and love she got from them all. However, she had to think of something to tell Simon. She didn't want to lie to him so decided to write him a letter that she has gone to Cornwall to speak to her Mother in urgent matters of Family, she would be back when she could and need not worry.

She was to stay the night at the Blue Anchor in Helston ready for the meeting Tuesday morning. Rebecca somehow felt good about going home to Cornwall and, the ten-shilling purse was a blessing to ease things for a while.

"Rebecca, thank you for coming and please let me say how sorry we are to hear of your Mothers passing, she was a good lady." "Thank you Mr Trevean," Rebecca replied. "Well, let's get down to business, as they say, I have here your Mothers Last Will & Testament." "Before you start, what happened and where is my Mother?" "We do not know exactly but we understand that she drowned somewhere abroad in Spain and her body lost. A memorial service is being held in the Church at Marazion this Sunday coming." Rebecca never really knew what her Mother did and although emotionally upset, the drowning and the loss of her body didn't surprise her at all. Mr Trevean went on to discuss the will and testament.

"Rebecca your late Mother Jeanne, her last will and testament is very specific, everything is to be passed to you including her cottage at Marazion. There is one proviso, that you should live there directly and receive a small stipend type pension of twenty pounds paid out of her Pension fund every month by the executor solicitors Trevean & Trevean in Helston."

Rebecca was quiet throughout and listened intently. "And what if I decide not to live in the cottage?" "Then the will is incomplete as your Mother wished and you get nothing." "Where will the cottage go?" "It will go to our good Queens Estate."

Rebecca hesitated and was silent as she needed to think clearly. Mr Trevean waited but after a long silence interrupted Rebecca's thoughts by saying "Ms Pendarve, I am sorry for your loss but we do need a clinical yes or no to proceed?" She looked back at Mr Trevean and realised that this could be the blessing in disguise for a better life she had been wishing for

She would have to leave Plymouth but there was nothing there anyway. "Sorry Mr Trevean, the answer is yes, however, I have my horse Lilly who is dear to me at my address in Plymouth and a person named Simon whom I live with, what am I to do with them?"

"Is it your wish that this person Simon live with you at Marazion?" Rebecca was silent and knew deep down this was the end of their so called relationship and a turning point in her life. "The answer to that Mr Trevean is no, I do not wish that but I do not wish for him to be left in limbo either unknowing if I will come back." "Very well Ms Pendarve, then we on your Mothers behalf will sort these things out for you and rest assured it will be done with discretion and respect."

With that Mr Trevean asked Ms Pendarve to sign in several places. "By the way Ms Pendarve there is a small footnote at the end of the Testament which I have been asked to read to you?" "Please do." "It reads, should you my beautiful Daughter meet a person who asks you to help a colleague, trust them."

Chapter 1c

In the Morlaix Tavern, South West France, the four of them sat together around the fire. "So what are we having?" Pierre Bouchier said, openly and joyous to all around him. Jacques immediately said "cognac', quickly followed by Zoe and then, "I will have a small shandy" coming from Pascal. Pierre then spoke the order for them all, "one large bottle of your best cognac please waiter with three glasses and a small shandy, oh and two pipes."

The Inn was nearly empty, apart from a few men at the bar and the fruit and vegetable wholesaler sitting in the corner that works his stall every day in the towns market and has done so for years.

With drinks poured and pipes lit, one for Zoe and one for Jacques's, Pierre raised his glass to give a quiet toast, "to the success of this new mission!" They all drunk back in one gulp then looked for refills except Pascal, he didn't like drinking, especially the way it made some people lose control of their brains.

With cognac now being drunk freely and at random, Pierre went over the plan again. In particular, he asked Pascal if he was confident, which he replied, "If the house you have put us in lines up with the geography I have described and calculated, then most certainly things will align correctly." Pierre Bouchier disliked this type of young arrogance. However, Pascal was not directly chosen by him but from his master Philip de Albret,

Count of Morlaix, for reasons of his mathematical type genius and family ties. Pierre also disliked the way he looked at Zoe as Zoe was his and his alone and they had a private agreement together.

Zoe on the other hand just didn't like Pascal. He kept looking at her breasts and smiling, licking his lips when she bent forward. She wanted to hit him about the head and for him to show respect but, she is street wise and plays the game, especially this game of cat and mouse. Sexually she would eat him alive and each time he leered at her she fluttered her eyelids as if butter wouldn't melt in her mouth.

Jacques's, older and wiser of them all and still extremely capable, thought Pascal impertinent and not up to the job, but Jacques's was tired and knew this would be his last task; he had to get a life.

"Listen you three", said Pierre, "your ship sails early tomorrow morning for the Cornish coast of Sennon and it's getting late, is there any final questions you have of me before I leave you." Everyone was silent knowing the long difficult task that lay ahead which may take one or two years to complete and, classed as extremely dangerous. Each of them looked into their glasses and said nothing.

"Good then let's raise our glasses once again to success." "By the way", Pierre continued, "you have not heard the good news of last week's encounter in which our Navy destroyed the English assassins."

Jacques's ears quickly pricked up on this news and was first to speak. "The word we got was that the English Galleon got away." "Indeed it did Jacques's but not before we destroyed the little boat in which they were escaping before reaching the Galleon. It was completely destroyed with a direct hit after only two rounds of range fire at half a mile, excellent firing and a credit to our gallant sailors."

"How can you be sure everyone died in the boat," Jacques's replied. Pierre, Zoe and Pascal looked at Jacques's wondering why he was asking question after question. "Because Jacques's, after the cowardly little English Galleon ran away, our Navy moved in to look for survivors and found none alive." Jacques's realised his questions of doubt had spooked some kind of distrust and loyalty conscience from him. "My apologies Pierre for questioning you but sometimes I hear these things and the truth is sometimes very different, I just wanted proof of our success that is all." This seemed to do the trick and took away the puzzled looks from the others.

Jacques went on, "so then, let's raise our glasses to our gallant and heroic Navy." They all obliged in unison except Jacques himself who shadowed everyone else with the raising of their glasses but didn't drink the cognac.

His heart had literally been cut in two as if that cannon shot had actually killed him.

Chapter 2

Throughout the year Joshua will go down to the beach. When he does, he sits on the rocks, watches the world go by and get the spiritual vibration of real life into his body. The weather is terrible, or glorious, depending on how you look at things. It's raining today with a very brisk forceful wind. If you leave your hands out of your gloves or do not pull down your woolly hat over the sides of your face, your fingers and cheeks will freeze.

He always sits in the same place towards the right of the beach near the old church where the rocks are most rugged. He sits there for hours until his body clock says enough, you have been rejuvenated through the power of the sea and the freshness of the air.

Joshua likes to think, he really likes to visualise things such as the spray of the surf, a leaf or a squirrel, watching and wondering how things are made or moves its muscles, or the way it's blowing or eating. He thinks life sometimes is just quite unbelievable.

Looking out the window inside his warm cottage above the cliffs of Gunwalloe, Joshua notices the wind outside is picking up and the rain is beating hard on the window glass but, the fire is good and the pot of water is on for a good strong cup of tea. He gets the tobacco out and prepares the pipe, ready for his first thoughts of the day. "The beach it is," he says to himself, and as he thinks that, he gets a weird feeling at the back of his neck that runs down the full length of his spine. His body shivers with cold but he puts it down to the weather outside. "Hmmm," he mumbles.

The little cottage is situated about a mile in land from the coast; set high around lovely greenery. From the front Joshua can see the sea and its beautiful aura of strength. There is one bedroom one work/utility room and a kitchen come rest room with open fire place and good chimney. The back garden is full of trees and shrubbery. The front garden is just grass with border flowers and slopes down away from the house. In the summer it's beautiful - in the winter it's beautiful.

The tea was good and with the smoke pipe finished he was ready. He pulls on his coat and warm woolly hat, made sure the fire was down and safe then puts on his boots and closes the door behind him. When he feels at peace and it is warm outside he would take along (Queenie and Cecil), or being more precise they, his two Jack Russell's, would gladly accompany him, but as it is cold and wet they stay by the fire and do not move so he leaves them by the warmth of the hearth to await his return.

He says in his mind he is ready for the day, taking a few long deep breaths of fresh air with some unwelcome rain mixed in, he fills his lungs, touches his toes, stretches both arms back and sticks his chest out. With the little exercise done, he is off. He starts to walk down the path to the little cottage gate which he opens and closes with a certain pride. At thirty-five years of age he feels pretty good and rather healthy he thinks to himself. He can see the beach and the rocks and, although he can strut a pace he is cautious as he has slipped over before and landed on his bum which immediately humbles one.

The beach is effectively empty of the human species, which he was glad of, as he needed this day to fully cleanse his brain and think. The old church sits quietly and never move's, always calm and thoughtful as though it's a part of the landscape and, you only need to enter it and the spirit of the Lord will talk with you.

The tide is coming in with an off shore wind so the spray is being tossed in the air like slow motion. Lovely, he feels, just how Joshua likes it. Sitting down on a smooth edged rock, which fits Joshua's posture just right and the feeling of being comfortable and relaxed, starts taking effect.

He stretches his eyes wide so he can get the full freshness of the chilled wind mixed with the cold wet of the rain deep into the eye sockets which feels like an injection of nature's medicine. Once this exercise is completed five or six times Joshua reaches into his pockets and brings out his new technology miniature type telescope which he bought from Bristol and now keeps on him most, if not all of the time. Why he purchased such a thing just seemed a natural thing to do.

Joshua spends an hour or so of digesting his problems in life, of which gladly most were now put into a better perspective. The cold isolation and freshness of the sea is giving him back the better feeling of patience, calmness and pace. As he smiles he notices a couple of tall ships out on the horizon. "What a beautiful life I have," he says to himself.

Drawing his legs up and resting his elbows on his knees he takes his telescope to his eye and steadies himself. He is trying to focus on the ships to get a better view but they are too far off to get any real detail. Just as he started excepting the fact, and still with his telescope to eye, he slowly started traversing the scope across the other side of the beach where the rocks have big caves with mouths as dark as the night when he notices a single person looking directly back at him.

Joshua immediately drops the scope from his eyes, rubs them and then raises the scope again on the human target at around three hundred yards away. Even sharpening the focus, he still couldn't see the face as it was shrouded in something and then he or she, Joshua wasn't quite sure, walked straight into the furthest and darkest cave.

"How can that be, what the, am I seeing things," he said to himself. Joshua works on logic but it felt to him as the person almost acknowledged Joshua seeing him. He rewinds his visual brain and runs over the sight again almost in slow motion and accepts the person did see him and, as he did, Joshua noticed the person's right hand fingers move like a crab. Like a magician who rolls a penny through the fingers. Was it some form of code acknowledgement? Joshua noticed the person, whoever they were, was not too smartly dressed but casual and appeared capable and confident but with no arrogance.

Joshua didn't move but started rubbing his chin in deep thought and squinting in almost disbelief. What was that all about? He wanted to roll a pipe and work this out but he was pre occupied in looking over the beach at the caves entrance.

All right I get it, thinks Joshua, let's wait this out then, I will sit here and you, whoever you are, you sit in the cave. "That's good Joshua; very reasonable solution" he said to himself.

Trying to act casual, Joshua decides to roll a pipe, flints it alight and takes a long slow puff. Joshua has also come prepared, just in case, with a hip flask of Cherry Brandy. So with his smoking he takes a lovely nip in between puffs. All the while he maintains one eye on the cave. Even when he moves his head out to the open sea, he manages to keep one eye on the cave.

Joshua's curiosity is on a high as when one hour passes to two he starts getting concerned, for the person should be out by now but, they have not. He was also getting very cold and thinking of heading back to the warm cottage. However, he was drawn to the cave, couldn't take his eyes off it but then instincts start kicking in, a trap? Overreacting doesn't do it for Joshua, calm and logic is his way.

However, he cannot hold back as his brain says it is not logical for someone to go into a cave and not come out especially, after all this time. He decides this is silly, gets up and walks confidently forward towards the lion's den. "Hello there!" He shouts as he was nearing the cave's mouths entrance. Nothing, so he moves closer, "Hello there!" Nothing, this cannot be, it's not logical. Someone went in and someone should come out.

Inching ever forward into its mouth he sees something shiny catching his eye on a large stone about ten feet into the cave. He carefully moves forward and sees it's just a bloody tin box. He starts to nervously chuckle to himself and thinks how innocuous a tin box is. However, if something means nothing, it must mean something, and that's what's drawing him ever closer to it.

Still very aware that the unknown person has simply disappeared, which cannot be, he gets himself to the tin box, bends down and see's written in bold lettering, 'Hello Joshua.'

Joshua stares in utter amazement at his name as though he is seeing things and then quickly looks around the cave for the other human being who, came in before him over an hour ago, but they have simply vanished. He has to get out. He quickly picks up the tin box and runs out on to the open sand. Once outside, away from the cave and standing in the middle of the open beach he calms down and takes' stock.

Alright he says, I'm in the open I have escape routes but he still feel's someone is looking at him. However, he notices that the feeling is not menacing anymore, more soft and observing.

Joshua decides to return to his cottage and so starts making his way back up the beach. Within a world of his own and continually shaking his head in bewilderment on what he had just seen and at the same time trying to make sense of it all, he arrived at his front gate, then, out of the blue hears a, "Hello Joshua."

Looking up he sees a woman with her arms by her side moving her fingers like a crab. Bemused he blurted out "Good day" as naturally as he could whilst trying to put his thoughts behind him at meeting this attractive lady. He always feels very comfortable around the opposite sex, fully believing they are better creatures than the male.

Maybe that's to do with his beautiful mother and her loving simplicity versus his past experience of brutal pub brawls and the knowledge that some males have attitudes and big ego's that he feels rather awkward in other men's presence. Nevertheless, he is on his guard. You never know.

As Joshua gets closer to this unknown lady she shows no sign of anxiety, in fact, she appears calm and friendly with a posture of openness. She is about five foot four with good body shape, strawberry fair hair and full featured face with lovely green eyes and full lips. She looks around thirty-three and, all in all, very attractive. The rolling fingers type motion is the one he saw the person on the beach do whilst looking through his telescope. What is this Joshua thinks, what is going on here? If she is the person on the beach, and he can see that she is, as she is holding the large hat and veil he saw through his telescope in her left hand, how did she get to his cottage before him?

"I apologise for surprising you at your cottage but have you time for a chat, it's very important," she asks in a nice tone of Cornish but with a hint of something else. "Yes of course, please come in and I will make us some tea. I hope you like dogs as I have a couple of Jack Russell's." "Thank you, yes" she says, "my name is Rebecca Pendarve", as with a certain sigh of relief.

"I am Joshua Pendragon," he said, with a certain formality of pride but it still came out warm and friendly. "Yes," she said "I Know."

Once both inside Joshua noted that although the fire was warm it needed building. Rebecca sat on the window ledge which is about two feet thick and as with most of the cottage, whitewashed. Joshua was going to mention the ledge being cold but she didn't seem to mind and was looking thoughtfully out of the window. Queenie and Cecil liked her immediately and were at her feet sniffing away, quite extraordinary thought Joshua.

Rebecca then calmly turned her head towards Joshua and said "I believe our families are connected in some way dating way back to our good Henry IV". "So we are distance cousins then, completely removed over 400 years" Joshua says with humoured confidence. "Cousins, no, not cousins," she says with a soft chuckle, "more, how can I put it, more related through a tight code of quiet cooperation and protection"

Joshua just shrugged his shoulders and said, "I'm sorry I am totally lost." He handed over the cup to her with a saucer. Funny that, he thought, with a man it would have been an old chipped mug but for some unknown reason he automatically made the tea with cup and saucer. He doesn't have much in the way of excess in the cottage since leaving Bristol, when his dear lovely wife went to the Lord whilst giving birth many years ago.

He had so many questions to ask he really didn't know where to start so he sat himself down at the old heavy wooden table and started lighting a pipe. "Ooops sorry Rebecca," he said like some school boy asking if he could go to the toilet, "do you mind if I smoke?" "No of course not, I like the smell, it actually reminds me of my Father before he passed to the Lord when I was younger." "And you're Mother?", Joshua asked. "Unfortunately, my Mother passed away two years ago somewhere in Holland, they said it was typhoid or something, but I was away in Plymouth, so I couldn't really get to understand the circumstances."

"I'm sorry Rebecca I didn't know, it's not easy sometimes." "My Father also passed away two years ago." "Thank you" she said, "yes it isn't easy and I still miss her every day."

"Rebecca may I ask why you are here, sorry, before I ask that, was it you on the beach by the cave earlier that I saw with my telescope?" "Yes, it was me." "Well at least I now know I wasn't seeing things, which is a relief but how did you get to my cottage before me as you never left the cave, or I didn't see you leave it?" "In fact, how do you know where I live?"

"Do you mind if I sit at the table with you," she said. "No of course not", he replied. She gently got up and walked over with the dogs following at her feet. Putting her tea down she looked around and then silently looked and studied Joshua and, he silently studied her.

"Before I answer any of your questions Joshua may I ask, do you own this cottage?" "Yes I do." "And may I ask how that came about?" He described his Father's last will and testament and the clauses therein.

"Hmmm," she said, "it's curious don't you think that my Mother and your Father also passed away at the same time two years ago." "Not really, maybe just a coincidence." "Ok, if I then said that my own small holding in Marazion was bequeathed to me from my Mother with the same clauses in it as yours, at about the same time as yours, would that be a curious thing?" "No not really, most parents do this."

"Please Rebecca, if you could just explain things clearly and in truth, perhaps we can discuss things a lot better." Again she started studying him as if waiting for something. Then she leant back, looked back out of the window then turned her head back again, breathed deeply and said, "Alright I will."

"Last week, while as I was sitting on the rocks on Marazion beach in the complete open air with other people about, a man came directly up to me. For some reason I wasn't afraid as he's demeanour was very simple, sincere and polite. He was well-dressed and politely presented himself as George Kernow. He then went on to explain why he was here, something about my Mothers work and how lovely she was. He further explained that the project she was working on was not finished and would like me and a colleague, being you, to help carry on this project to completion."

"Did you say 'Colleague?'" "Yes I did Joshua, that's what I mean, it was mentioned in my Mothers will that should someone say this to me, do not be afraid, trust them." "That's what was said to me also in my Fathers Will."

Rebecca nodded and continued, "I was to go to Gunwalloe beach this very day at around 10.30am and wait outside the furthest cave on the left; he will meet me there and introduce me to the colleague in question. He said he knows it all sounds a bit hush hush and secretive but assured me that in fact, it is. I believed him" she said.

"I got the ferry to Porthleven and then rode over here this morning and did as the gentleman suggested. When I was about twenty feet away I noted that he was already standing inside the cave, out of sight. When he saw me, he loudly and in a bright and cheerful manner said 'good morning Ms Pendarve, please stay where you are, if you would kindly look over to the other side of the beach you will spot a man looking through a telescope. He then started motioning his fingers on his right hand like a crab and said, 'once the gentleman looks over, please copy what I have just done with my fingers as it is a sign of identification,' again I did, as asked."

"He then invited me into the cave and said, 'well done Rebecca.' For some reason I just wasn't nervous of this man. We then went to the back of the cave to the top where a sealed hatch was opened and I followed him upwards through a neat symmetrically square tunnel, all the way up here. He talked all the way in reassurance that your name was Joshua Pendragon and your Father worked with my Mother. I was to wait at your front gate for you to arrive. I was to introduce myself, explain what had happened and what was said and, if you are in agreement, we are to meet this same gentleman later today in the same cave at teatime this afternoon, meaning 3.00pm."

Joshua's jaw dropped in utter disbelief all the time as Rebecca was talking but once she had finished he simply said, "would you like another cuppa?" With a seemingly sigh of relieved tension she smiled and said "yes please, thank you, I need one."

Whilst making the tea an atmosphere of quiet came about which felt uncomfortable but Joshua's brain was deciphering everything which she had said, trying to work it out into some logical form and sense. He also felt this lady Rebecca didn't like the quiet atmosphere either but she gave him the time and space he needed.

With refreshed cups of tea in hand he said, "Rebecca, you believe this man?" "With what he knew of my mother and the openness in which he talked then Yes I do believe him, and may I add that since meeting you only half an hour or so ago, I feel that you also are a good man but, what you make of my tale is yours to do as your will dictates."

Studying her through his silent thoughts, Joshua twists and turns his brain to try and give a comprehensible answer but just says, "Thank you Rebecca and you too seem a good woman also and may I say a brave one at that, what would you like me to do?" "What do you suggest?" she responded.

"I say we try and eat something, gather our thoughts and be outside the cave for tea, we'll then both find out exactly what these people want with us." He then added, "however, this time when we meet these people I will have my loaded pistol with me, primed and ready."

Chapter 3

So there they both were, Rebecca and Joshua outside the cave at the appointed time. When the tide is in, this particular cave's entrance is unapproachable, however, the tide had receded just enough. Being brave and a gentleman Joshua went in front of Rebecca and then stopped about fifteen feet away from its mouth.

Suddenly and unexpectedly out of the other cave next door came a voice. "Good afternoon Rebecca, Good afternoon Joshua, please both come over if you will."

Joshua looked at Rebecca in puzzlement but together went over and entered. Just as they got inside the man came forward and gave Rebecca a kiss on the cheek then turned to Joshua and, standing a little more firmly, extended his hand. "Joshua, I am George Kernow, good afternoon, thank you both for coming." Joshua felt immediately relaxed with this man and could see how Rebecca wasn't afraid; this fellow oozed confidence but with not a shadow of arrogance. In fact, when Joshua looked straight into his eyes he felt warmth.

George then said, "I do apologise for the little deception about not being in the right cave for this meeting but one cannot be too careful, by the way, that person over there," he pointed to someone in the shadows at the back of the cave, "that is a good friend of mine as are a couple of other persons located on the cliffs outside."

Joshua and Rebecca were both surprised that others were involved and felt a dread of fear so Joshua immediately went to feel for his pistol as a means of protection and comfort. "Please do not worry yourselves," the man said, "they are only here to advise and protect us." "Do the one's outside have telescopes?" Joshua bluntly asked. "Yes of course," George replied.

"Ok let's get down to business," said George. "Please both take a seat on the rock over there and I will sit here opposite you both."

Once all seated, George looked over to the person at the back of the cave and with a nod of approval turned to Rebecca and Joshua and with openness and full clarity said, "We require your help, both of you, and hope that you will accept." He continued, "we have reason to believe that enemy sleepers are in the towns of Newlyn and Mousehole and are executing a plan of hurt towards our good people of the Cornish in the hope of softening our defences before a full scale attack. Their success would increase the probability of them winning future attacks and also reduce their casualty rate. We do not know exactly who these people are but believe them to be French or Spanish, with help from some so called English hands who have heavy anti sympathies towards us and our beautiful Queen Anne."

Joshua kept his mouth quiet and listened intently as George went on. "You may wonder why I have been so open in such a very short space of time. The answer is, we trust you both as we trusted and worked with your Mother and Father, God rest their souls." "You worked with my Mother?" Rebecca asked in confusion. "Yes, we did." "How can that be?" Rebecca responded. Joshua was all ears and listening with keen interest.

"Rather than go into full details now" George responded, "I promise that all will be made known to you Rebecca in due time, with full courtesy and respect, as your Mother always gave me." Joshua was going to ask the same question about his Father but expected the same answer so said nothing and carried on listening.

George continued, "The information we have is that these so called sleepers have been in place for some considerable time and appear to be dug in deep. We therefore, wish for you two, using your intelligence, logic and life experiences to find them and flush them out. Time is not on our side and our departments only objective is keeping this realm safe for our hard working and loyal people, guided by our good Queen Anne, God Bless her." "And your department is?" Joshua interrupted with a sense of calmness, which rather surprised him. "Hmmm," George hesitated, turned his head to his shadowy friend for a sense of support but got nothing, so turned back and said, "The Diplomatic Department based in Whitehall."

George carried on, "with the wars in France, Spain and America, our defences are stretched to the maximum, that is why we, in keeping things close and tight, have personally come to see you as well as sort some other things out here in

Cornwall. Penzance, Falmouth and St Austell are very strategic places of importance to us and to the enemy as they give excellent bridging status, close to their shores."

No one said anything as no one quite knew what to say so silence prevailed until George again took the lead. "I don't mean to rush anyone on such an important matter but we do need to get going quite shortly and ask you both that on the brief information I have given, will you help us? Money, authority and good people will be on hand to help where necessary. You only need to say yes at this stage and a date and time for initial briefing will be suggested and coordinated to you both for sometime early next week, at Mevagissey. You will of course have time to ask questions, which I would assume you have many."

"One question to you Mr Kernow before I give my answer; did my Father trust you?" "Yes, he did and I him Joshua," George said with conviction and truth.

"I also have one question Mr Kernow; did my mother work with Joshua's Father?" "Yes she did," he replied.

Again silence but Joshua felt an endearing feeling to his lost Father and the thoughts of him working with this man, Mr George Kernow. After rubbing his chin in thought and weighing up the logic of the loss versus gain of the yes versus no answer, Joshua decided to go first by saying "Yes, I will help you, subject to verifications on further questions and answers." Not long behind came Rebecca with a yes as well.

George got up and said "Thank you both. Now let us please say our goodbyes and let you both enjoy the rest of the day. We will hopefully see you both again in Mevagissey next week, God willing. If you would both like to exit the way you came in, myself and my friend will wait a little while in here."

When Rebecca and Joshua were out of sight, the supposed George Kernow turned to the shadowy figure at the far end of the cave and said, "Well Mr Kernow how was that?" "Very good Henry, I truly believed you were me, now let us be off from here and move to our next rendezvous." Once Henry had gathered his things he asked Mr Kernow, "When would like me to deliver the information about the meeting at Mevagissey?" "You mean St Just, Henry?" "I thought you said Mevagissey?" "I did Henry but we must keep one step ahead at all times, just in case."

George then said "Oh and by the way Henry the meeting is not next week its tomorrow."

They both then went to the back of the cave to a side access point leading through to the adjoining cave but then the real Mr Kernow stopped and turned to Henry and asked, "What are your initial thoughts of those two Henry?" "I believe them to be good people and once I advise them on their parents, I think they will be trustworthy and capable of doing a good job. Joshua is strong and logical and Rebecca is wise and thoughtful." "Just like their parents then," said George. "I think Rebecca's Mother was a little more head strong, but other than that yes you are right."

"Good," George replied, "please get a message to them both within the hour that we will see them both again tomorrow at the Star Pub, St Just, at ten o'clock, a room will be made available under your name. I will see you Henry this evening in Helston at the Red Lion at 8pm. Now let us get through this damn opening and back out through the tunnels away from here."

Once through the opening and into the main cave, both men stood at the back opposite an access door to the tunnel leading back up through to the cliff tops, the one Henry showed Rebecca to go through a few hours ago. Henry couldn't help but think how very simple the Cornish tunnel workers code of direction was. If the main access point to any tunnel had a carved single digit, it was a straight tunnel. If it had a carved V type impression, it was a tunnel with a single fork. If it had a carved trident, it had two forks, right and left, not left and right, and you knew where the forks were by a large square indentation on the tunnels left wall, always in intervals of one hundred steps. So no torches were necessary, simple but extremely effective. This particular tunnel had a V and George said, "We take the fork," pushed the access door and up they went.

On groping the left wall and reaching the first hundred steps George felt the walls large square indentation then barged to his right and the fork access opened and on they went. Speaking softly with each other and holding on to one another's shirt tails does very much help lessen anxiety, Henry Hosking thought to himself, with merciful gratitude.

Once Henry and George were both safely out of the tunnel they turned and waved to their two protection lookouts who, acknowledging their signal to join them, withdrew to their tethered horses.

Joshua opened the front door to the cottage and waited allowing Rebecca to go first. On entering Queenie & Cecil came rushing up happy as can be. Joshua said to Rebecca, "please make yourself comfortable, I will take these out for a quick walk and maybe then we can talk further on my return?" "Alright" Rebecca said, "that sounds good 1 will boil some water and make us a nice cup of tea."

Rebecca looked about the cottage and noted how manly and bare it was, no creature comforts, more workable and simple. However, the cottage did have a warm feeling she thought and by the hearth sat two snuggly type armchairs right inline of the fire.

With Joshua and the dogs now back and seemingly refreshed the dogs laid back down where Rebecca was sitting and not the usual spot by Joshua. It seems they would prefer Rebecca than him Joshua thought. However, he accepted the rebuff with a smile, took a deep breath and said. "So what do make of it all Rebecca?"

"I'm not too sure Joshua, my brain is trying to make sense of it all, only early this morning I was in Marazion thinking how lovely and simple my life is and now I am all over the place.

One thing I do know is, George Kernow knows an awful lot more about us than we about him."

"Hmmm," Joshua mumbled aloud, "and what about the person in the shadows in the cave, do you know anything of him?" "Nothing," she replied, "in fact I didn't really get to see him so I have no idea why or what he was doing there."

Once again "Hmmm" came out of Joshua's mouth. Joshua needed to make sense of the situation. "Shall I run through the facts as we know them and we start from there?" "Alright, that would be good", Rebecca replied. "However," she said, "I can see this is not going to be a short conversation and I have left my small gig and Lilly, my horse, back on the beach behind the church as I then walked to the cave from there this morning."

Joshua, realising he had forgotten his manners, apologised and suggested they now walk back down to the beach and fetch her horse and gig and bring it back here in safe surroundings. He then said, "we can then relax and talk openly and when you feel you are ready you could ride home or, if it gets too late, I could either escort you home or you could make my bedroom yours for the night and I will rest by the fire."

"That's very kind of you Joshua, I have no one really reliant on me in my cottage for a night or so but my chickens would need attention soon. So let's see how we get on and if it's not too late I will take you up on your escorting me home." Rebecca didn't mention the other option of staying the night.

Getting to the gig Rebecca allowed Joshua to sit next to her as she instructed her horse Lilly to, 'push on,' heading them back to Joshua's cottage. Joshua hadn't been in a riding gig with a woman for many years and found it strangely tamed and calm.

Back inside and with tea and pipe, Joshua started, "now let's look at the facts. We are both about the same age, both live alone in cottages given to us by our parent's last will and testament and who both passed away two years ago. Since then we have been pretty much living by ourselves, is that right Rebecca?" "keep going she says." "So, this afternoon we meet an unknown person called George Kernow." "You didn't say stranger then Joshua," Rebecca says. "That's right Rebecca I didn't, how strange, hmmm. With George was another man who we couldn't see, and also two other observers on the cliff tops with telescopes. George said he had worked with our parents and knows of a plot to hurt our good people and we are to flush them out."

Joshua paused for a while and Rebecca carried on. "We also know, which we didn't yesterday, of these secretive tunnels, an odd way of moving one's fingers for whatever rhyme or reason and that this George not only worked with our parents but trusted them and, what is more to the point, we both believed him!"

Rebecca and Joshua both fell silent and together like twins mumbled in harmony…"Hmmm."

Whilst looking at the fire in silence and trying to make sense of what was happening to them, both Queenie & Cecil suddenly leapt up, ran over and jumped on the window seat and with both looking outside started growling and waging their tails at the same time.

Quickly glancing at each other, Rebecca and Joshua got up in unison to see what the fuss was about. Coming through the gate was George Kernow who tipped his hat and carried on walking to the front door. Like an aged wedded couple, Rebecca instantly and comfortably said, "I will boil some water." Joshua went to the front door to meet George. Queenie and Cecil went with Rebecca as if not a care in the world.

Standing at the door step, Joshua greeted George who responded by saying, "Hello again Joshua, may I come in and talk. I trust Rebecca is still here?" On confirming both, George entered whilst taking his hat off at the same time.

Rebecca had already moved a chair from the table to the fire area as the dogs started sniffing George but got bored and went back to Rebecca. All was pretty quiet whilst Rebecca wrapped the course towelling around the handle of the kettle pot, sitting on the metal grill over the fire, then pouring the contents through the strainer with the tea leaves into a cup, casually asked "milk and sugar?" To which George replied, "both please and thank you Rebecca." Joshua sat back quietly and pleasantly looked at her.

"I suppose you have both been wondering what is going on. I have come here to truthfully explain to you both as best I can, with the information I am allowed to advertise, should you both wish?" Joshua took the lead and suggested, "we are all ears, as they say."

"I am not George Kernow, my name is Henry Hosking. George Kernow is the person who was sitting at the back of the cave when we last met. I have worked for George these past many years and can safely vouch and say he is a good man but with heavy responsibilities. He takes his position very seriously and yes he does work and report to a government or royal office department; very nice tea, may I say Rebecca." "Thank you Henry, if that is your name?" Henry then squared a little and realised that they were only listening out of courtesy and, now not believing as before. He realised that before he carried on any further he would need to reassure them both in believing in him and, really take stock in what is happening.

"Alright," Henry said, "let me go back and explain why all three of us are here, drinking tea in an old cottage overlooking Gunwalloe Cove with the pretty Church, how's that?" "That would be a good start Henry", Joshua said and Rebecca followed by saying, "Yes please do Henry, if you would."

It was time for Henry to be clear and precise. "Jeanne, your Mother Rebecca was a beautiful woman with strawberry blonde hair and fiery spirit." Staying with Rebecca he continued, "Richard, your Father Rebecca, was some time in the Royal Navy and you all lived in Saltash." Rebecca stayed silent then Henry turned to Joshua. "Joshua, your Father John, was a good man and Captain, also sometime in the Royal Navy when he married your good Mother Charity and, you all lived in Plymouth." Joshua stayed silent and then Henry turned to them both. "Rebecca and Joshua, both your Grandparents lived in these cottages after serving the crown in the Royal Navy.

Your Grandparents, and Cornish bloodline forbears, have a written alliance with Charles 1st and to his heirs and successors for their loyalty and support in times of need. However, in verbal terms, your families' quiet loyalty dates back to Edward the fourth."

Still looking at them both he carried on "For reason of communications, both your Grandparents, including the wives, were ordered to London and unfortunately all died tragically of the virulent plague in 1665. At this time both Richard and John, both your Fathers, were young and away from these shores serving in the Royal Navy and, when home from duty were both working out of Plymouth. The Cornish cottages you both now live in then became vacant and were passed and demised to your Fathers. Shall I go on?" "Please do" they both said. Joshua and Rebecca were listening intently and taking it all in.

"Your Fathers became good friends and on return from duty, were together secretly briefed of their family's obligations and duty to the safety of the realm, outside of their front line Royal Navy services. Both then were delisted out of the Navy service, given a pension and brought into the services in which the real

George Kernow and I work. Richard, your Father Rebecca, married Jeanne, and John, your Father Joshua, married Charity. The rest you probably know but I feel I need to carry on reaffirming to you both of our close relationship and bond of communication. You Rebecca and you Joshua are both single children having no brothers and sisters and both Richard, your Father Rebecca, and Charity, your Mother Joshua, passed to the good Lord through ill health in 1689.

Rebecca you were around nineteen years of age living and working in Plymouth and unmarried. Joshua you were around twenty-three living and working in Bristol and married. Your Father Joshua, immediately informed us that his best friend and confidante in this service had passed to the Lord and was subsequently advised by us whether Jeanne, his wife, could step in and help in continuation of their work.

With John's positive report back and blessing, Jeanne was duly enlisted and all ownership of everything that your good Father Richard had, was transferred directly into her name."

Henry, feeling exhausted with recalling all this information said "Have I now successfully convinced you both that I am genuine because I really do need another cup of tea and am conscious of time as we all have a rendezvous tonight at 10pm in St Just with George Kernow?"

Joshua and Rebecca looked in disbelief and Rebecca said, "You said this afternoon, it was to be at Mevagissey sometime next week?" "I know I did and I apologise. It is what George

Kernow asked me to say and then, when you both left, he changed the time and venue for tonight in St Just. He is very security minded and always likes to be ahead, just in case. Although intrusive and irritable, he plays these quick moves all the time and assures everyone that it saves lives and, I am positive it does."

With a pause in proceedings they all then heard a muffled voice from outside and Henry quickly got up and looked through the window. "Just a moment," he said, "I think this is for me" and with that walked quickly to the door and out he went. This gave Rebecca and Joshua a quick moment to discuss what had been said and quickly ascertain what they wanted to do. Rebecca was first to say "I am intrigued and want to know more, my life has been very quiet these last years since returning from Plymouth and have pretty much kept myself to myself living off my Mothers inherited monthly allowance. What say you Joshua?" "I also am interested, like you I have done pretty much the same since coming back from Bristol and wish to know more of what they expect of us."

The front door opened and Henry walked back in and looking at them both said with a huff, "the venue is not St Just at 10.00pm anymore, it's now The Blue Anchor in Helston at 7.30pm, if you are quite happy with my communications so far we best quickly finish off here and be on our way as time is moving on."

Before they were just about to leave Henry turned around and said, "are there any last quick questions on your mind you wish to ask before we all ride to Helston?" "Just quickly," Joshua said, "you know an awful lot about our parents and grandparents, what do you know of Rebecca and I?"

"Quite a lot actually, and in brief, what I can and am allowed to say is that you Rebecca, while in Plymouth worked for Samuels Ship Builders Devonport as secretary/operations to Mr Samuel Junior. You wrote frequently to your Mother and returned here in fullness nearly two years ago. You Joshua, after ten years in the Royal Marines resigned your commission and moved to Bristol where you worked in Avonmouth Munitions Company. Apart from your initial wayward and public fighting hiccups, we shall say no more on that subject, you met your good wife, settled down and returned here, living quietly for the last two and three quarter years. Now can we please get going?" Rebecca and Joshua looked astounded and realised these people are for real.

While Henry went outside, Rebecca contemplated asking Joshua a question or rather not, as it may be a little too delicate, but she quickly weighed it up and decided to ask it anyway as it would bother her continually if she didn't. "Joshua, are you married, where is your wife?" "Unfortunately Rebecca," he replied, "when working in Bristol my lovely wife died giving birth to our beautiful still born daughter, I must say Rebecca, I loved her deeply and still feel the loss to this day, although it helps to know she and our daughter are with the Lord." Standing together alone inside the front door Rebecca laid her hand on his and said with tender compassion, "I'm so sorry Joshua I didn't know."

It was then that she looked at him differently and more deeply, being six-foot-tall, black short length hair, strong shoulders with a lovely determined type face, straight nose and clean shaven and for all his show of braveness there was something of a child inside. Quite nice she thought, beware.

Chapter 4

Joshua knew where the Blue Anchor lay so Henry bid his farewell. They had about an hour to prepare before the probable hour's ride in to Helston town. Rebecca decided to take up Joshua's offer of staying the night as it would be extremely late when they got back and so started making herself at home in the bedroom with the minimum amount of sundries a lady could work with. Joshua took Queenie and Cecil for a walk and when returned made something quick for them to eat and rolled a pipe for a smoke.

"I think once we get this meeting out of the way we can then fully evaluate what is what and decide what to do, what do you think Rebecca?" "I agree," she said "but I will need, if I can, to sleep on things before any decisions are made one way or the other. I think that's my Mother or Father talking."

Once Joshua's horse, named Harry, was bridled to his larger gig and everything checked, they set off at a nice slow pace. They were pretty much quiet all of the way except Joshua asking questions which kept cropping up in his mind. This in fact was Joshua all over, facts, analyse, objective, consequences, which all mean taking the right actions which equal's solution. Hmmm he thought.

"Rebecca, something really has been bothering me all day, you said you went through a tunnel to get to my cottage which I understand, but could you explain what is was like and where it exited?" "I was thinking when you were going to ask that", she said "as I would have asked you hours ago."

"At the back of the cave there was an entrance to a tunnel that led straight, no bends at all, straight as a dye with a gentle slope upwards coming out just behind your cottage in the back garden with loads of shrubbery and brush all around." Rebecca carried on, "I have heard so much of these so called tunnels and smuggling tales that I just accepted it as natural, how odd is that?"

"That's really interesting" he replied, "so my cottage is the proud owner of a tunnel, I will have to search it one day. But like you I don't feel the least surprised something like this is around the family especially here at the bottom end of Cornwall and, the cottage so close to an isolated cove."

On arriving at the Blue Anchor in Helston, a young boy employed by the Inn asked if he could guard the horse and gig. These boys are supplied by the publican and therefore must be reliable or, their lives would not be worth living. "Yes thank you" Joshua replied, "how much?" "Penny an hour Sir paid on exit," he said confidently. Outrageous he thought but then again what else could they do. "That will be fine, thank you", Joshua replied.

As they went through the front door of the Blue Anchor they noticed the place was buzzing with drinkers but then caught sight of Henry to the right at a table with two other men. Henry got up and waved them over, pulled out the end bench and invited them to sit. As soon as they both sat down one man immediately got up and walked to the bar which left Joshua, Rebecca, Henry and one other.

Then the other man at the table turned his head and looking straight at Rebecca and Joshua said, "Good evening to you both and thank you for coming on time my name is George Kernow." Rebecca said good evening back and Joshua followed. He carried on, "I will not take much of your time, would either of you like a drink before we begin?" They both asked for a small cider and with that, Kernow waived his hand to another man, who then went to the bar to order and collect.

No one said anything until the drinks were laid on the table in front of them. Then this man who was the real George Kernow spoke again, "Now I am going to say and ask some things of you both tonight, please could you answer individually with Rebecca being first, is that acceptable with you both?" Quite naturally Rebecca said, "that is fine" and Joshua followed saying the same. "Good, then let's start as we have only eighteen minutes before things happen in here." Rebecca and Joshua didn't get the eighteen-minute thing but didn't pry and let it go.

George then continued "On the information you have heard today do you believe what we say and advertised to your ears is true and, extremely confidential to ourselves?" Rebecca and Joshua acknowledged as agreed. "Do you also recognise that what I am probably about to divulge is one hundred percent secret and you promise to keep it that way?" Again, both agreed yes with their reply.

Taking in their positive responses George paused looked at Henry and said, "so be it, we would like you both to work together on behalf of the department to flush out these enemy sleepers and the turncoat traitor in the area of Newlyn, possibly Mousehole or Sennon, not fully confirmed. Once you have found these heathens with categorical evidence on who they are and what their dastardly plot is, then and only then, report this to me, understood?" "Yes Rebecca said but how?"

Then waiting and expecting the same response confirmation from Joshua, came nothing, so everyone went silent. Joshua then noticed that all three were looking at him. Realising his mistake, he apologised then copied the same answer as Rebecca and with that George nodded in bemusement and carried on.

He picked up on Rebecca's last question, "that is up to you and Joshua my dear to work out and implement your own strategy to achieve the desired result. Henry here will assist and be the go between but will not work in the field anymore as he once did with, your good Parents. Now, we have done some homework for you both and surmised that these sleepers would not have been installed more than two years ago and hence we have checked the subsidy and parish rolls and found that many unknown families have moved and working in Newlyn area within this time frame. However, saying that, we also know that many unknown other families have moved into the area without notifying the authorities also." Well that cancels that information out thought Joshua.

George continued, "we are not saying any of these families are the people we require but it is somehow a start. I apologise for being sparse and vague but exact information is rare and extremely hard to get in our line of work. However, we do believe these sleepers to be three in number either all male or one female and two males. As for the traitorous heathen, we believe him to be a Cornishman and of the old faith with very deep sympathies towards the French."

Rebecca and Joshua listened in total stunned silence as George carried on, "As for money and tools required. Trevean and Trevean Solicitors, who you already know through your Cottage Title deeds and monthly pensions, will advance you fifty pounds each and raise your monthly income from twenty pounds per month to twenty-five pounds from immediate effect. How does that sound to you both?" They both nodded and Rebecca said calmly "Thank you Mr Kernow", in which, Joshua concurred.

"Then we are all agreed, I believe that then does it for tonight", George said, and went on by saying, "please do not under estimate the enemy and be very careful and diligent. This assignment is categorised as dangerous so use all your skills and inner tact in achieving the results we need. We believe you have a one to two-month time window. Good luck to you both."

George then advised Rebecca and Joshua to look to their left. They shall see three men and a woman at the bar drinking together. The largest man will turn to face you in a very short while and please do the same to him. Please do not take your eyes of each other for at least one minute. Just as they thought nothing was going to happen the man turned around and eyed balled both Rebecca and Joshua without a flinch.

After what seemed an eternity and an embarrassing one minute, the man turned back to the bar. Joshua noticed the others around him didn't turn away from the bar and, understood what this man was doing. Surreal but professional, he thought.

George then said "we are finished, if you both could just wait one more minute before leaving that would be appreciated. Henry here will make contact shortly," and with that, as if on cue, a commotion started over the left side of the bar and the lady with the three men started shouting abuse to some other men and all hell broke loose. George with a glee in his voice said, "the diversion is in progress, if you would both like to slip out now the way you came in that would be good and once again thank you, and take care."

Chapter 5

The chateau Morlaix, near Brest in Brittany, is owned by the Count Philip De Albret, a model in charm and richness. The Chateau oozed money and extravagance. Only the very best attended here. The gardens were delightful and cut to perfection like a razor. The foliage colour, even in winter, was beautiful. All carriages that visited Chateau Morlaix passed through massive front iron gates then travelled along a mile of gravel driveway, cut finely, through the massive lush green estate, giving the occupants a feeling of self-importance, whilst, acknowledging that the owners had truly made it in the highest of French society and, its nobility. The owners, in fact, were cousins of the Duke of Brittany with friends and associates at the very heart of the King and its protectors.

Time was moving on and Philip Albret had to get back to the cards. The three men sat again in silence in the sombre smaller inner room adjoining the library. Philip had left his card game and entered the room through the main library, the other two had entered from a back door away from any persons.

Philip broke the ice, "so, are we saying we are not ready?" "Not exactly," said Pierre Bouchier, a man of medium height, jutting chin and teeth. Bouchier also had a receding hairline but a full brown beard, thinking it made him look virile to the ladies.

Bouchier is Count Albret's right hand man on the ground and, has only one interest, and that is his self-impoitance, always shown when he away from his master. However, saying that he gets the tasks done whatever Albret asks him to do and, he is ruthless. Bouchier continued, "We have, after long investigations into the geography and lay of the lands, now identified the initial target and worked out how it will be done. However, due to hitting an unsuspected heavy granite seam, our sleepers have had to move locations, which is dangerous, but necessary to achieve success. We also understand our sleepers have implemented phase one in opening up an entrance in readiness to proceed on receipt of your approval tonight."

Seemingly content with Bouchier's response Philip then turned his attention to the other man, "and what say you Sir? Are you ready with your participation?" The alchemist was an older man of bald head and tubby features but known as an expert in chemicals and worked out of the Abbey of Landerneau, in which Philip Albret is the main sponsor. "We will be Sir," he replied, in a confident manner. "Enlighten me where exactly you are then?" Philip asked. "As you know, we experimented with some scoundrels and paupers in Paris, at your request, and the germ worked well with no suspicions even through autopsy. However, the cloning agent required to be attached to the germ achieving zero status in smell, colour and taste for the larger scale operations, needs more work and I anticipate completion ready for delivery in enough quantity in a month or so."

Philip was listening with a quiet confidence and then asked, "How much of this so called germ agent is required for this initial target in Mousehole and how are you going to transport?" The alchemist didn't answer, instead turned his head to Pierre Bouchier, who then took up the discussion. "As you know Sir, there are many disgruntled people in Cornwall who are true believers and are prepared to fully cooperate with our ambitions to rid their country of the new faith and return them to the true way, irrelevant if it costs lives of their own." "Yes I am aware of this," Philip responded.

Pierre continued to answer Philip's questions; "we have recruited a reliable agent called Mr Ashley Ward, a pig farmer in a very satisfactory position near Sennon, to receive goods from the sea and then transport inland to the new location for the sleepers. Mr Ward has worked for us before and proven very reliable."

"We also have another favourable agent in Penzance who is being considered as a backup. This so called germ agent will be delivered in false bottoms in our brandy kegs. For every four-gallon keg of brandy, half will be the agent. We believe we require two hundred gallons of agent and therefore one hundred kegs. This should be achieved in a one and only delivery, minimising risk exposure."

Philip Albret once again fell silent and contemplated the situation. He then spoke to the alchemist. "How many people are aware of your work?" The alchemist replied, "You asked me over a year ago that the work I was undertaking was for the defence of France by the King himself and that success would bring the true faith back to us all, if done in absolute confidence."

The alchemist continued, "therefore, the answer is only one and that is me, apart from my two apprentices, who know nothing of the reason for my work, believing only that they are experiments of the sciences." "Good," replied Philip, who then glanced at Bouchier, who looking directly back into Philip's eyes and without moving a muscle gave the very slightest of nods only the keenest of eyes would have seen.

Philip Albret answered Bouchier's ever so slight movement of the head by saying, "Agreed." With that a door in the wall behind the Alchemist opened and a large able man appeared who simply walked up behind the alchemist's chair and without so much as a word, garrotted him to death with clinical and clean brutality. Once completed, Philip said very calmly, "Thank you, now take him away and dispose."

Once the body was removed, both Pierre and Philip looked at each other with calm satisfaction of their professionalism and knowing brutality of the game they were in. "Now Pierre," Philip said, "having listened to all information and however much I do not like chemicals and germs, this is the future, and I and my family will make history in its first ever use over the enemy, then Pierre, we will have our first successful bridgehead in England and I will be made the highest knight in the land. My decision therefore, is to proceed."

With that, Pierre responded, "It will be done Sir, we will now make contact with the sleepers and Mr Ward immediately. The germ will be completed on time with activation in a few weeks and with the bigger primary target set, subject to this initial success, early summer 1708, as projected."

"Good" said Philip, "that fits most nicely with our ships time tables and rear echelon supply schedules. Our dear beloved King will be most pleased. By the way, how is my prisoner?" "She is safe Sir, as you requested." "Thank you Pierre, now I must get back to the cards, I am on a winning streak." They both chuckled.

Chapter 6

Everyone's attention in the Blue Anchor was on the fight and total chaos at the other end of the pub, so Rebecca and Joshua simply slipped out unnoticed into the brisk cold night air. The young boy, who had attended to them on arrival was there holding the gig and quietly talking to Harry, Joshua's lovely black stallion which Joshua bought some two years ago.

"Thank you," Joshua said, as he helped Rebecca up into the seat. The young boy handed Joshua the reins and then slipped his hand into his pocket and reached out a sealed envelope saying to Joshua, "I was to hand this to you directly Sir, on you leaving the Blue and only, if you and the lady were together." "Thank you, may I ask who you are and who do you work for?" "My name is 'Little George' and I am in the service of Mr Henry Hosking." With that Joshua pocketed the envelope and jumped into the seat next to Rebecca. Once they had both blanketed themselves warmly, ready for the off, Joshua flipped the reins and nodded to the young boy in respect.

The ride home was quiet as they were both tired with the day's events and much to think about. Harry seemed to be enjoying the exercise in trotting very graciously through the town and out towards the direction of the lizard, where after a couple of miles, they changed direction heading due south for Gunwalloe and Joshua's comforting little cottage.

Queenie and Cecil were pleased to see them and once they had taken their hats and coats off, Joshua stoked the fire and asked

Rebecca would she like a little glass of brandy in which she replied, "Yes please I think I need it."

Sat around the fire, they began to relax. Rebecca suggested they both need a good night's sleep to take in what has occurred over this last day and to wake early and discuss their thoughts then. Joshua agreed and mentioned that he will get his things out of his bedroom in readiness to make it her's for the night. On returning, Rebecca was staring into the fire with both dogs by her feet and looking very thoughtful. When Joshua had finished moving things about he said, "I have done my best to make things a little more comfortable and have lit the candle and trust it will be acceptable." Rebecca turned and smiled and said, "I am sure it will be fine, thank you, where are you going to sleep?" "I shall pull out some rugs and lay by the fire, it will be most comfortable", he replied.

Rebecca said her goodnight and got up, with Queenie following her. Cecil didn't really know where to go so reluctantly stayed with Joshua with his eyes on Rebecca but Joshua felt this little Jack Russell also wanted to be with Rebecca.

Once everything had calmed and the night was silent, Joshua felt the fire looked especially spiritual with its flickering flames and spits of crackling sparks against the dark cold granite walls. He then he drew in an ambience of the peace and how comforting and protective he felt knowing that a woman was within these walls and sleeping. He then remembered the envelope!

Knowing he couldn't wait till morning to find out what it said, he got up, went to his coat and retrieved it and then sat on the chair by the table. Having relit the lamp, he opened the envelope.

R & J

You are good people with experiences of life to achieve success.

Look in both your scrub area's to find a stone slab marked V which is yours to use as with your Mother and Fathers.

Respectfully yours

A Colleague

He flipped the page over looking for more writing but that was it, short and sweet. Joshua replaced the letter in his coat pocket and realised that whatever is in the slab V can wait till the morning, his mind was all over the place and he knew he couldn't, at this hour and being extremely tired, think straight, he needed sleep. Lying back down by the hearth and covering himself over with rugs, he released his thoughts through quiet breathing then stretched his body as though dispelling any tension, laid his head down and was gone.

Cecil woke Joshua up by scratching at the front door around 7am. He hadn't slept that well, with constant dreams of trying time after time to swim through a torrent of water and getting nowhere. Throwing back the rug, he got up and let Cecil out to do his business. He then stoked the fire up and put on some water to boil to make some tea and wash his face, leaving enough spare for Rebecca. However, there was no sign of Queenie or Rebecca.

While the water was boiling he took the envelope out of his coat pocket walked over to the bedroom door and knocked gently. On hearing Rebecca's sleepy voice acknowledging his knocking, he asked if he could enter.

Rebecca was under the bed clothes with Queenie by her side, snuggled up, and Joshua felt immediately very protective of them. On rubbing her eyes and attempting to wake up, he walked over and handed her the note and explained that she should read it and suggested he would bring in some tea and a bowl of warm water and, that once she was ready, perhaps they could both discuss what it means. Rebecca read the note with a quizzical look and then said, "Thank you Joshua, you are very kind." On leaving the bedroom, Queenie jumped down and followed Joshua out, wanting to join Cecil outside. Joshua obliged and let Queenie out.

On delivering both the tea and the bowl to Rebecca, he went with the remaining warm water in to the scrub area of the cottage. Trying to discipline himself not to look until they were both together, he couldn't help but roam his eyes across the whole area trying to spy the V slab. Eventually, pouring the water into the bowl and refreshing his face with the warm water, he started to dry himself before noticing in the left corner of the floor, tight up against the outer wall, a slab marked with a single deep scratch. The iron bath tub was covering the rest of the mark so pushing it aside he saw the full mark of the V; unbelievable!

He wanted to shout eureka! but thought better of it, then heard Rebecca walk in and ask, "have you found it?" "I believe I have," he said. "Shall we investigate?" "Where are the dogs, maybe we should bring them in first?" He agreed and Rebecca went and opened the front door and called them in.

They were now standing side by side, both looking at the slab wondering what they should do. Rebecca suggested they clean all around it and then try and get it raised. Opening the back door, Joshua found an iron bar next to the privy and on his hands and knees started scratching and digging at the slab. Rebecca helped by brushing all the debris away. Once completed, he jemmied the slab up, leaving a two by two foot opening with a much larger chamber below. Rebecca fetched and lit a candle for him, as if knowing he was going to go down first, which in fact, he was thinking that anyway.

The chamber was very well lined and dry, about ten feet long by six wide and six feet high, so Joshua could just about stand up but what he saw was amazing. Everything you could imagine to be self-contained in times of extreme trouble, including swords, muskets, flintlock pistols, maps, wine, water, food, all types of clothing, all up to date, including a most beautiful long range micro telescope. Once he understood what was down there he pressed himself back up the gap and suggested Rebecca see for herself, and handing her the candle, she slid easily into the chamber.

On helping Rebecca up, they dusted themselves down and moved into the front room with the fire to sit down and decipher what they had and what they were going to do. The time was now, to set and agree the plan!

On feeding the dogs with their left over meals and themselves with fresh porridge, they sat down by the hearth and began to chatter about what has happened, what is happening and how they are going to do things going forward.

They agreed on three critical points; one they should not work alone and isolate each other but work together at all times. Two, they should alias themselves together as husband and wife, and three, as the targets may probably be in the Newlyn area, time wasn't on their side, they would need to be closer and move today to Rebecca's cottage to make their initial base. Queenie and Cecil will have a holiday with Mrs Stephens's family in Cury just over the way.

Being in the marines and working in munitions, Joshua knew about weaponry and self-defence but he was worried about Rebecca. With that thought, he turned to her and said, "Rebecca, have you any experience in weapons or fighting?" In which she laughed and looked at him as if he was on a different planet, even Queenie and Cecil looked at him in a strange way. Rebecca replied, "Joshua, the closest I have ever got to hurting something is preparing a rabbit for a stew. As for guns and things, I have never fired one in my life. Now Joshua, if you ask me what I can do apart from not killing people, I will tell you. I can organise, read, write, understand mathematics, stitch, have sex and understand that life is about agreed discussion by cooperation, not by female subservience!"

Nearly choking on his pipe, he said, "I think I get it and thank you Rebecca." Joshua quickly thought that Rebecca comes across as a quiet lady until such time as she feels undermined or threatened, then watch out! He will remember that in future.

However, as they were going into dangerous territory, he felt it necessary to convince Rebecca that she should at least learn how to load, prime and fire a pistol and to wear both a dagger and pistol on her person at all times, just in case. She looked at him square in the eyes, but knew that his warning made sense, if not for her protection but for his as well, and therefore she nodded with agreement.

Not knowing what was needed or not needed, they decided to load the gig with pretty much most of the stuff from the V chamber. Once completed, Rebecca chose a fine dagger and sheath for herself that fitted snug and not too heavy and Joshua chose a small flintlock pistol for her, with the latest all in one ball and powder cotton bag, for ease of loading and reloading. Taking five cotton bags and moving away from the cottage overlooking the sea, he set out a bucket for Rebecca's first target practice about twenty feet away below the wall.

Rebecca was a very receptive trainee and took immediately the seriousness of what was happening and listened intently to getting it right quickly.

Rebecca got it straight away and didn't seem at all conscious that ladies don't do this sort of thing. Steadying her grip and aiming with both hands on the butt, she missed. With a bit of encouragement and two musket balls later, she was on or near the target and completely understood the loading procedure.

On finishing up, Rebecca casually strapped the gun under her skirt, attaching it to a skeleton strap holder just above the knee. Joshua didn't know where to look. Rebecca then said, "Pity Anne Boleyn didn't have one of these." He just looked on in bewilderment.

With everything ready, Queenie and Cecil jumped up beside Rebecca in the gig. Joshua decided to also take his own horse and so jumping up on Harry, they both left the cottage with Joshua leading. On arrival in Cury village, Mrs Stephens was glad to see Joshua and pleased to take the dogs of his hands for a few weeks as if it was of no bother to her whatsoever.

Explaining to Mrs Stephens about Rebecca was another matter and Joshua sort of stumbled his way through it, as if they were already married, not married, engaged or betrothed. In any case, Mrs Stephens was lovely and just cuddled him and said, 'you two go off and have a lovely fun time together.' "Thank you Mrs Stephens," he replied.

Jumping in the gig next to Rebecca he asked if she was ready and she replied, "Yes, I am ready Joshua, let's do this and let's do it well." With Harry tethered to the back, they waved to Mrs Stephens, turned the gig around and went off to Marazion.

They kept a good steady pace and the countryside passed by crisply with rugged beauty. Helston lay slightly to the east of their route to Marazion and it wouldn't have taken much to pop in to see Trevean Solicitors and ask for their monies but Joshua thought better to head direct to their destination as agreed.

On heading North West along the country paths, they soon hit the main Penzance road. Passing through Breage and Rosudgeon they were now only a few miles from Marazion. A couple of quick miles later they met the turnpike road where Rebecca announced they should bear left and then a half mile on advised taking the next track on the left. With a little pull here and tug there, Joshua guided the gig well.

A couple of minutes later they could see the track coming to a dead end when Rebecca pointed to her Cottage on the right. She jumped down and opened the gate and Joshua pushed the gig forward. With Rebecca walking ahead and taking the lead, they slowly came to a halt by the front porch area. "Welcome to my home Joshua," she announced. "Leave the gig there and come in while I get the fire lit and put the tea on." Joshua did as was told, jumped down and tied his own horse Harry to the bench pole. However, before he went in, he quickly got some water for both horses.

Joshua thought the Cottage was lovely, very much like his own with granite build but bigger with two bedrooms. However, the main difference was the soft furnishings. Joshua's cottage was just the bare minimal requirements whilst Rebecca's was a home just like he had had in Bristol. A woman's touch just amazes him. He decided to help Rebecca with the lighting of the fire and ask if there was anything else he could do to help. However, she seemed to have it all under control and suggested that he could unbridle her horse and put her in the barn then come back to rest and await the tea. Once again he did as was told and then took Harry in the barn also.

While Rebecca was organising things Joshua decided to stand and look out of the window. Although the cottage was tucked high above and away into some trees about half mile west of the village, he could see the beautiful wide bay of Marazion with St Michaels Mount to its left, off centre, and Penzance and Newlyn off to the far right in the distance, about three miles as the crow flies. "What a lovely view," he said. "Yes isn't it just lovely," Rebecca replied.

Once settled down with tea in their hands and the fire looking brighter and catching well, they started to relax somewhat. "Joshua, I know we are going to go about as husband and wife but I have two bedrooms here and one should be for you and one for me, I just wanted to get that out of the way now." Joshua started to laugh and said, "of course Rebecca, I understand completely, but, when we are out and if staying the night somewhere as husband and wife, we would have to share at least the room, do you not agree?" "Yes I understand that, but that is different, that's business."

"By the way Rebecca, talking about husband and wife, would you have a couple of spare rings for us both so we can display to others?" "I do have a small jewellery box and am sure I could find us something suitable," she replied. "Thank you Rebecca," he said sincerely. Even though they were acting, Joshua didn't like to belittle the sanctity of marriage. With that Rebecca left the room and after a little while came back with two rings.

"How about these," she said. "They are not wedding rings, more for decoration but I think they will pass" and with that she passed one to Joshua. She waited for his response, as if knowing that if they put the rings on together at the same time, it would not be demeaning to the Lord. Joshua's felt a little tight, but he squeezed it on and then they both looked at each other really not knowing what to say, so they said nothing.

On contemplating his surroundings Joshua found himself quite comfortable looking at Rebecca's work in making the place feel very warm and cosy. He was quiet whilst Rebecca also seemed to be deep in thought.

Time was moving on and Joshua felt he should go out to Harry and comfort him a while and start bringing in the belongings when Rebecca said, "If you want to bring things in I will put some supper on and tidy your bedroom to make it comfortable for you, how does that sound?" "Sounds good to me," he responded.

With all the baggage in and supper eaten, with candles lit and fire roaring they sat down quite exhausted. Although the atmosphere had been calm and pleasant, Joshua had always been thinking how and when they are going to achieve their mission. Analysing this and visualising different scenarios his mind was working overtime and he believed it now to be the right time to ask Rebecca what she was thinking and, how she saw things.

Rebecca's response was thoughtful and calm. "I may look as though I am quite happy with this but I am worried, we are amateur's, we have no plan, no strategy and what's more how do we get the information back to Henry or George. I am also concerned for our future, as if we succeed or fail, do they just leave us alone and we get on we our lives as normal?"

Rebecca's response, Joshua thought, was a good one which left him quiet. "Then let us together start building a plan step by step. I think the first thing I shall do tomorrow is ride into Helston and talk with the Solicitors about the monies we are owed and somehow find out how we contact Henry."

"Agreed," she said, but one thing I have learnt in life is confidentiality, not to say too much Joshua, people only need to know what we want them to know. If you go to the Solicitors and start asking questions about Henry too soon, the whole of Helston will know we are on his payroll, so may I suggest you hang about by the Blue Anchor, no drinking mind Joshua, find the boy in his service and say that we need to talk to his Paymaster and arrange a meet."

Joshua was a little taken back by Rebecca's suggestion that he might talk too much but even after over ten years in the Royal

Marines with all the fighting, bitching and biting, he knew she was right to remind him of the importance of working undercover.

"By the way," she said, "earlier on, when we first arrived and while you were giving water to the horses, my curiosity got the better of me. I have been to the scrub room and think I found the slab with the V scratch mark by the back door in the corner but the iron tub is on top and I couldn't move it to find out more." "Shall I try?" "Yes please Joshua" With that they both got up and went to the scrub room and on pushing and shoving the heavy water butt aside they uncovered the full V.

Same as Joshua's, they jemmied the slab away and with candle in hand, found the underground chamber to be full of equipment usable for tasks of their pending adventure. "Unbelievable" she said. "Quite!" he said.

They both agreed that what was found in the chamber should stay in the chamber until tomorrow, as what was important now was for both of them to get a good night's sleep and be fully refreshed for a busy day tomorrow.

Rebecca showed Joshua the outside privy and the alternative wash area, away from the main inner scrub room, then wished him a pleasant good night's sleep, as Joshua did her.

Stripping off his clothes and getting into his new bed, he found everything to be much more comfortable, unlike his own bare bedroom and much harder bed. Even the blankets felt softer and warmer. Laying still and letting his mind wander on what was happening he drifted off into a much needed sleep.

Chapter 7

Waking early, Joshua got up and used the outside privy but then came back inside to wash in the scrub room. It was once again very cold both outside and in. Rebecca was still asleep in her room so he lit the fire and got the water on for the morning tea. Whilst the water was on he checked on Harry.

Coming back into the cottage Joshua walked up to the windows and admired the view. He thought he had a great view at Gunwalloe but nothing quite like this. Gunwalloe was a cove, this was a massive bay with ships of both the line and merchant and on the far right side was the fishing fleet of all shapes and sizes.

Joshua made the tea and was starting to make a pipe up when Rebecca looked in and said "Good Morning." "Good morning" he replied, "the water has boiled, would you like a cup of tea?" "You and your tea! By the way, I really don't mind if you want to smoke." "Thank you, Rebecca."

Rebecca got herself ready quite quickly and they both sat down by the fire. Joshua spoke about the agenda for today, as agreed by them both yesterday, and said that he should start making tracks shortly. Rebecca suggested he have some warm porridge before setting off. "What will you be doing while I'm away in Helston?" he asked. "I want to give this place a good clean then go through all the things we found in the scrub chambers and better organise them so we can identify exactly what we have and store them accordingly."

"By the way Rebecca, I have been thinking, it would be a good cover if we could start our closer move in to the target area as a couple who wants to celebrate by the sea town of Penzance. We could find ourselves a room at an inn and work the area from there for a while, how does that sound?" "I Think you are right, it's a good simple cover story but maybe tonight when you get back from Helston we could go through and practise things so we are both singing from the same hymn sheet. "Agreed Rebecca," he replied in an approving way.

With the day's itinerary established, Joshua set out. With the gig ready and Harry bridled, he flicked the reins and trekked off. Rebecca had already opened the gate for him to pass through and as he did they waved to each other.

The weather was cold and the ground very hard so Harry was moving steadily but assured at a relaxed walking pace. Joshua anticipated that the journey to Helston would take at least two hours. The ride was lovely and relaxing and gave him time to think. Although he saw some people walking and riding it was in the main, a quiet journey.

Joshua saw the sun was now up trying to make some sort of effort to heat the earth but the cold freshness of the air was having none of it and wasn't giving it a chance. However, it was a nice thought that the spring was coming. Reliable Harry kept his pace well, in a strong controlled manner.

He thought about Rebecca and her composure of the situation and really did admire her courage and fortitude. It was then that he promised himself, he would use all his skills and Marine's experience, to achieve what was needed and more importantly protect her. He felt good about that.

The village of Breage was coming up ahead when Joshua noticed a steady rider heading towards him. It was the boy at the Blue Anchor. "Good morning Mr Pendragon," he said, as they both stopped side by side. "Good Morning Little George, how are you?" "I am well, thank you. I went to your cottage at Gunwalloe but you were not there so I thought I would push on to Ms Pendarves in the hope that you were there, as I have a message to give you from Mr Hosking."

"How did you know I would be at Ms Pendarves?" Joshua asked curiously. "Mr Hosking said if you were not at Gunwalloe then I was to push on to Marazion to Ms Pendarves. Am glad we met halfway as Suzy my horse is getting a little puffed out." Suzy was a lovely looking well-kept horse. Joshua's stallion Harry kept trying to get a better view but Suzy kept her stance ignoring him.

"Well then, that is good we met," Joshua replied, "what is the message?" "Could you meet Mr Hosking for lunch in the Coach Inn at Breage?" Joshua knew there wasn't enough time to get to Helston and the Solicitors first and then get back to Breage. Weighing things up he decided to forsake Helston and head directly for the Coach Inn and wait if he had to. Little George waited politely for his response when Joshua eventually acknowledged the message, that of course he will go directly.

"Thank you Mr Pendragon," Little George said, "Do you mind if I accompany you as my master Mr Hosking is already there?" "That will be my pleasure Little George but I would not get Suzy to close to my Harry as he sometimes thinks he is our good King Henry the Eighth when around young fillies." Little George had a nice soft laugh and they escorted each other to the Coach Inn

The Coach Inn was a large fronted white washed Inn, set back off the road and appearing ready and able to accommodate any traveller. Little George volunteered to look after Joshua's gig while he went in and met Mr Hosking. On entering, he saw Henry by the fire with another man whom he recognised as the man that created the havoc at the nod of George Kernow at the Blue Anchor in Helston.

Henry noticed Joshua coming in and waved him over. "Good morning Joshua, let me formerly introduce you to my friend, Bull." With that the man called Bull got up and held out his big hand which Joshua shook and said, "Good day Sir" and he responded likewise with a heavy Cornish accent.

"Right," said Henry to Bull, "I think our business is completed for today, have you any questions?" "None Mr Hosking, I get the situation and understand my responsibilities and bid both of you good day." Still standing, Joshua again shook his hand and then nodded their approval to each other as if somehow knowing their paths will cross again.

Henry then turned his attention to Joshua. "Right Joshua, I am famished, shall we eat? Please take a seat and I will order us an early hearty lunch and then we can talk." This, Joshua accepted gladly, as he was also hungry. Henry waved to the maid who took their order whilst pouring Joshua a large cider. Henry also refilled his wine glass.

"Before I forget, these are for you and Rebecca." He handed over two heavy looking purses containing fifty pound coins each. Joshua took them both and laid them by his side and said, "they are heavy but you have just saved me a trip to Helston, thank you." Henry nodded and continued, "I presume you got my message about the underground stores." "Yes we did and found both. Rebecca is at this moment, organising things."

"Good, one thing you may find strange, if you haven't already, are the undershirts and shifts made of cotton, with a mix of plated iron and tin plate sewn in strategic areas to protect the vital parts of the body. They are light enough to wear and I assure you they are very worthy garments and can stop a blade or a glancing musket ball." "I have not noticed these items yet as we have been a little rushed, but I'm sure Rebecca will come across them, thank you."

Joshua explained to Henry their plan to enter Penzance as husband and wife tomorrow and then to evaluate the situation and work from there. "Good," he said, "I will make arrangements for a room to be ready for a happy couple at the Turks Head in the town." Joshua looked at him quizzically as he felt it important that they work alone. "Don't worry Joshua; I know it's important to work quietly and alone but let's use the resources we have and not leave things to chance. I will send Little George over now to arrange things." Joshua couldn't but agree with his logic and therefore, Little George was tasked.

"Now, there has been some further information come in from abroad, a person related in some form to this espionage plot has been killed or removed. I bring this to your attention for two reasons, whoever is behind this is deadly serious for its success, and do not under estimate their brutality and ruthlessness to achieve their goals." "I completely understand" Joshua said.

"Also Joshua, we are no further forward with information on this planned scheme except for what you know. So, while we eat you can ask any questions of me and I shall answer as best I can."

The stew was delicious and whilst eating Joshua capitalised on the openness to ask questions. "Who is this man Bull you introduced me to just now?" "Bull, is of extreme reliable character and has an enviable reputation in a fight, especially in defence of our good Queen. He is what we call our 'backup in times of need'. If you are in trouble or need help, Bull and his compatriots will be there." 'That's fine," Joshua says, "but how do we communicate if we need to get word to you?"

"Yes of course, good question. I have a house at 10 Lemon Street in Truro, you can always leave a message there. If not, find Little George who is usually found at the Blue Anchor working both for the Landlord and on my behalf." "By the way, who is Little George?" "Little George and his not much younger sister Christine, entered into a pauper's house five years ago and three years before that their Father died at sea fighting the Spaniards. When their Mother passed away it was when I saw them begging in the streets. I could see they were decent and very polite children and immediately took a shine to them both. I took over parental rights to get them out of the pauper's house, made them comfortable in mine, and looked after them ever since. Christine works and has a room at the Turks Head in Penzance, where you and Rebecca will be getting a room."

Joshua continued his questioning "Henry, may I ask what is the setup, I mean who are you all?" Henry smiled nicely and understood the question completely. "As you know we are now called Great Britain. This is a great Country but being great, we relish and thrive on information. George Kernow is responsible for the complete South West internal security and reports into London direct. As you know, I was like your Father and Jeanne, Rebecca's Mother, doing the frontline stuff. After that George Kernow asked me a while ago if I would manage Cornwall and come away from frontal activity. I agreed and was asked to handle three cells, one of them being you and Rebecca. I also have some support operators, loyal to the Crown, who help in the field, as and when required, one of them being Bull whom you have just met."

"Thank you Henry, now it's all starting to fall into place. And, what about the tunnels?" he asked. "The tunnels are a long standing asset to our means of success. There are many more around Cornwall and only known to us. As time goes on, you will know more of them." "Has Rebecca a tunnel?" "No, Marazion bay is too busy, we like secluded coves like Gunwalloe. Any more questions Joshua?"

Joshua continued, "I have loads more Henry but one which keeps coming to the forefront and that is, what if we get caught or injure someone or even kill anyone in our work?" Hosking's nodded, he understood where Joshua was coming from. "The Cornwall justices are aware of our presence in only the vaguest of forms, in other words, they know we exist for the benefit of safety to the County and Country but have no idea how or who. Should you or Rebecca maim or kill anyone whilst working, it's as if you were back in the Navy. The only difference this time is, it must be formally asked by the injured party or, by proxy if death occurs, which rarely occurs."

Henry continued, "We well understand this may come to pass and if it does, we will support you both. We will have a discussion to find out what happened and get on with things. However, if you are caught doing things which are illegal but feel must be done to gain the information, be conscious the local Constables are not aware of you or your work. Should you be caught and cannot get out of it then you must do what you have to do."

"I understand," Joshua said then carried on, "one last question Henry I promise, what of this rolling fingers thing I saw from you and Rebecca?" Henry burst out with a laugh. "That, that was brought in three months ago on the advice of someone in

London, something to do with secretly knowing each other. We tried it but made a decision yesterday to throw it out as it's just too Walsingham and doesn't work, and furthermore, in Cornwall we either very much know each other or we don't. So if anyone does it, as from this moment on, I would run."

With that they chatted idly about the weather and then parted. Joshua needed to get back to Rebecca and explain what he had learnt and deliver her money purse.

Chapter 8

Joshua arrived back at Rebecca's cottage mid to late afternoon and once he had looked after Harry, who he thought had done really well apart from his boyish behaviour with Suzy, went in to the Cottage only to find that Rebecca wasn't at home.

The cottage looked really clean and walking on through he entered his bedroom and noticed that the gear from the scrub chamber had been laid out across the bed, floor and even in the cupboard, all in an orderly fashion. He went into Rebecca's room and found her things also laid out in the same way. He decided to make a cup of tea, have a smoke and sit and wait by the fire, which was still alight, and only needed a couple of logs to flare it up.

It was thirty minutes or so when he heard the door and Rebecca walked in offering a nice "Hello Joshua, I wasn't expecting you back for quite a while, did everything go well?" "I didn't get to Helston as we planned, shall I make you a cup of tea and explain all?" "Thank you, that would be nice," she replied. Making another cup of tea Joshua explained everything in full detail on what had happened and handed over her purse of fifty pound coins.

"I'm glad," she said, "it reassures me that Henry and George Kernow are who they say they are and that we are operating within a team, albeit a very small and quiet team across Cornwall. It makes me feel part of something, as over the last couple of years I have been quite lost as to what to do with my life. How about you Joshua, how do you feel?" "I feel the same, I also have been at a loss of what to do with mine."

With that Rebecca explained where she had been as though he needed to know, which to be truthful, he was curious on where she had been. In truth she had gone to the small village a couple of miles away to fetch milk and bread for supper and breakfast for them both.

Rebecca continued, "By the way I found some more interesting things in the scrub chamber like a smaller lighter pistol with a holder that will fit into the small of my back rather than my thigh." "That's a pity' Joshua said cheekily with a grin, at which Rebecca laughed.

"Also, I found strange intertwined under garments with yards of material, maps, a compass and curiously an outfit for a man that would fit me. I instantly tried them on and with my hair up, hat pulled down and thought, with a bad light, I could quite easily pass as a man which we may find useful Joshua, what say you?" Joshua said, 'yes, anything that can give us an edge, no matter what, is good."

"Rebecca, you are really quite something" he said in a proud way. "Thank you Joshua, I feel my Mother's streak of adventure is coming through me."

With that they decided to pack the things they needed in to the luggage cases, ready for loading in to the carriage gig, ready for the morning off. Rebecca suggested Joshua sort Harry and Lilly, her mare out, ready for the morning trip to Penzance. They thought it best to bring Lilly with them as an extra means of transport if required.

Once everything was completed and they were happy they had all the things relevant, they sat down to discuss and agree their cover story. They met in Exeter three years ago at a dinner party whilst Rebecca was working in Plymouth and Joshua working in Bristol.

It was through a Charity, they both supported for ex-Navy personnel, that guided them together. Also finding out that being both Cornish was another sign. They kept in touch and met as frequent as they could and decided to marry only a few weeks ago in Exeter where they first met.

As their parents lived in Cornwall they decided to carry on tradition, hence their first vacation of being man and wife would be by the sea. Rebecca reminded him that knowing the Cornish, they will delve and pry further as to where our parents lived and if we stutter or stumble in reply they will know something is not stacking up. Therefore, they weighed things up and agreed they will mix truth with lies and except that their parents did indeed live here in this cottage and Joshua's at Gunwalloe and came down often to stay with them. However, as they have passed to the Lord they now manage the cottages between them as best they can until such time as they know exactly what they want.

As they had both pretty much kept themselves to themselves, people in their respective areas would know them by sight but would not really know the full details of their lives and therefore, the scenario they have created would probably pass any basic scrutiny.

However, they changed the traditional bit to being their first real time away together by the sea, to having a break from managing both the cottages. It didn't seem so cavalier, more boringly unadventurous which, sounded good to them as if they were bored then it will bore the inquisitor even more.

They went on discussing their likes and dislikes and the reason they are not in full work at the moment, which was agreed due to the monies left to them in their parents will.

One thing they left out of the cases were the weapons needed. Joshua knew how his pistol worked and thought it wise to question Rebecca about her new pistol and had she tested it yet. "I have only put it around me for fitting purposes but no I have not fired it yet." Joshua felt the risk of her not practicing was too much of an unknown certainty and said "we need to be sure Rebecca" and as it wasn't too late they got the pistol and cotton charges with ball and went out back as far away as they could to quickly practice. Rebecca did well and both pistol and loading went smoothly as with the tree she hit on her second attempt.

Going back into the warm the only thing to be done was to try on those protective under shirts and shifts. Joshua took off his tunic and under vests so he was then bare chested. Rebecca was looking at him as if it was natural for a man stripping off in her cottage. She passed him the protective vest and he awkwardly tried to put it over his head. Rebecca jumped up laughing and came to his rescue. "Maybe if you undid the shoulder straps it would be easier Joshua?"

Once the vest was on and the straps tied down it fitted him quite snugly without much weight at all. The protective plates were over the heart, each side of the kidneys and in the back behind the heart. "Now it's your turn." Rebecca got up and went into her bedroom and said, "I will be two minutes."

She came out with the vest over another cotton vest. "I put an under vest on as the metal plates rub a little under the heart side but what do you think?" She done a little twirl and Joshua could see the plates were all in the right places and settled, except the front one which was protruding slightly, due to her bosoms being, he believed, more firm. He tried to say something about this but started to go a little red when Rebecca said, "I know Joshua, we need to bend the metal slightly in the front to blend in with my body but other than that it feels like a garment I could wear without too much fuss."

So with the protective vests eventually sorted and mended accordingly, they both sat down each with a large glass of brandy and Joshua lit his pipe.

The morning was fresh and they arrived at the Turks Head in Penzance around midday being met by Little George and his younger sister Christine. They had been waiting for them. Little George introduced his sister who they found to be delightful and liked her instantly. Being at the end of the street, The Turks Head had good stabling facilities to the side of its buildings. Christine showed Rebecca to their room while Little George and Joshua did the stabling and the transfer of their belongings. They agreed to meet the girls in the bar area when they had finished.

The room was on the first floor to the side and away back from the front of the Inn and its main drinking area. On entering they found a cosy main room, warm with fire already lit, a little wash basin area and one bedroom. The main room had one window overlooking the stable yard with a small waste land in between. At the bottom of the stairs heading away from the bar and towards the main stores, was a locked back door.

Little George had selected their room well, knowing they would need access and exits without being seen anytime through the day or night. Joshua said, "well done Little George and thank you, you have chosen well." "My pleasure Mr Pendragon, Oh and by the way here is a duplicate key for the back door." Joshua thought for a young lad he is very bright and a good asset to have.

They then both went to meet Rebecca and Christine but only found Rebecca sitting at a table close to the large open fire. The bar was quite busy with a few men getting jolly. "I'm glad you've arrived as I was being eyed up by a couple of men over there," she said. "That's because you're very pretty Rebecca."

"That may or may not be the case Joshua, or it could be, I am the only woman in here, which is more likely."

Joshua asked where Christine was and advised that she had to get back to work which somehow he thought a prudent move from this young girl. Little George did not sit down and Joshua could feel him getting slightly anxious when he said, "Would you excuse me, as I also have work to attend?" "Before you leave Little George, how long are you staying at the Turks?" "Until tomorrow, my sister and I are to head for Truro to be with Mr Hosking for a couple of days. However, we are to return here after and assist my sister for a short while in helping you and Ms Pendarve. I am to share lodgings with her here in the Inn and if necessary work alongside her, which will benefit the landlord Mr Rosevear." On hearing this, Joshua asked if they both could come to their room early this evening.

Joshua and Rebecca had drinks served and a lovely mutton stew. The men at the bar were drinking further and getting rowdy with song. Joshua suggested they should get their coats and start the process of their mission in getting to know the layout of Penzance and also to practice memory skills of everything they see or notice and anything which seems untoward. "Are we to go as husband and wife or would you like me to dress as a man?" Rebecca said with a smile. Joshua couldn't tell if that was a real question or a subtle way of saying calm down but he replied, "Husband and wife."

They drank up and went to fetch their warm clothing from their room before this first part out together. Joshua thought it funny that when he was in the Navy, how easy it was to say there is the enemy, this is how we fight, this is how we fire our guns and these are our tactics. However, seeking out an enemy of sleepers completely embedded into a civilian population is a different ball game. He had never done this type of work before and neither had Rebecca so he was taking things seriously. Walking arm in arm with Rebecca like two newlyweds, felt very interesting to Joshua and he thought anyone who was watching would be totally unaware that they were not. Appearances can be very fooling he thought.

Rebecca played the part like an experienced actress on the stage. He chatted to Rebecca on what he was thinking and how easy it was to see the enemy when at war when he was in the services. She replied, "yes I can understand that, I am also at a loss on what we are looking for and how we find whatever we are searching, maybe we need to sit down and start working things out and maybe put ourselves in the enemy's position and work from there."

Rebecca was right. "Alright," Joshua said, that sounds a really good idea, let's walk around a little more and get the layout of the town, clear our heads and then go back to the inn for tea."

The town itself was a bustling place as was the quay area; it only started drifting into a more peaceful place the further out you went. The main industry being fishing and a port for anything else you care to name. Unlike Truro, which seems prosperous and fine, Penzance was a working town and the sea was a major player in the town's life. Again, unlike Truro, which now had tea shops as the main sort of refreshment, around here was beer and brandy served in busy inns and, Penzance seemed full of them.

However, there were still some lovely spots which they could sit and watch the world go by. Joshua thought the place itself had around two to three thousand people with about three to four hundred houses and cottages, in all sorts of shapes and sizes and most, in small streets of tightly packed rows. 'Hmmm' he thought, 'there is no rhyme or reason to any of this, just a busy town trying to grow'. But one thing he did notice, there was a roguish element.

Getting back to the Inn, they were greeted on the way in by a well-dressed but slippery looking man. "Good afternoon Mr & Mrs Pendragon, I hope your room is satisfactory?" "Very nice, thank you," Rebecca said, "are you the Landlord?" "Yes, Mr Rosevear, he said, at your service. I am just on my way out but my wife is serving, if you require anything."

Joshua said, "We are off to our room but may come down this evening for refreshment." "Good, Rosevear replied, "then we may see you both later, have a good afternoon."

"I do not trust this Mr Rosevear at all" Rebecca said, as they closed the door to their room. "I tend to agree" Joshua replied, "There is something not quite right about his manner, however, maybe we are a being a little too sensitive at the moment." "Joshua, we need to be sensitive and use all our skills including spiritual and inner feelings if necessary, do you not agree?"

"Yes," he responded, "I agree Rebecca we can question him a little further this evening and discuss our thoughts again once we have returned here."

They also agreed they would like to ask Little George and Christine a few questions so Joshua went out to find them. He found them cleaning the yard and Little George suggested they should be with them within the hour, when they had finished their chores.

Joshua went back to the room, stoked the fire and put some water on the boil to make some tea for them all. Rebecca was unpacking and organising the bedroom as she felt it was needed. Joshua sat by the fire and let his brain wonder then cross wonder and basically came out with a mix of things no better off than he started. He needed to get a grip on this and start focusing.

It wasn't long before Rebecca joined him. Joshua asked if she had any ideas about finding these sleepers and the traitor. "Not really Joshua, and to be honest I am looking and trusting you to lead us. Don't get me wrong Joshua, if I feel that your decisions are questionable, then I will question." Somehow Joshua felt relieved as his tenderness and protectiveness towards Rebecca was blurring his decision making, and they badly needed direction. However, to meet Rebecca half way and to ease his conscience he said, "Rebecca, your right to question, really is important to me, especially in these circumstances; we are amateurs so I feel we must tread carefully."

With that they went over what they knew, which wasn't a lot. They agreed there was only three people they could trust, being Henry Hosking, Little George and his younger sister Christine. The vague information from Mr George Kernow suggested that the unknown families are in Newlyn or Mousehole, not Penzance where they were. Also, they didn't trust this Mr Rosevear, their Landlord.

There was a knock on the door and Little George and Christine entered and were welcomed with tea and a soft seat. Rebecca went first with questions to Christine on how she knew Mr Henry Hosking. Her reply mirrored that of Hosking's evaluation. Rebecca went on and further asked why she was working in the Turks Head in Penzance, not some place closer to Helston.

Little George interrupted and replied on Christine's behalf. "My sister and I work and are boarded in this inn as well as the Blue Anchor in Helston. Our guardian Mr Hosking explained to us that in his work, information is very important to him and asked us both, if we were willing to be his eyes and ears in two places where drink loosens the tongue. Christine and I discussed it and due to Mr Hosking's kindness, after our Mother passed to the Lord, we agreed."

"How old are you both?" Joshua asked. Little George said, "fourteen" and Christine said, "twelve nearly thirteen." "Do you enjoy what you do?" They looked at Joshua strangely, then Christine replied, "Mr Pendragon, we are not silly children and if it wasn't for Mr Hosking's offer of us being useful, with lodgings and food included, would still be begging. So whether we enjoy it or not we had no other choice. However, to answer truthfully, I would prefer to be at school or an apprentice in sewing and I know my Brother Little George would like to be an apprentice in the stables or Blacksmiths, anything to do with horses."

Joshua was silently pleased that this little girl was like her brother, Little George, they both had that grit when needed. Rebecca asked them about Mr Rosevear, the Landlord, and what they thought of him. Little George said, "We do not like him or trust him but Mr Hosking says he is valuable to him and we must stay close as we can without endangering ourselves."

Joshua continued, "In that case, what do you think of us?" Christine immediately responded and said, "we find you both very favourable." Little George echoed by saying 'Hear Hear." "And what do you know of our visiting Penzance?" Christine said, "We do not ask, only that Mr Hosking has said that you are both to be trusted, are loyal friends and we are to help in any way we can but, we must keep Mr Hosking informed."

"In that case," Joshua said, "I must tell you that we feel we have made a mistake coming here to the Turks Head and must head further into the Newlyn, Mousehole area. We have decided that we will be leaving as soon as we can, probably in a couple of days. We may possibly require some help while we are there. Would, one of you be able to do this and maybe act as a son or daughter or something?" Little George looked at

Christine and said, "Yes of course, however, we will have to explain to Mr Hosking tomorrow of your intentions."

Rebecca didn't say anything about Joshua's explanation about their planned move so he took that as a good decision made. With that Joshua got up and made them another brew of tea and lit his pipe.

When Little George and Christine left the room, Rebecca said She was tired and wanted to lie down for an hour. Joshua decided to go and check on Harry and Lilly and go for a walk around the town again. He next wanted to go to the quay and see and feel what was happening. He sat on an old large piece of granite seating which he presumed was meant to be some kind of artistic design, in the so called art world.

The only ships in the quay were various fishing ones. It seems the only activity here were the pubs behind him with the sailors and fishermen enjoying themselves. He got out his telescope and scanned the bay ahead, not really looking for anything in particular and found nothing, as all was quiet. With that he strolled back to the inn and to Rebecca, thinking of their meeting this evening with Mr Rosevear.

Rebecca was already awake and moving stuff about as only women can do. "How's the town?" she asked. "Quiet and empty, except in the public houses," he said. "You look cold; I will boil us some water for a nice hot cup of tea." "Thank you Rebecca, that would be very welcome."

Once rested it was nearing time to go down stairs to eat and drink and meet the landlord. Rebecca was ready and looked fine. However, Joshua needed to change his shirt and asked if all was clear and ready in the bedrooms, in which Rebecca replied "Yes the bedroom is ready and all your belongings are laid out on the far side of the room." The bedroom was indeed prepared and he must admit, Rebecca is well organised.

He found the shirt easily and put it over his protective vest which he was now getting used to. He noticed that Rebecca had put a big wooden divider in the bed which he could only inwardly chuckle at, 'she thinks of everything this one'. Coming back out of the bedroom he asked, "Rebecca, you are wearing your protective under vest?" "Yes Joshua, we agreed that we would always wear it, thank you for asking."

Before they left to go downstairs they looked at each other and Rebecca said, "Remember Joshua, we don't trust this man, or the people here so let's be on our guard." Joshua nodded and said "we are also husband and wife."

Mr Rosevear couldn't have been more inviting, reserving a nice table by the fire away from the other drinkers. Christine came across with a pewter of cider and bade them good evening and mentioned that Little George was putting Harry and Lilly down for the night.

On chatting about nothing, a lady came across with two plates of lamb and roasted potatoes and introduced herself as Mrs Rosevear and said, "should you need anything, just holla"

Joshua's initial gut feeling was, she was a likeable good woman blinded on working hard and, whatever is going on outside in the real world, including her own husband's interests, is of no interest to her. They also realised that the Rosevear's had a young daughter about Christine's age who was working hard cleaning the tables and serving the meals.

Viewing the customers around them they noticed several small parties all chatting or whispering then laughing loud and ordering more drinks. This very much reminded Joshua of when he was in the service going abroad with his mates to fight the French or the Spanish or indeed any other country we had an argument with. But that was then and this is now.

They ordered another jug of cider and even started to enjoy the atmosphere. Someone brought out a harmonica and a fiddle and started playing tunes and people started joining in the songs. Joshua looked at Rebecca expecting some sort of unhappy face and told to go home to their room. Instead she just smiled and started tapping her feet and started humming along with them. 'Is it me', he thought.

It wasn't long before Mr Rosevear came over sat down with them and immediately started asking questions, such as how was the meal, how is the room, how long have you been married, what was Rebecca's maiden name, where do you live etc. Both answered alternatively as practised and it sounded good, and it sounded real.

However, one question which they hadn't practised was "So how do know Christine and Little George?" Rebecca, to her credit and calmness, responded straight away with, "Oh we were friends of their Mother's family, such a pity, lovely children." "How do you know them Mr Rosevear" she rebuffed. "Hmmm," he said, "I know their guardian and help them out as best I can." "That's a really lovely thing to do Mr Rosevear you are good man," she replied with sweetness. Not knowing where they were going with this, Joshua decided to ask how long he has been the Landlord here. "Nine years, we moved in January 1st 1699."

"Why do you ask?" "No particular reason just thought I would ask as you seem to have a healthy amount of clients." "Hmmm yes we do, they seem to like my beer and my wife's cooking."

"Joshua," Rebecca butted in, "Stop asking silly questions and let's have another drink, I'm enjoying the singing, we are on holiday you know." She then leant across and kissed him on the cheek, turned her head towards Rosevear and rolled her eyes. He laughed and hollered to his wife who brought another jug across. "I'll leave you two love birds alone, enjoy the evening," he then got up and went behind the bar with his wife.

With more songs, drink and merriment, Rebecca turned to Joshua and said, "Joshua I don't feel very well, would you please escort me to our room." Joshua was just getting into it, taking Rebecca's lead in smiling and singing. "What's wrong," he asked. "I think I am drunk and I need to be sick." And on that they retreated to their room, worse for wear, but having achieved their aim in not saying anything untoward and no curiosity laid to them, other than two newlyweds having some fun.

Joshua let Rebecca be sick in the bed pot and then rolled her into bed fully clothed apart from taking off her laced boots. She was out like a candle light. He then went down to the privy and emptied the pot and washed it out. On coming back in from the backyard he bumped into Little George. "Hi Little George," he said. "Good evening Mr Pendragon, is everything alright?" "Yes, thank you Little George, Ms Pendarve, I mean Mrs Pendragon has had a little too much cider for her own good and has been ill." Little George, although young, identified Joshua's error but chose to say nothing and simply said. "I am sorry to hear that Mr Pendragon; I hope Mrs Pendragon gets well soon." 'What a quick intelligent young man' Joshua thought.

Joshua went back to their room and decided to get dressed ready for bed. On checking Rebecca, and due to that blasted big wooden bed divider, had to walk back around his side to climb in.

With candles out, the room was very dark, he could hear Rebecca's quiet breathing which sounded reassuring and somehow really nice. Joshua hadn't slept with anyone for many years and definitely not a drunken woman. That made him smile. He leaned back and put his arms behind his head and started thinking. Rebecca got him out of a little hole tonight and he must remember to say thank you for her quick wit.

Chapter 9

"Ashley we are not going to get into trouble, are we?" "Of course not woman, how can we when we are doing the Lords work." "I was just thinking that was all, you know how I fret and worry." "My dear all will be well, we have assurances that no harm will be done and that by assisting our friends back to the right way, is a good thing to do. What you say woman?" "Yes of course Ashley," she said and then went back into the kitchen. He shouted, "They will be here soon, make ready the refreshments and the ales and make sure the brandy is to serve." Nothing came back but he assured himself that she had heard. He hadn't told her about the five hundred pounds and a small settlement all of his own, as reward for his gallant work in letting his farm at Sennon be the pivot of their plans, for a successful operation.

Pierre was getting nervous as he disliked having to go into the frontline, but he had no other choice. Philip Albret, his master, would not take failure at any excuse and he needed to get his message across and find out first-hand what the holdup is. The three-gun sloop had sailed round the coast off Lands' End and was now laid off at Sennon. The ship's Captain was very able and like Pierre, won't take chances when he doesn't have to. Therefore, he laid back the ship a little too much from the shore for Pierre's liking but would not budge on getting any closer, leaving that to the small rowing boat crew having to row a little more.

Pierre was in the rowing boat with a devout priest of the right way and had briefed him exactly what he wanted to happen. Two other men were rowing hard and two marines with muskets were also in the boat, just in case. When Pierre did something, he did it right and took precautions. He had learnt the hard way.

Whilst Pierre was coming from the sea, his team of sleepers were coming in land from the west. He was looking forward to seeing them again and praise their courage, especially Zoe. She was a fine woman he thought and one day she would be his. As for the other two, Jacques and Pascal, well they need a kick up the arse. The meeting was arranged for midnight at the Farm.

"Why is this meeting necessary?" asked Pascal, in English. "Because that was what the message said," replied Zoe, also in English. They were disciplined in their speech, when in England, they spoke English, when in France, they spoke French. Zoe and Pascal lived in a cottage in Mousehole, which they had only recently moved to, appearing as Brother and Sister and were awaiting Jacques to come so they could all ride together to Sennon. Jacques, on the other hand, had taken residence in Penzance and lived alone as this gave him freedom to move about without notice to anyone. When Jacques finally appeared they all rode at pace to the rendezvous at Sennon.

Ashley Ward looked at the clock then went outside to give the signal. Both parties were waiting in their respective places. Zoe, Pascal and Jacques were in the woods to the east. Pierre

Bouchier, Priest and marines were on the dunes below, by the sea. On seeing the signal for the 'all clear' both parties made their way forward and entered the farm from their opposite sides. Ashley Ward greeted them as they came into the Farm House and escorted them to the large room with a roaring fire and cool refreshments. The two marines stayed outside on guard.

On seeing the Priest, Ashley knelt down and kissed his hand and said, "thank you for coming Father, thank you." Mrs Ward was not to be seen.

This was the first time all had been together and everyone was looking at everyone else, but really not knowing what to say. Pierre took the lead. "Thank you all for coming, we will all take Mass and then I will talk to you individually, as instructed by my superiors. Mr Ward, would your wife like to join us for the Mass," Pierre asked. "Thank you Mr Bouchier I am sure she would be delighted; thank you so much, we have waited for this for so long."

With that, Ashley Ward led them all to a private underground chamber. When the service was over Pierre took Mrs Ward to one side and thanked her profusely for her hospitality and friendship towards the right way, and the strength she gives the Cornish people. "Thank you" she replied. "Now Mrs Ward," he continued, "we have some business to attend, so may I ask you to tend to my friends while I discuss things in the large room with that lovely fire?" "Yes of course" she replied.

On settling down in the arm chair, Zoe was the first to enter. He immediately got up and kissed her on both cheeks. He wanted to do more. "Sit down Zoe, how are you?" "Well that depends on how you look at things Pierre," she replied. "If you mean how the project is going, I would say slowly. If you asked have we have embedded ourselves in the community, I would say excellent." "Good Zoe, Good" he said. "And what of the project, why is it going slowly?" "Pierre you know I am not responsible for the project's success or what it completely entails, only to act as cover and use my wit and knowledge in helping both Pascal & Jacques achieve theirs." "I understand Zoe; is there anything you need?" "Money as always, Oh and tell that bloody Pascal, we are brother and sister, not husband and bloody wife." Pierre didn't like Pascal and this type of behaviour increased that dislike.

"Zoe, when this is finished you will be rewarded as you know, with your very own holdings of your choice and, I will make sure that you are looked after in every way." "Thank you Pierre, but when will it be finished as I can't hold on much longer here with these savages, who only eat things called pasties and drink bloody cider all day, bloody savages they are." Pierre could not help but chuckle and said "I would say not too long now my dear, just get us to early spring then all will be done and you can return to our lovely France and we can dance forever." Before she could reply Pierre lowered his tone and said, "you do have the poison Zoe?" "Yes I do and will use it on him as ordered when the time comes, as we agreed." "Well done Zoe, now take this purse of one hundred pounds." They got up and he kissed her on the lips. The meeting finished.

He saw Pascal and Jacques together and listened then questioned them thoroughly. They were professional in their own ways. Pascal is a geologist in mining and Jacques was them leader. What really concerned Pierre was timing and the audacious move to another cottage, which could have raised eyebrows in the community and jeopardise cover.

In Pascal's opinion, the move was absolutely crucial to achieve the necessary results, as the mining became impossible due to an unforeseen massive layer of granite. The tunnel direction also needed to be changed and recalculated to exactly match the underground river in accepting the chemical germ correctly. "So are we saying, we are now on course?" "Yes, most definitely," Pascal replied. "Good, I needed to hear that directly from your own lips Pascal."

"Jacques, please tell me why now have you moved to Penzance?" Jacques, replied, "When Zoe and Pascal left the last cottage in the middle of Mousehole and went further north of the town, Penzance becomes a little closer and its bigger population and size offers far more cover for me to move freely. Also, it's a little more direct and quicker to Sennon using the main road." Pierre seemed convinced and responded with a simple "Understood."

"Is there anything you both need?" "Money," they said in unison. With that Pierre handed each a purse of one hundred pounds. Pierre then went on to discuss how and when they are ready to receive shipment of the chemical germ mixed in Brandy Kegs, they must send a message through the same channel as before, and give two weeks' notice in preparation. "By the way Jacques, is this farm under Ashley Ward, still the best place to receive this chemical consignment?" "Good question Pierre, I have been looking at alternative places for this drop and thought I found one at the Turks Head and am still working on it."

Jacques continued, "The owner has smuggled before and is still doing it but whether he can take a hundred barrels cleanly and move them on quickly without risk from the authorities, I would say I am not sure, if he can, then the Turks Head would be ideal. If I feel he cannot, then the Farm would be best. Either way, I will get word to you once I have my conclusions."

Pierre got up and whilst shaking their hands said, "Thank you both, you are very brave men and doing your Country of France proud, your rewards will be waiting when the project is completed and successful, may God be with you." The meeting finished.

Pierre went to find Ashley, who all this time had been with the priest, and once he found him made sure he went over the top in thanking him for his duty to the Lord. "We will be in touch soon with the cargo required to spread the word and thank you again Mr Ward, is there anything you need?" "I would like to buy some pigs for the farm" he said with a wink. Pierre dipped into his pocket and handed over the purse of a hundred pounds saying, "I trust this may go some way to help?"

Pierre, the Priest and the guarding marines then set off to the boat waiting at the sea edge for their voyage back to Brest.

Chapter 10

The night passed quietly and Joshua slept well, maybe the drink helped. As he leaned over the bed divider, he noted that Rebecca was already up and noted her side of the bed was all neat and tidy.

Rebecca was in the arm chair with the fire alight and was looking refreshed he thought. "Good morning," he said. "Good morning Joshua, the fire's aglow and the water is boiled," she replied. "Lovely, thank you Rebecca, what a beautiful way to start the day, how are you feeling?" "Well, I have felt better that's for sure but the sleep was good and I have had some tea and am feeling much better, thank you."

Once settled in their seats and watching the morning fire, Joshua said "I think I owe you a big thank you for getting Mr Rosevear off my back last night." "I had to do something Joshua and although it made me ill in the night I was quite enjoying myself, seriously though, Mr Rosevear was probing for information and I could sense something was not right."

They discussed last night in a little more detail and apart from a few ominous characters in the bar and Mr Rosevear's questioning nothing really was out of place. However, they agreed that moving away to Newlyn or Mousehole as quickly as possible was the right thing to do.

They decided to stay until Little George and Christine returned and, until then, keep themselves to themselves except for eating in the bar area. They practised with their flintlocks with dry loading and unloading. Joshua also wanted to make sure that Rebecca was comfortable wearing it in the small of her back and started helping her adjust the straps so she could take out and replace easily without hindrance. The daggers were also practised and it was agreed that Rebecca's be strapped to her lower left leg, as she is left handed and with her dress or skirt would cover all.

Once lunch was taken in the bar, they walked the town in a leisurely style. They were wrapped up well and enjoyed the walk and fresh air. However, unlike before, when a walk was a walk, they now started taking everything in and learning what they had seen, what was fine and what was slightly not. Joshua found this to be light hearted fun but it was good training and Rebecca bought into it as well.

The day passed rather quickly and after dinner, which they shared with a small diluted cider, they went back to their room with a bottle of brandy. Mr Rosevear was not there and so they were served by his wife and daughter. They asked Mrs Rosevear about the whereabouts' of her husband and she said, "talking and drinking with his so called friends at the Fisherman's Inn, as he always does on this evening, he will be back in a while."

Joshua felt an inner shudder and didn't like it and had learnt that anything, anything that just doesn't fit, alarm bells start ringing inside him. Once in their room he shared his gut feeling with Rebecca who, bless her, said, "Joshua I agree it didn't and doesn't feel right, I feel that something is going to happen to us, what do you suggest?"

"Discretion is best part of valour, I say we pack up and get out of here quickly and quietly and leave through the back door which I have a key, thanks to Little George." "Where do you suggest we go." "I do not know Penzance well enough, so I say we head for the forest and sleep outdoors tonight." "But its bloody freezing Joshua!" "Yes, I know, we can take the warm blankets we have here and with our other stuff we will be safe, rather than wait here any longer unknowing our fate. We can then assess the situation in the morning, what say you Rebecca?" "I say let's get on with it."

They packed quickly and quietly, luckily having the room at the farthest end of the Inn gave them an exit to the stable yard without distracting anyone. While Rebecca was finishing off, Joshua went to get their carriage ready and Harry and Lilly sorted. While he was at it, he took as much horse feed as he could carry.

Rebecca came down wearing double full clothing, looking like a puffin that has eaten too much. "Don't laugh Joshua because I am not going to get cold for anyone, especially the likes of Mr bloody Rosevear." Joshua did as he was told and hurried back to the room to get the remaining bits and pieces. Once satisfied they had everything, he glanced around the room just in case. He decided to lock the door and take the key.

With Rebecca safely in the gig with all their belongings, he gave a gentle tap of the reins sounding a quiet shhhhh, which Harry seemed to know means tread softly and they quietly left the inn. On studying the map beforehand, his decision was to head west by northwest towards the cross junction. Once there Sennon will be due west and Helston due east. Going south cuts down to Newlyn and North to the safety of the forests.

Mr Rosevear was indeed at the Fisherman's Inn with a belly full of beer and mouthing off about his beloved Turks Head and only the best in society stay there, unlike this place, which is the pits. The Landlord and fellow drinkers were all loudly agreeing with tongues in cheeks and laughing, especially two of them. Quietly through all the loud banter, Rosevear gestured the Landlord to come closer and then whispered in his ear, suggesting a young couple who had just booked in his place, had money and informed him of the room number. During the agreed hand shake, Rosevear slid the back door key into his hand, he drunk up and left.

The Landlord took the key and after a quiet chat handed it over to one of the two men at the bar. As he was just about to take it, the Landlord held back and said quietly but assertively, "fifty, fifty?" The man nodded, took the key and put it in his pocket. The Landlord then gave them more free drinks in anticipation of his cut.

Jacques, a tall able looking man sitting quietly in the corner, was watching and listening to all what was going on but said nothing. He always drinks cognac and lives alone as this gave him freedom, which he likes. He doesn't mix, just gets on with things and comes in when he wants and leaves when he wants, no time table. He causes no trouble but people feel he is capable so simply leave him alone, apart from a nod here and there.

After an hour or so the two men at the bar left the Inn, got their burglary tools, including iron bar and daggers and headed for the back stable yard of the Turks Head. "Bloody fool that Rosevear, thinks he owns the place," one said to the other. "He didn't say much about his smuggling mates though, did he," the other responded.

The key went smoothly in the back door and turned without a hitch. The men looked at each and smiled. They went upstairs to the room furthest from the main entrance. Ever so gently and quietly they picked the lock knowing at this time of night the lady and gentlemen would be in the back bedroom and wouldn't hear them until it was too late. The lock clicked open and they entered. The main room was empty, as thought, so they moved over to the bedroom door but this was already open and again nobody was inside. Empty, bloody empty, 'That bloody Rosevear!'

Rebecca and Joshua got to the main road. It was now past midnight and really cold. They saw the forest over the other side but couldn't find an entry point wide enough for the gig, so they carried on towards Sennon and just before the road branches off south west to Newlyn, saw a good enough but tight entrance to the woods.

Joshua urged Harry onwards, excepting the fact it was dark but the clear night allowed visibility albeit not full. Harry pushed forward through the woods keeping centre of the track as best he could and Lilly followed obediently.

"This should do Rebecca." Rebecca didn't say anything but Joshua felt she realised and understood there was nothing else they could have done and although cold, they were alive and far away from the danger they both felt at the Turks Head.

"If you would like to unpack the warm gear, I will get a fire lit and see to Harry and Lilly," he said. Joshua didn't feel they were being hunted, more getting out of the danger zone so going covert tonight without warmth was just not worthwhile. Rebecca replied, "I will try and make some sort of cushioning for sleeping." They both got on with it and after a few swearing words got themselves sorted. Joshua said "as we are newlyweds, we have a great excuse should we be found, in that we are exploring the wilderness of love." Rebecca replied, "As long as I am warm, I don't care what excuse we use but the tale sounds plausible to me."

The fire was small but done its job and Rebecca declared the bed was ready. Around the fire and listening to the woods all around them, it was a very earthy feeling. In other circumstances, Joshua would think it would be quite romantic. Rebecca said, "Joshua do you have that brandy bottle?" With that they both had a good couple of nips and once warmed inside, decided to retire to the so-called bed of warmth.

When Rebecca woke, they were huddled together like bear cubs. Without a word, she unfurled herself and got up. It was early and very cold but thankfully dry. Joshua also started to wake and got on his elbows to look around when he saw Rebecca walking away past the trees. With a smile on his face, he got up and checked the horses and gig.

On her return Joshua announced "Morning Rebecca, sleep well?" "Good morning Joshua, let's put it this way, I have slept better and a lot warmer but I must say I feel a lot less anxious than last night."

"I also," Joshua said, "Shall we freshen up and get dressed as best we can and I will relight the fire, so we can then consider our next move?" "Sounds good," she replied.

Although they had nothing to eat or drink they sat by the fire warming themselves and with minds now coming alert Joshua began, "I feel this thing we are on Rebecca, is just starting and we need to get closer to find our enemies. Therefore, I think we have to go into the belly of the beast and with the vaguest of information we have and supplied to us, I still don't quite know whether that is Newlyn, Sennon or somewhere else."

Rebecca answered, "George Kernow mentioned Newlyn and Sennon and Mousehole so let's concentrate on these for now. Like you, I thought we could move to and fro from the Turks but even if we could, I now realise we wouldn't gain the information we require and so I agree we need to get closer." Rebecca continued, "I have also been thinking that if we are to find these so called sleepers, we must work smart rather than brawn. What I am trying to say is that if these people have embedded themselves into the community then we must play that game as well. The only thing we don't have on our side is time." "I'm impressed," he replied, "any suggestions?"

She replied, "Every time I come up with something I imagine may work, an obstacle blocks that idea out, so no, I haven't any suggestions at the moment on how to progress, other than try to play their game better."

"So," he said, "What we need is a way to mingle with the local people, ask questions without raising suspicion and when we have the required information we engage the enemy." "I agree with the first two bits" she replied, "but as to how to engage the enemy, I think we should wait until we achieve phase one and two." "Rebecca are you sure you were not in the Army or Navy?"

"Joshua, if you asked me to explain about armed conflict and combat in battle, I would not have a clue, as you know, in fact, I don't think I could lift a musket for longer than a couple of seconds. But, this is different, these people are using mind games and tactics to mislead, convince and manipulate Cornish civilians of which I am one." "Point taken," he replied. They then both looked at the fire in silence.

After quite a few minutes, Rebecca broke the ice. "Maybe we should go to Newlyn and get ourselves some accommodation with a view of renting a property on a short term. This will allow us to get in and probe and start asking questions about the town and its people, as any normal people would do if they were thinking of moving into the area." She continued. "We could also enquire into setting up a little business there, so again, not to raise suspicion. In fact, we could say that as newlyweds we are selling our cottages to fund the move as a new opportunity for us both."

"That sounds good to me Rebecca. What sort of business were you thinking?" "Well Newlyn and Penzance are up and coming, the fishing industry is booming in both towns, so money is becoming more free. Don't get me wrong, I fully understand that this is not London but something like sewing or embroidery. I also understand that coffee and tea shops are becoming popular in Truro so why not here. It's not as if we intend to do it long term, just as cover for the very short term."

Joshua suggested that Christine and Little George are important and very useful, as further cover, and could have them employed by us as apprentices in the business sense. "Yes, we could, that would fit' but we would need Henry's approval first as he may have other things he wants them to do," she replied.

Both in agreement Joshua poked the fire and said, "Shall we make haste and find some suitable accommodation then?" "I am ready when you are Joshua but why don't we enjoy the warmth of the fire for a while longer as it's still very early." "Agreed," he replied "I will make ready the horses and gig and pack away our things including our lovely bed and come back."

Whilst Joshua was busy packing it gave Rebecca a chance to think things over. Although she was confident in front of Joshua she herself was really unsure about all of this and where exactly is it leading. Joshua she now knew was a good man albeit a little alien and insecure around women but was sure he could very much hold his own against other men and at that she felt safe.

She also thought that their communication together was equal and nice without fear and a warm little smile came over her. She looked around at the beautiful silent cold forest and suddenly felt a sturdy resolution come over her to protect Joshua and, get the job done.

Joshua returned and said, "All packed and ready" then sat down to warm himself and relax a little. "Are you alright Rebecca, you look deep in thought?" "Yes I'm fine, just thinking about things and how they are going to pan out, I am also starting to enjoy the silence and solitude of these woods."

She continued, "I have also been wondering about Little George and Christine and how we going to get a message to them?" "Yes I have also thought about that and think that sending a message to Christine at the Turks is a little risky so maybe once we are settled, I will gallop over to Penzance in the night and get word with her myself." "That would be good Joshua as I have an endearing feeling for those two."

Joshua also mentioned that early tomorrow they ride out to the Sennon coast as although Newlyn or Mousehole is thought to be where the main problem is, in the back of his mind Sennon kept nagging at him and he felt the need to go there sooner rather than later.

Having got everything ready, Joshua helped Rebecca up and once she was comfortable, decided to take the reins and carefully lead Harry and the gig out of the woods on foot with Lilly bringing up the rear.

Nearing the clearing but still just in the woods, he caught sight of a rider off to his front left galloping fast along the main road about hundred yards from his position. He halted, turned his head towards Rebecca and put his finger to his lips. The rider carried on without noticing, forcing the horse faster. Joshua watched waiting to see which track he would take at the cross junction assuming it would be either Newlyn or Sennon. The rider took Newlyn.

Joshua scratched his head and thought two things, one, it's very early to be riding fast and two, the rider looked familiar not his looks but the manner of posture or something like that.

Waiting a little more, just in case, Joshua pushed forward into the clearing then got up beside Rebecca. "What was all that about she said?" "Don't know, I just feel we need to be careful and something in me decided it was wiser to not be seen. Funny thing though is I thought I recognised the rider in some way." With that he gave Harry a quick tap of the reins and they were off. "Don't forget Joshua, first thing is accommodation and warmth!" He liked her when she was in this jovial authoritative mood.

It was good to be on the move and once at the split, guided Harry left on to Newlyn. About fifteen minutes Newlyn appeared and they slowed to a walking pace. Newlyn itself was definitely a fishing port and the town itself very tightly knit and compacted with granite cottages and houses close together in no specific order. The town is also on a slope heading downwards towards the sea. Newlyn was on the up and other roads and houses were being built. Newlyn and Penzance have never got on but both of them were prospering but, Penzance still act's like the bigger brother.

They were looking for an inn to take them all, including the horses and Little George and Christine, if needed. On seeing a couple of Inns on the way, they both shook their heads knowing they didn't seem to fit what they were looking for. Maybe it should be something in the centre where it was all happening. Getting closer to the quay they came across the Sailormans, which was a large substantial building offering all that they needed.

Although they stopped, they decided it was too close and too busy without any good exits in emergencies so they pushed on. Just as they were coming out of the town heading towards Mousehole they spotted the 'The Anchor Inn.' This seemed the perfect place with a few minutes walking distance into town and good exits away from the town and with stables.

The Landlady seemed very nice and efficient and she had rooms available. Holding hands, they explained their situation and their need to be alone away from the main hub of things. Being a romantic, the Landlady understood without any questions and as Joshua went into the bar area for refreshment, she showed Rebecca the room.

On her return, Rebecca asked for a small cider and they both warmed themselves by the fire. Breakfast had already been served but some bacon and fresh bread rolls were brought out especially for them, which were heartily eaten.

Rebecca had chosen wisely the furthest rooms away, on the first floor, with a back door on the ground floor close by the stairs, very similar to the Turks. She had rented two rooms next to each other with an adjoining door that could be locked. Asking for a fortnightly term, Rebecca paid in advance explaining that her sister maybe joining them. "Sister," Joshua said. "Joshua, we must be cautious and not mention Little George and Christine as we don't know where they are and how they are going to help. The important thing is that we have a room for them and I am sure the Landlady wouldn't mind if it were my sister, brother or nieces." Joshua understood her caution and suggested another cider and then he will organise the horses and start bringing their things in.

Little George and Christine arrived safely at Mr Hosking's house in Truro and were enjoying the couple of days' rest with their master Henry who lived alone except for the housekeeper and maid. His job to the crown didn't much allow a loving relationship but that was his decision and he accepted it. He had only loved one person and that person was gone but he thought about her often which gave him peace. He knew he could never love another as he had loved her but she never knew of his intentions of heart, as he never had the courage to tell her.

His thoughts passed to the last time he had seen her and the three of them together, John Pendragon, Jeanne and himself, trying to get aboard the ship in the early hours of that dark morning with a savage and treacherous wind in the little rowing boat, rowing for their lives.

They had completed their operation in Morlaix and had ridden quickly north to reach the waiting ship in the early hours, arranged by Kernow, where they would sail home safely to Cornwall.

The covert operation had gone well and the mole they went into France to find, and if necessary kill, had been achieved. When they had eventually found this so called patriot, he was in the services of one Philip Albret. John had eventually shot him dead whilst he had held Jeanne in front of them both, with a knife to her throat, threatening to kill her in his bid to escape from us. Although he, himself, had his musket aimed at the traitors head he couldn't fire the shot due to his emotional loving intent for Jeanne, and his aim was shaking terribly. John had no hesitation.

It was only when they entered the open sea on their escape phase and seeing the French Galleon coming around the west coast, they knew they were in trouble. The French knew their jobs well and literally didn't make haste to catch their escape ship, rather they slowed to balance their ships for accuracy of fire. Henry remembers John Pendragon shouting, "They are targeting us for range, hurry up." Attaching the little boat to the ship Henry rushed forward to get up the ladder first to steady it for Jeanne and remembered thinking, at least now they were safe. Then whoosh! Why didn't he let Jeanne go first, was it his cowardice, as if he did, she would be alive now and this guilt he lived with every day, would be no more.

He thought they should never have gone there in the first place. Their job was to protect the Cornish people on Cornish soil, not go in to foreign territory but George Kernow insisted they finish the job, whether it be here or there across the waters.

John Pendragon, his friend, knew he had strong affections for Jeanne but as they were not lovers in the sexual side of things, accepted it as flirtation and said, 'If it doesn't affect their effectiveness to work together he had no problem with it.' Henry also thought that George Kernow may also have known but again, had never said anything.

The problem when Henry reminiscences it becomes deep and thoughtful and when he comes out of it, he honestly can't remember how much time has lapsed. Not only does he miss Jeanne, he also thinks he has some form of shellshock, which was becoming a little known issue with men coming from these battles of warfare.

Henry shook himself out of his thoughts and went down to see if Little George and Christine were up for breakfast. Both were sitting at the table as they said their good mornings. Henry sat down and advised them both, as his wards, that he had indeed thought things through and it was time for them to head back to Penzance and help Rebecca and Joshua.

Little George and Christine had debriefed Henry straight away on their arrival a couple of days ago. Henry had been silent and listened intently to what they had to say and said he would think on it. Little George and Christine, although young in age, accepted this type of working methods as a way of life and knew that utter confidentiality and any intelligence gained must be delivered accurately and without passion. They had learned well.

Henry continued, "You are to be careful with this Rosevear man, do not put yourself in any danger. We understand that he is double crossing for his own gain. Act as brother and sister and nothing more. I want you both now to concentrate on what Rebecca and Joshua are doing. Although they are a little naive they are purposeful and loyal. For your protection my lovely children, I have put our friend on alert that we may be of need of his services in the near future. I also will move into the Blue Anchor tomorrow so you can reach me more speedily. I have a letter for you to give the Landlord there before you push on to Penzance."

Little George and Christine listened intently taking everything in. Henry was extremely proud of them and how they respond with affection and loyalty towards him. However, he was concerned about their tender age but knowing the alternative to helping him in his line of work, although sometimes dangerous, was the work house, and that made him feel better.

After breakfast Little George and Christine got ready with the help of the maid, whom Christine adored. Little George packed himself as he was nearly a man. With the morning moving to lunch time they were ready. The housekeeper had packed them both food and drink.

Although Henry knew that Mr Rosevear would not dare jeopardise the safety of his wards, for if he did, he would hang him, pure and simple, but he is a slippery fellow and could quite easily organise something away from the Inn for something to happen to them, should they overhear or see something they shouldn't.

With Suzy raring to go and saddle bags packed, Henry helped Christine up on her back behind Little George. He handed him a note to give to Joshua and just like he had been trained, tucked it into a slit in the reins. He shook Little George's hand and kissed Christine on the back of her clutched fingers and said, "I am very proud of you both, take care and be wise, you know where I am and see you in a few days, no more."

Pushing Suzy on Little George felt very proud of himself and his sister. Christine looked back and saw the maid waving which she thought was really nice and made her feel warm and wanted.

Once out of Truro they made good to Helston where they stopped outside the Blue Anchor. Christine got Suzy some water and Little George went into the inn giving the Landlord the letter from his master Henry. He thanked Little George and requested that Christine come in too and both have some refreshment.

On leaving, the Landlord said "Make good speed, keep your eyes sharp and do not stop for anyone that you do not know." This they understood as the Penzance road was becoming quite horrid with people getting robbed by highwaymen.

Although Christine was the youngest, she was bright. Holding tightly around Little George's waist with Suzy gentling trotting out of the town, she said, "If I was going to rob someone on the Helston Penzance road I would do it in that horrible dip going through the woods at Porthleven by the brook, I never liked that place and it gives me the creeps." Little George, being the bigger brother squeezed her wrist and said, "yes I agree, I don't like the place either."

A couple of miles out they reached the area where Christine had mentioned. Surrounded by a forest on both sides Little George reined in Suzy and stopped. Christine waited. Suzy hesitated and her ears were alert.

The feeling wouldn't go away, something was not right. He could either hear something or feel something but whatever it was made him nervous. He thought of Henry his master; never ever put yourself at a disadvantage and always listen to your inner feelings.

With that Little George turned his head to Christine and said, "hold on." He turned Suzy sharply right to the north and galloped quickly across the heavy shrubbed area as fast as he could. He was taking a chance and all their safety depended on Suzy dodging scattered granite boulders and pits as best she could. They carried on for over two miles until they came across a narrow clearing heading west towards Penzance, which they took.

Steady galloping brought them eventually into the known village of Breage. Little George was disappointed as he thought they would be further on than that but at least they were safe and far passed the brook which caused so much doubt. Without stopping Little George got back onto the familiar main road. He would remember that de tour route, just in case.

They arrived at the Turks Inn later than anticipated, just after tea and the night was drawing in already. They met Mrs Rosevear who greeted them with kindness and suggested to put away their things and then Christine to help out in the bar area and Little George to help in the stable yard as quickly as they can.

This they did and it was always the same feeling of sadness that they were away from the big open house at Truro and now back in a dark room which was small and just fitted the two beds. But it was clean and they were working for Henry which pleased them. Christine went off to the bar but Little George decided to check on Mr & Mrs Pendragon.

When he got to their room, the door was open and the place was empty, cleaned and ready for any new arrivals. Little George hurried to the yard but again found no sign of Harry or the gig. They had gone but where and why, they said they would be here waiting. Little George was confused. He didn't like being confused but couldn't get to understand any reason.

Christine came running into the yard and saw Little George sitting down upset. "They have gone haven't they Little George?" "Yes they have and I cannot understand it." "Well, Mrs Rosevear said they just got up and left yesterday evening and no one has seen or heard from them since. However, Mrs Rosevear was quite jolly as they had paid a week in advance and the room was clean and, wished all guests could be the same."

They sat down together and cuddled each other and knew they just had to get on with it but what to do was something they didn't know. So they decided they would be brave and carry on as usual, say nothing and give word to their master Henry in a few days, as he advised.

Rebecca and Joshua were concerned about not being at the Turks when Little George and Christine returned and knew they had to get word to them. But things weren't that simple and had to prioritise the importance of their next step. They decided that staying low and to rest was the most important. Therefore, with a day or so holed up in the Anchor they decided to walk around Newlyn and get a feel of the place, arm in arm of course. However, Joshua would go to the Turks tonight and find them.

Like Penzance, the village town of Newlyn was busy but not as dense. Again, it overlooked the large bay of Marazion which is nice if you could see through the mass of sails in the harbour.

They agreed to go to the Sailormans for refreshment and start their investigation. The place was crowded and conversations loud. A few men pushed themselves aside to make room for the lady, Rebecca, and Joshua to sit by the fire.

They ordered wine and listened to the chat. Rebecca leaned across and said in a quieter voice, "We need to get some soothing cream for my back as this pistol is chaffing my skin horribly." Joshua smiled and said "of course my dear." They then chatted about nothing with more intent on listening and looking.

Joshua suggested he go to the privy and whilst there check out the stables, as he wanted to look at the horses as he felt it important if he could start seeing identification marks which could be of use later in some way. "Don't be long," she replied, "I feel I am the only woman in here who is spending money, rather than making money."

"So he's left you then as he?" said a man who just came up to her side as bold as brass and smelling of liquor. Rebecca ignored him and kept looking at the fire knowing that conversation would only encourage him, which she didn't want. He leaned further into her space and said "Excuse me madam, if he can't afford you, I can, what sort of money are we talking and what do I get for it?" Again she stayed focused on the fire. Tapping her on her front shoulder, he said in a louder voice "Have you no tongue woman?" She wanted to punch him on the nose because not only was he rude, he was ugly.

"Leave her be" one of the other men said, who had earlier moved up to make room for her and Joshua. "Her hubby has gone to the privy and will be back shortly." "Who's talking to you, bird brains?" Both men squared up to each other in silence. After an eerie long minute, both males looked away from each other to their respective corners of support. In no eagerness to confront each other yet, at this early time of day, they all laughed and more drinks were ordered.

Joshua came strolling back in and smiling to Rebecca, offered her another drink if she wishes. Rebecca couldn't wait to get out, got up, took Joshua's arm and led him about turn, out of the front door. Once outdoors a big cheer erupted inside. "Bloody heathens," she said.

"What's happened?". Rebecca explained what went on inside while he was away and how she felt like punching the loud mouth on the nose. Joshua didn't say anything and just smiled protectively.

Walking together a woman passed and Rebecca asked if she knew of a place that sells soothing ointments. "Yes my dear, keep going straight and you will find Mr Pendricks shop, the last on the left, he sells all that sort of stuff." With thanks they moved on.

"You're new to the town I guess?" Mr Pendricks asked. "Yes," Rebecca replied, "We are thinking maybe of selling our cottages and moving into the area and are presently on vacation, I suppose you don't get many new faces here?"

"No, not really, everyone wants Penzance; it's the place to be. They got another approval for 'Market Town Status' and I also heard they have got the royal approval for building some sort of coinage mint. We get the fish; they get the gold."

"Apologies" he said, "there's me carrying on, who do I have the pleasure?" "Mrs Pendragon," Rebecca replied, "and this is my husband Joshua. So you do have the soothing ointment?" she repeated. "Yes I do; may I ask what exactly is it for?" Rebecca explained about her lower back and how she had been carrying some iron goods home and it rubbed greatly, leaving it red raw. "Arrr yes, I know exactly what you need" and handed over a small pot of cream to be rubbed in twice a day.

They paid for the lotion and turned to leave when Mr Pendricks said, "where about are you staying?" "The Sailormans," she lied, "it's a bit rowdy but it will do." "Well, if you are looking for something a little homelier, I am renting out my little cottage?" "Thank you," they said, "but why are you renting it?" "Well business here is doing well and I have rooms upstairs, for my bed and things, and I get a little lonely in the cottage, as my good wife passed to the Lord over ten years now." Joshua said, "we are sorry to hear that and thank you we may well take up your offer." They went on to discuss agreeable terms and said they would come back with their decision on the morrow.

They found Mr Pendricks single story little cottage a mile or so on the western side of Newlyn, just off the main road to Mousehole, but closer too, which seemed a very appropriate location.

The front looked very nice and pretty but lacking in love and care. The back had a stable yard exiting onto a lane heading north out of town and south edging back down to the quay. They could enter through either back or front but the back access was especially important and was glad that access was large enough for the gig and horses.

Returning to their rooms at the Anchor they discussed that although things hadn't gone very far, they were achieving their initial goals in moving into an unknown area, without raising any suspicions or questions and that their language and stories are being believed as just a new loving couple moving in.

This was good but they now needed to keep their ears and eyes open and play the quiet patient game and probe where they can. Rebecca showed Joshua her small of her back and asked could he rub in the lotion. Joshua smiled a cheeky grin and got the jar. She laughed and said, "just the back Joshua." He also adjusted the pistol holder and strap to make it more comfortable for her. They both agreed taking on the cottage was a good idea and would move in the following week. There they could have a base to operate more freely without prying eyes everywhere.

The afternoon ran into early evening and Rebecca said, "What time will you be off to see the children?" "I was thinking mid to late evening as I want to catch Little George on his own so we can talk." "Be careful Joshua, I have a funny feeling about the Turks Head and will be well pleased if they agree to come to us." He decided to double check his pistol and knife making sure all was correct, just in case. Rebecca now accepted these checks as wise and sensible. Once finished they went to have an early supper, he also needed to get Harry ready.

The Turks Head came into view and was about a couple of hundred yards away when Joshua decided to dismount. It was important not to be identified as he wanted to get in and out quickly with no fuss.

Walking the long way round and coming to the back of the stable yard seemed to take ages. Joshua waited quietly in the shadows just outside the yard for an hour but still no sign of Little George, or in fact anyone. Harry was being very good and liked the calm stroking. 'Patience Joshua, be patient and silent, he who waits will win,' he said to himself.

That's fine he thought but he couldn't wait all night and decided to give it another thirty more minutes and if nothing, had no option but to go into the Inn and find them. Time passed and nothing so nervously he entered the yard and loosely tethered Harry. Remembering he may need a quick exit, he left the back yard gate open.

He could hear the singing in the bar but crept in walking smoothly to the rear quarters were Christine had her room. Someone was coming his way. What to do? No time to run or second guess. Front it out, he thought, and carried on but his tension was up and so slid his hand to his back, as he approached a corner, ready to draw the weapon. It was dark and when he turned the corner, he was facing the daughter of Mrs Rosevear. Funny, he thought, how he was so tense and extremely nervous and she didn't seem to have a care in the world. Get a grip of yourself Joshua!

"Good evening sir," she said, and was going to walk straight past. "Good evening," he replied, "have you seen that boy Little George, he was meant to be looking after my horse" "He is in the bar area helping Mama with the drinks and food." He convinced her to fetch Little George as he wished to talk with him only very briefly and will make sure he is back within the minute.

Joshua then went back to the stable yard and waited outside by the door. Soon enough Little George appeared and when seeing Joshua, rushed up to him and hugged him. Joshua bent down and hugged him back. He then explained to Little George the situation, as best he could, and asked if he and

Christine would come to them. "Yes we will," he replied and pulled out a letter saying, "This is for you, from Mr Hosking."

Joshua told him not to go back in but get his horse Suzy ready to ride and he will find Christine. "Christine isn't here," he said, "Mr Rosevear has taken her to the Fisherman's Arms." "Alright, get Suzy ready, I just need to read this with some light."

Joshua went back in where the light was better from a wall candle in the hallway. It read;

R & J
Get out and take the children.
Respectfully yours
A Colleague

So they were right, that bastard. Think Joshua, think. He put the letter back in his pocket and went outside to find Little George.

Little George was ready and without further delay he got onto Harry, noting he acts with a more confident strut, every time that Suzy was near. They were heading for the Fisherman's Inn.

Reaching the Inn, Joshua told Little George to stay outside on Suzy ready for a quick off. He will go in and fetch Christine. The Inn was loud and heavy drinking seemed to be going on all around. Joshua knew, as he had been in this situation many times before, there was literally only one way to achieve what he wanted and that was swiftness and directness with a clear exit, found before he acted. Rebecca's words of caution were gone out of the window, for now.

Little George looked worried as he also knew what had to be done. Joshua said, "Hold Harry and keep ready as when I come out we are off. If I am not out in ten minutes, ride to Rebecca who is at the Anchor Inn west of Newlyn as fast as you can."

Joshua entered the bar area through the front door and sized the situation immediately. His life depended on it as he knew from past experience. Rosevear and his cronies were at the other end of the bar, which was good. He caught sight of another man sitting quietly in the other corner closer to the entrance. This man looked very capable and noticed his jet black hair and icy blue eyes but, for some reason, Joshua did not feel any threat from him.

The exit route Joshua confirmed was the entrance, the way he had come in. He saw Christine serving ale, looking tired and worn. Joshua was ready. "Christine" he shouted. She and everyone else in the bar looked round. Nobody moved, the place went silent. She went to go to Joshua but Rosevear said strongly, "Stay where you are girl." Stalemate, just what

Joshua didn't want. The exit is still clear, good. Then Rosevear started, so all the pub heard, "What are you doing here Pendragon, why don't you go to that new little wife of yours and get her to warm you some milk for bed, with the big divider."

A gaggle of laughter came from everyone at the bar but it soon died. Joshua didn't say a word but moved slowly forward with the exit firmly in his head. Shall he pull the gun, shall he not, shall he pull the knife, no not the knife. If he pulls the gun people will be aware for future problems, he needed to act smartly as the seconds of silence ticked by.

Smash! Someone had thrown something heavy through the outside window were Rosevear was closest. Everyone looked around in amazement which gave time for Christine to run to Joshua, who grabbed her and ran out with her under his arm. He saw Little George getting back up on Suzy and knew it was him who had diverted Rosevear.

Joshua put Christine on Harry as he jumped up behind her. Joshua was in two minds. He was tense and alert to the violence that this Rosevear brings and was ready to do it, but he knew that he had achieved getting Christine out, albeit with Little George's help, but nevertheless Christine was here. It hurt his pride but knew he had to run with the children. One day he will get Rosevear, one day he will get him without anyone around, one day.

The man known as Jack was still sitting quietly in the corner drinking his French brandy and saw everything but didn't move. He too didn't take kindly to this Rosevear, or his thugs for friends, but he had been useful in the past with some stuff he wanted shifting and may be useful later so, he will now keep him at arm's length with nods and smiles. However, this man Pendragon, whom he had never seen before quietly impressed him with his courage and calm. He took another sip of the French brandy and contemplated things.

They were off just as the Rosevear clan were coming out and jeering loudly. Harry led the way and Suzy followed. They were soon on the main road to Newlyn and in keeping up a good pace of gallop meant it wouldn't be long before they could ease up and relax a little.

They got to the cross junction where the road split and as they went left to Newlyn they slowed the pace. Christine was shivering so Joshua took off his doublet and hugged it round her. Little George seemed good and was keeping up well.

They got to the Anchor west of Newlyn and entering through the back, they left the horses in the yard and all of them went in to find Rebecca. The horses were breathing heavy and needed a rub down. Joshua would do it once the children were safely with Rebecca.

Rebecca had locked the door but once opened and seeing them all, she made a big smile and both children ran to her where she cuddled them like a mother hen. Christine said she had no clothes or anything. Rebecca said lovingly, "Don't you worry, tomorrow we will go out and buy you a new wardrobe and you also Little George, now tell me what has been happening and why do you both look so worn out."

Joshua started to cough in a gesture that he was also here. Rebecca responded by saying, "Joshua, you can tell me all about it when I have the children sorted and put to bed." "Have you the brandy bottle?" he asked. "Yes, it's on the table." "'Then I will just tend the horses and come back and get tipsy if that's alright?" "Joshua, that is fine, I can see things haven't gone to plan so I will also make you a pipe."

Sometimes Joshua thought he wished he was born a woman as they always seem to say the right things at the right time making you feel lovely, even though he had to go back outside again without a mentioning of a thank you, women, unbelievable.

Chapter 11

Jacques, as he was known to his compatriots in his beloved France, or Jack, as they say in English, was getting tired of this cat and mouse game. Twenty years he had fought for his Country behind the scenes. He knew he wouldn't get recognition as the Generals do, with their sabre rattling prances but he was good at what he does and he knew it.

But this new undercover germ of mass type killing was not his style, especially when it was not against frontline troops, more the underbelly of its supply chain. However, he was trained to do a job and the job he will do.

It didn't seem that long ago when you gained information and supplied it to interested parties at the best price. He was told that times are changing and we must all change with them and this type of warfare was the way forward. He tried to convince himself that this was right but knew he was fooling himself and that he was ready to quit or retire as he liked to keep telling himself, after this Cornish thing.

Bloody Cornish, bloody savages and all in bred. All they do is fish, bloody fishing, and dance around some bloody pole with soot on their faces and men in dresses prancing around like prats. With those thoughts held, he took another large nip and chuckled inside.

He started to weigh up Rosevear of the Turks head and the advantages and disadvantages of choosing him to take the germ. However, after the Pendragon thing and his attitude with his louts, he decided he was too much of a security risk and therefore wouldn't use him. He was also a loud mouth double crossing cur who thought he owned the place.

No he wouldn't use him for his barrel running. Decision made. That means he would not switch his tactics, as he suggested he may. He would keep with the trusted sympathisers of the Wards, at Sennon, so he needed to get information to Bouchier, as quickly as possible. However, getting that message away secretly was easier said than done.

Taking the last swig of the brandy and feeling a nice glow of warmth run down in his belly, he thought about his boss Pierre Bouchier.

Bouchier, he thought deeply. Jack had been drafted in to lead this project in Cornwall and really didn't know too much about him, only that his reputation preceded him as a ruthless man who had contacts up and down the chain ladder. However, they had got on alright together as Jack didn't like being twisted and lied to and preferred facts, in which Bouchier gave or, believe he gave.

But again, Jacks experience quickly came in and knew that he doubted Bouchier's loyalty to people like him and didn't at all doubt the man's will to get a job done, no matter what. In other words, Jack could be wiped if Bouchier thought necessary.

Jack got up and put his hand up to the barman in a salute that he had finished for the night and left the Fisherman's in deep thought.

Jacks place wasn't too far away located in the middle of the town as he liked it. With the hustle and bustle and everyone and everything going on about, he could be invisible. He rented a room in a mediocre house where he could come and go as he pleased and tonight he wanted more brandy and a good sleep. He was on mining duty the day after tomorrow which didn't inspire him at all and knew, this had to change as well. Everything was taking too long.

His room was small and sparse and as soon as he entered he immediately laid down on the bed, fully clothed, with pillows puffed up and bottle in hand. Taking large swigs and making the effort to hold the drink in his mouth then slowly letting it slide down his throat to the pit of his stomach, he felt the effects of drunkenness which is what he wanted. Too long he has been here and too long being too much.

Jack drifted to thinking about his home and the women he had had. He wished he had a women waiting for him like every good love story he had been told about but, he hadn't. His job didn't do it for them, or him.

But again when this one is finished he would go home to his little small holding in South France and which he owned outright. He would somehow find a woman to settle down and take care of him. His heart and soul just couldn't and wouldn't let him think about his real love. He was just dozing off when he awkwardly remembered to take out his pistol from the inside of his doublet and laying it on the floor, when full sleep took him.

On his waking, Jack felt drained with a heavy head. He made the decision last night about not using Rosevear and nodded inwardly that it was correct. When he worked on the mainland whether Austria, Netherlands or Germany, it was much easier to give and get information to his home land but here in this bloody England, there was a massive channel of sea in between them and, eyes were everywhere. He had to get to Mousehole and meet his contact. He needed to get to Bouchier quickly with minimum fuss.

He washed and went to the market in the town and bought a couple of pies. He then went to the local blacksmiths to pick up his horse, stabled, at a cost, but was looked after well. He was a big chestnut with a white patch on his rump and called Arc. If people here asked why he named him Arc, they were given the beautiful soft answer of, 'due to the rainbows in the sky' but in truth, it was in remembrance of his heroine Joan of Arc.

Once on Arc he felt the brisk air run through him, which was what he needed. Once on the main drag to Lands' End he opened Arc up to full gallop and enjoyed the thrill. After a mile the speed had done its job and so steadied Arc to a canter. The cobwebs were shaken off both man and beast. Getting to the cross tracks he turned left on through Newlyn then pushed over through to Mousehole.

Mousehole was a funny little place. It didn't know if it was a town, village or port. It was a bit of everything. He knew where his contact would be if the ship was in. Reaching the wharf, the ship was indeed in the dock being cleaned and waiting to be loaded with sardines ready for the mainland European markets.

It didn't matter which country they landed at, Jack thought, as once he was abroad on land it was only then a matter of distance for him and Arc to ride. They could take which course they wanted in which circumstances permitted. Jack knew that having to expose himself in a small village like Mousehole and trying get a ride to France, or as near as he could, was dangerous but it was the only way. The problem is the enemy know these sorts of things.

Cautiously he went into the Smugglers and ordered a drink and some stew, then took a seat trying to mingle as best he could in being just another person.

His contact was already there and although they saw each other, they did not acknowledge one another. Then after about ten minutes had lapsed Jacques got up to go to the privy. Once there his contact came in next to him.

"I need to get to the mainland," Jack said quietly. "When?" "As soon as possible both for me and my horse." "We set sail for Calais day after tomorrow at high tide around five o clock." "Calais!" "Take it or leave it," the man said. Jack thought, quickly realising that Calais was hundreds of miles from where he wanted to go, but it was at least the mainland. "I will be here." "That's fifty pounds paid now." Knowing the exorbitant rates this man charges Jack paid and left without going back and leaving his stew.

Jack needed to be careful now. He would need go back to his room in Penzance and lay low. He was up very early tomorrow as he always was, on these particular days of the week, but especially now after meeting a contact, it was always wise to withdraw for a while. Experience Jack thought, which made him proud of what he did for a living.

He got back to the stables in Penzance where the blacksmiths apprentice took over Arc and his needs for water, food and a good rub down. Jack told the apprentice that once Arc was done to take him to the usual place next to his accommodation and tie him up for the night. The apprentice was used to this and was paid accordingly on top of the stabling costs. Jack went off to his accommodation and lay on the bed.

Like clockwork he got the brandy out and drunk himself to oblivion. He knew he had a problem but always justified it once the first drops started down his neck.

Zoe and Pascal were in the cottage as always never leaving only in necessity and this day was a necessity. There was hardly any food and the water buckets needed filling. This was Zoe's job. Pascal was underground tunnelling as usual with his weak arms but intelligent brain. He wasn't built for digging, he was built for thinking and being romantic and thought all other men were cavemen in comparison with worm brains. How could women refuse his intelligence.

Zoe left the cottage to go down into the market and get the groceries, nodding to people as she went. She spoke perfect English without an accent and people accepted her as a recluse type person and as she always paid her way with good cash no one pried. She also knew that with her being sultry tall with blue eyes and jet black flowing hair she caught the eye of many young men, which she could do nothing about but inwardly enjoyed the way she rejected them.

Heading back up town through the narrow streets the cottage was found at the very top at the end of the terraces on the left with a little yard attached to the side, just enough for a few horses to be tied.

It had been chosen by Pascal through his so called intelligence of navigation to achieve the best results for the job in hand. The previous cottage was too far off and the veins underneath the deep earth were found to be granite and ran in the wrong direction, which he said no scientist could have foreseen, hence the need to move, which gave some curiosity but no one said anything.

Next step for Zoe was the water so after dropping off the food supplies, she went back out to the nearest well. This was relatively close and in line with Pascal's new judgement of the cottage location. Filling the buckets was easy, it was the bringing back that caused her the aching back. In fact, on numerous occasions people would say to her, why don't you get your Brother to do the water run Sue, as she was called. She would always reply with a roll of the eyes 'Oh you know what men are like?' Then she would carry on without further discussion. In her mind she would think, 'bloody fools.'

She knew she had to be especially careful as she was the only one of the three who had to mix with the locals every now and then and, didn't relish this close contact. This Cornish contract sounded good in France but never ever has she felt so on edge.

The thing that kept her here was the loathing of the English enemy and what they have done to her people in the wars gone by. She was doing her bit. But like Jacques she felt it was easier in France were she could mingle much more freely.

Maybe it was a confidence thing. She didn't know but what she did know is that this was dangerous and Pierre better reward her as he said he would, otherwise she would kill him. As for his advances, she played him like an instrument for her own gain as she loves another.

Once back in the cottage she felt more secure. They had weapons loaded and gunpowder ready to fire in strategic positions by all windows and doors. The bolts on all entry points were extra strong, just in case. The horses were again always ready to go in a minute's notice. Zoe however was tired. She recognised that this new method of warfare was taking a long time. She prefers movement over long distances, not stuck in one place working covert in an overt way and especially not working with smelly bigheads like Pascal.

She also prefers to work alone specialising on single entities as her best forte. But the reward for this Cornish job will out way the cost, she thought hopefully.

The day was moving on and Zoe was working hard to move the rubble and crap into workable heaps coming up from the ground from Pascal's digging. They would have to start using the front room and kitchen area if they don't get to the target soon. Pascal decided he had had enough for the day and will let Jacques carry on early tomorrow when he arrives for his shift.

Zoe had made some stew and she and Pascal ate together. One thing Zoe was good at and that is stringing people along and letting them believe she liked them until such time when they are of no more use. Pascal talked about how wonderful he is and how his own precise bearings and measurements are proving very beneficial to success. In fact, he wondered how on earth any other team could have done this without him. Zoe agreed all the way like a doting pet, preening his ego all the way.

It wasn't that late but Zoe was too tired and wanted sleep. Jacques would be here early and he liked a cup of tea before he started work. 'Sounds like an Englishman' she thought. Pascal too was tired and so they went upstairs together but entered separate rooms.

Jacques waited and watched. The morning was very early around two thirty. The place was quiet and dark. He was just inside the front door slightly ajar. On seeing and hearing nothing after five minutes he went for Arc. Gently without a murmur they left Penzance. If people had asked why he was up so early he gave the answer that he was a fish cutter in the fish station at Newlyn and the hours were crap. They always laughed at the end bit and never queried.

The cottage in Mousehole soon enough appeared so he stopped and dismounted. Pulling Arc and himself into the shadows he again waited and watched. All was good. The time was early around 3.30am as Zoe heard the rat a tat tat – pause – tat – pause, rat a tat tat, on the back door. The code was correct and timing right. She pulled back the bolts and Jacques quietly slipped in.

With the door bolted behind him, she hugged him and he responded. The water had boiled and Jacques took the tea and sat down. "Pascal's still asleep upstairs," she said. "Good and long may he stay there." Jacques didn't do Pascal and knew the feeling was mutual. Zoe on the other hand, he liked but was cautious. He knew that a woman to do this type of work was very resourceful in many ways. He considered telling her that he was off to France to speak with Pierre tomorrow about the delay and the time this mission was taking. He also wanted to tell her that the role he was being asked to do was crap and above all the cursor was swinging above the acceptable risk of being killed, versus getting the job done and surviving. While they chatted he thought more on the subject and decided he would not tell her.

Changing into his digging clothes he went to the hole located in the back room and climbed inside. The tunnel was small and went away from the row of terrace cottages into an exact direction he knew not, somewhere he thought between north and west. It didn't take him long before he stopped and saw the end of the tunnel. 'That bloody Pascal' he thought.

'That idle bastard. If he thinks I am digging to make up for his bloody idleness he's got another thing coming. Bouchier is going to be informed of this. Things have got to change.' He decided to dig but he was totally fed up. Filling the buckets which lay in a line he dragged them back to the entrance and decided to rest. Zoe realised something was up and asked "You seem fed up Jacques, what are you thinking?" "I'm thinking that idle bastard Pascal." He was going to say more but remained silent, something was telling him that Zoe was probing for something or, was he being paranoid. Either way he needed to talk with Bouchier first, that was the important thing.

"Yes, I agree with you Jacques, all he says is he was built for intelligence of the romantic and field of science." "Well he can go to a bloody field for all I care and use his intelligence with the cows, this job is taking too long and the tunnel is not as far as it should." "What do you mean it's taking too long?" Jacques realised he had said too much, Zoe had friends and knew Pierre had a thing for her. "Nothing" he said, "it's just that I'm not feeling well this morning, I think I'm coming down with something. I will work through this day and tomorrow as best I can."

Zoe then thought that Jacques was up to something. He was cagey and edgy. She was used to this type of character but knew when it was out of place. "Jacques, do you still believe in this mission?" "Yes I do, I am just not feeling well that's all." She left it at that but her inner defence mechanism shivered a little. 'Be careful 'she said to herself.

Pascal came down middle to late morning. When seeing Jacques, he said "Good morning Jacques, how are you this morning?" "Terrible actually," he replied. "He is not well Pascal, he thinks he is coming down with something," Zoe added. "Anything I can do to help Jacques?" he said. Jacques was just about to say 'Yeah dig faster and work bloody harder' but instead said, "No that's fine, thank you Pascal."

Pascal then went on defending his work rate over brain power and how he was not built for being a miner. They all nodded in agreement and acceptance of his dilemma, or so he thought. "How long will it take until we reach the target area?" Jacques said. "At the rate of which we are tunnelling and using the formula of time equals distance over speed, I anticipate the first point would be three weeks." "What do mean the first point?" Jacques said. "I mean once we hit the centre of the first point of ninety feet, we then turn eighty-seven degrees for forty-three feet at a fall ratio of one inch in three feet and that will take a further three weeks. Altogether, I would say eight to ten week's maximum and within the time scales of Mr Bouchier's directive."

Listening to this entire baffle, Zoe butted in and said, "then what?" "Then we inject the germ into the current and allow that to feed itself into the mix and 'Voila'!" "And how long will that take before we reach 'Voila', as you say?" "It will take three days, from point of pouring the chemical germ into the ground, enough for us to make our escape and let nature take its course."

Two months more of this back breaking work and then keeping these guys safe and watching for the enemy outside was just not good, thought Jacques. He also saw Zoe's face frown about the length of time it will take and seemed to take a reality check on her safety that this was pushing things. How long before someone got curious or a mistake was made? The only one not to feel threatened or at risk was Pascal and that was because he hasn't and doesn't have to mix with the local people or, he is too stupid to realise the position he is in. They may be Cornish, Jacques kept thinking, but one slip could be the rope for us all. Bouchier has to be told of our fears of safety. Again he wanted to inform Zoe but something inside, yet again, stopped him.

The day went fast and the digging slow. Jacques finished around six o'clock and said to himself that was it. Zoe had made a good stew for all and Jacques gulped it down. Pascal didn't drink but Zoe did and liked a brandy and knew secretly of Jacques love of the drink. Pascal took over the digging duties for an hour or so but Jacques and Zoe hit the bottle. Come late evening Pascal took for his bed and his books. Much later after finishing the bottle, Jacques and Zoe went to bed together.

Zoe turned to Jacques after she had told him she loves him time and time again, that he was the best she had ever known and asked, "Two more months is a long time here, we may not make it Jacques?" "I know" he said, "that's why I'm off to France tomorrow to speak with Bouchier." "Well done Jacques, you clever thing but how?" "Contact in Mousehole, bloody expensive and can only get me and Arc to Calais." "When tomorrow, or more to the point when today?" as time had pushed by midnight. "We set sail at about six this evening with the tide and so have got to be there for five. It will still be daylight as such, which I don't, like but it's the only way."

Well he had told her now, she knows exactly when and when not to ask things and he fell straight into it. "So how long will you be gone?" "I would say a week to two, why will you miss me?" He said curiously. "Yes of course I will miss you my little my sugar pumpkin," and then she thought what a bastard for not telling her. "You be careful Jacques my dear" she added warmly.

The morning came too soon and Jacques was thinking about the trip to Calais. Although he wanted to take Arc with him he really knew that moving in daylight hours wasn't good, especially boarding a ship with an expensive looking horse like Arc. Weighing up the risk he would have to buy a horse at Calais market and leave Arc here at the cottage. He would also have to dress down.

Pascal, as usual, entered the tunnel periodically throughout the day doing little digging and more talking. Jacques found the gunpowder keg and set a cord to it then placed the whole thing on the floor inside the entrance. Although tight, there was still room for manoeuvre. He said to Zoe and Pascal that he would be away for a week or two and if anything should happen, light the fuse and get out. They understood.

He explained to Zoe she would need to follow him to Mousehole Harbour and bring back Arc. Once again she unbolted the back door into the yard and both waited five to ten minutes. With the all clear they ventured out, took the horses and rode quickly away from the town. It was further going round the town than going through the town in Mousehole but Jacques preferred this indirect route, just in case.

Getting to the small wharf the contact and boat were there as promised, ready for sail. Jacques, looking like a pauper walked to the wharf. exchanged greetings and got aboard. The contact briefed him that the wind was favourable and should reach the destination very early morning which suited Jacques well.

Zoe was on her way back to the cottage with Arc in tow. She went the long way round mirroring the same way as they went. Like Jacques had taught her, once the cottage was in sight, she got off her horse and waited. Feeling comfortable she walked the horses to the back yard and gave the customary double with pause rat a tat tat on the door.

Pascal wasn't there, no one answered. She waited and knocked again. Nothing, so she gently pushed the door and it opened.

Cautiously she called for him and tip toed in but nothing. She went upstairs and there was Pascal fast asleep. He roused when she shouted at him and said, "sorry Zoe, I must have dropped off." "Dropped off, dropped off!" She just looked at him in utter amazement.

How could he lack the basics of covert working within a team? This guy was a serious health problem who has one concern on his mind and that is, his bloody self.

Zoe went downstairs and thought about the consequences of Pascal's non interested attitude towards security. Anyone could have come through the door and seen everything and then she would have been lynched. She raced back out the door, jumped on Arc, who was faster than her filly, and went directly through the town heading for the wharf.

People noticed her but she didn't care, that bloody stupid Pascal. She was in time as the ship hadn't sailed yet. She asked a sailor at the plank where her friend was. He replied that her friend had gone for a drink before sail and pointed to the inn on the wharf. Hurriedly she went over and entered finding Jacques with another man. They looked at each other and he got up. "What's the matter, what are you doing here in broad daylight?"

She told him about Pascal and the breach of security which, could have been a catastrophe. "Kill the idle bastard, I will square things with Pierre and get this sorted." She nodded, but just as they were about to part he whispered, "before you do this, you must get his book of coordinates first, do you understand Zoe?" "Yes," she replied. "I will get back as quick I can Zoe, don't you worry."

With nothing more said she turned and left. Jacques will tell Pierre and Pierre loved her. That should bring some new ideas to help her quicken her goal. Zoe got back to the cottage via the long way round but feeling more relaxed, as she knew what had to be done. She didn't bother doing the waiting thing just entered the back yard, tied Arc up, opened the non-bolted door and sat in the kitchen. Pascal was up digging in the tunnel but that cut no ice with Zoe.

Zoe decided to clear things up and relight the fire and get this cottage into some sort of order. Her defence mechanisms were kicking in and she knew it. She felt alive with excitement. She made dinner and put fresh water on for a brew. She made Pascal's favourite dish.

It was an hour or so before Pascal's head came out of the tunnel. Once again he apologised to Zoe about his lack in their security in a way like a child to a parent. Zoe played the game well and said, "That's fine Pascal, you have been working very hard and on top of that you have to somehow work out all the coordinates for success, it should be me who ought to apologise. I have made your favourite skirt stew with dumplings. Go now and get freshened up and then come down and relax, let work go today you have done more than enough for any man and, I am very proud of you."

Pascal couldn't believe his luck. He knew one day she would understand and that day had come. Feeling good he went upstairs as advised.

Having set dinner by the fire the two ate in a seemingly refreshed feeling of like and understanding of each other. Zoe chatted about her young days and Pascal responded with his days at college and how he had passed all exams and the girls he wooed. "I always thought you were clever Pascal but was too afraid to say it as I am not that learned as you and you may think me dim." Pascal accepted this, nodded and said, "I understand Zoe."

Zoe had changed her dress for dinner and was now showing a little bare leg above the ankles and her blouse was a little more open than usual, showing off her breasts. Pascal kept looking at both areas.

"So how can a simple girl like me learn something like direction and coordinates of mining?" "You can't, you haven't the basic skills of mathematics," he replied. "Then teach me," she responded. "It's not that easy Zoe and it would take years." "Oh I see, never mind, it was a silly thing to ask of you, more tea?" "Yes please," holding out his cup.

Once Zoe had tidied everything up, leaving Pascal to relax in the chair, she decided to head for bed and get an early night. She said her goodnights. "Goodnight Zoe and thank you for your new understanding of me and the extremely difficult job I have been singly tasked to do." And with that she went to her room.

Getting into bed she relaxed her thoughts and dwelt on Jacques trip to France and her method for getting rid of Pascal. She could use the poison or more simply the blade. Either way she needed first to know his coordinate workings but every time he left his bedroom, he locked it. She heard his footsteps outside her bedroom and then stopping outside. She knew what he was thinking and waited. After a minute she heard him move on to his own bedroom. Tomorrow it is then.

Chapter 12

Rebecca put the children to bed in their own room and stayed with them until they were asleep. On her return, Joshua was quite tipsy and feeling sleepy. "That bastard Rosevear," she said, "putting young Christine to work not only at the Turks but in the Fisherman's too. She had to scrub the privy every hour then clean and clean until her fingers bled, poor little mite. As for Little George, he worked him harder, taking over the duties of his own daughter as well as the stables. If it wasn't by the grace of God that you went over tonight they would still be there. My God it doesn't bear thinking about." She finished by saying, "that bastard." "Would you like a nip of brandy?" Joshua asked after patiently waiting for her to finish. "Yes a large one please."

Joshua discussed the letter he had received from Hosking and what had happened at the Fisherman's. He explained how Little George had bravely caused the distraction which allowed the stalemate to be broken and give time for Christine to get to him and escape. They both agreed that the children were resilient and very loyal to each other. "Why would Rosevear do such a thing, knowing that Hosking is their guardian?" "I have no idea," Joshua replied. "Ego and greed and thinking he owns the place may have something to do with it and also, he knew the children wouldn't say anything and just get on with it."

Rebecca said, "Well it stops now, I won't have it anymore, these children are staying with us and I will speak with Hosking myself. I will talk with the children tomorrow and ask if they wish this to be. If they do, Joshua are you in agreement?" Without even thinking, Joshua just naturally said, "Yes Rebecca, of course." "You're a very good man Joshua."

With that Rebecca smiled and poured him another drink and reminded him that they have a busy day tomorrow so they had better turn in. Rebecca went into the children's room and got into their bed and cuddled them as they all snuggled up like three peas in a pod. Joshua put the candles out and leaving the adjoining door ajar, went to bed. He thought about the whole situation and realised how a person's life can change course from a single moment and you either go with the wind or not.

Joshua woke early and still in thought about what to do. It was coming apparent that he would have to take more control of the operation in which they have been tasked and more to the point, both of them had accepted. Christine he thought needed Rebecca whereas Little George needed a little more guidance as a man. His strategy started taking shape and he decided to put his thoughts to Rebecca for approval.

He got freshened up and sorted the horses out ready for the day. On his return all three were up ready and dressed with smiles on all their faces. He was just about to say something when Rebecca said, "right Joshua, what you say we all head into Helston and have a day out shopping, we can also see Hosking and discuss things. The children have decided they wish to stay with us." "I couldn't agree more" he said with a broad grin.

Little George helped Joshua with rearranging the gig to be pulled by both Lilly and Suzy side by side and Joshua would ride on Harry up front. He felt that two people and two children in one gig were a little too much for one horse. Once the gig was completed and the horses seemed happy with each other, Little George and Joshua met the girls in the downstairs breakfast room and once all were satisfied with their full, they were off. The day was freshly cold and clear but the smiles on the children were glowing with warmth and happiness.

Harry took the lead and it wasn't long before they were on the main route east to Helston. Helston is a Market type town and tries to compete with Truro. Although there are shops, Truro really was the place to go. On arrival they split up and it was left to Joshua to talk with Hosking alone. They decided to meet up at the top of Meneage Street for a small late lunch in the new tea shop. They left the gig and horses in the saddler's area.

Reaching the Blue Anchor Joshua asked for Henry. The landlord told him to wait. He then came back and escorted Joshua through the Inn, up the stairs to a back room. On knocking, Joshua was asked to enter. Henry was sitting at his desk with quill in hand and the man named Bull sitting opposite. 'That's the second time I have seen these two together', he thought.

Bull got up and shook Joshua's hand and stated he needed the privy, mentioning he would bring back some refreshments. With Bull leaving, Henry and Joshua were alone which he thought was very discreet and polite of him.

Henry put the quill down and once Joshua was seated asked what was on his mind and how things are going. Joshua explained everything in detail on what had gone on. Henry asked how the mission was proceeding. Joshua went over their plans about moving into the rental cottage west of Newlyn on the outskirts of Mousehole to work from and once in, they would have a base in which they can work more quickly and thoroughly. Joshua also explained their strategy that a night and day observation type rota was needed to understand movement of people and then work from there with the information gained.

Timing was another question, as it always is. However, Joshua's answers seemed to be making Henry satisfied that they were working cautiously.

They also went over the facts of what Rosevear had done which begged Joshua to ask the question, 'why Rosevear?' Henry apologised and explained the situation and it became apparent that this Rosevear fellow was a friend of a friend which allowed Henry to insert Christine into a place that was being suspicious in its activity.

Henry continued, "I know you may think me cruel to put a young girl at risk but I thought she was safe and believed she was in no danger plus the information she gleaned was extremely useful. Joshua, we now know for certain he is double dealing and our intention is to raid his place very shortly, covered and disguised, as we do, as a nasty bar brawl. In fact, that's why Bull is here to discuss tactics. My advice Joshua is to stay away from the Turks Head for the next two weeks until our job is done there."

"What about the Fisherman's?" Joshua asked. "Joshua you have been away for a long time being in the Marines and working in Bristol. The Cornish, as you know, are hardworking people and very much like to trade and smuggle, it just seems to be in their blood. Nearly every Inn across the county is doing things not quite right, including the Fisherman's. However, I will let the sheriff's sort that out but Rosevear has pushed the boundaries over this limit of acceptability and, if my information is found true, a traitor to boot."

They went on to discuss the children, and Henry, after listening to what had happened, reluctantly agreed with Rebecca's thoughts. One thing about Henry, he is practical. He knew the children needed more but his job just didn't allow this commitment type of love and attention. He also sincerely praised Rebecca as like her Mother, she would treat the children well and keep them safe.

He wanted to keep his title of guardianship as he felt a loving responsibility for them but confirmed that they could live with them for the foreseeable future. Little George and Christine would be a loss in his gaining of gossip information from around this town and Penzance area and so, would need to recruit quickly.

They shook hands and Henry said, "Well done to you both for getting into Newlyn and Mousehole and establishing a base without any noise or commotion and good luck with the strategy, it will work Joshua, I know it will. Whoever they are Joshua, they are imbedded so be patient and diligent and together we will get them." "Thank you Henry, and thank you for your kind encouraging words."

On leaving the Blue Anchor, Joshua passed Bull with tray in hand heading back to Henry. Joshua nodded his appreciation in now understanding that his job was as difficult as his and, they were on the same side. Bull responded the same.

Rebecca wasn't at the new trendy styled cake shop so Joshua ordered tea which seemed slightly strange not ordering a beer in an Inn but like everything, times are a changing and to be honest, Joshua felt strangely pleasant and dignified. However, it wasn't long before they entered and seeing Rebecca and Christine with new bonnets and Little George with a new hat made Joshua smile inside.

Joshua quietly discussed his visit to Henry with Rebecca. The children were not really listening, being too absorbed with the shop surroundings, until Joshua got to the point of the children living with them and in which Henry had agreed. They then became all ears and beaming smiles. Rebecca put forward a suggestion. They should all this day push over to Truro and stay the night in a well to do Inn, then wake up early and shop all day and enjoy themselves together as a family. What could Joshua say but, "Agreed."

The evening and following day in Truro went too fast but they all thoroughly enjoyed themselves. Rebecca was thinking ahead and taking ideas from both the tea shops and linen shops as to which area she may want to go into, if and when, setting something up in Newlyn or Mousehole. Christine was very attentive.

They started back early afternoon and decided on a quick detour to Rebecca's cottage in Marazion and, although it had been quite a while, the chickens were still there babbling away. 'Hardy little fellows' Joshua thought. Having checked out the cottage and taking a few extra bits they decided to take the few chickens with them and give them to the landlady of the Anchor, where they were staying, in thanks.

Rebecca and Joshua talked a lot about the children and although this was nice he felt that they were drifting and being a little too comfortable, when they should be alert and diligent in trying to find these dangerous people. Rebecca accepted this observation and so agreed that this indeed seemed to be happening and they did need to sharpen themselves up accordingly. However, she suggested that let today be for the children's good spirit and once they were back at the Anchor they would revert to their low profile working until such time as they were all safely in their new cottage.

The following days leading up to their move into their new cottage were intentionally quiet playing cards, talking and discussing things. Having the final terms of the rental contract agreed with Mr Hendricks, they could now move pretty much when they wanted. Two mornings later, that time had come and all having a hearty breakfast and with Little George and Joshua packing the last things up, they were off. The move went well albeit taking a few trips backwards and forwards due to the extra stuff they had collected along the way.

Although the cottage had only a ground floor, it was pretty spacious with one large room come open fire and three other rooms. Two bedrooms and spare for all the clutter, tools and other things they had bought, and a scrub room.

Whilst settling in, Joshua's mind was on their next move, which was to come once they were settled, probably in a few nights' time. He needed to get an understanding on the sort of movement coming in and out of Newlyn and Mousehole. He also needed to get a better feel of the area and more importantly any unusual practices, that became a pattern, in which he could follow up.

Rebecca and Joshua were now getting used to wearing their protective underwear as Joshua made it standard practise between them, that although it be slightly uncomfortable it was imperative they get used to it, until such time as their mission was completed, as with the pistols. Both weapons and protective clothing had to become natural parts of their day to day living. Little George and Christine, being so close, observed these things in their stride and knew it was part of their business. 'Bless them both', thought Joshua.

Rebecca made everyone a lovely stew with bread which went down a treat. Rebecca, with the help of Christine, also prepared dried food for Joshua's next move. They went over all the equipment they had gained to complete the tasks ahead and tonight he needed the warm weather and covert clothing gear. The musket and scope were also going to be needed. It was agreed that Joshua's task tonight be done alone with Little George helping only in the insertion and extraction.

Little George got Harry and Suzy ready. Harry would take Joshua and his gear and once in position, Little George would then leash and lead Harry back to the cottage.

Once the horses were ready Joshua said his farewells and he and Little George left the cottage quietly, out through the rear yard into the dark lane leading away from the town. The time was midnight and so if all goes well, Joshua should be in place by no later than two.

They slowly and quietly walked the horses for about half a mile before jumping on their backs and speeding on. After about twenty to thirty minutes later they got to the main cross section of the Helston to Lands' End road, which forked north to St Just and south to Newlyn and Mousehole. They got off their horses and waited and listened for around ten minutes. The night was fresh and the stars out. The cold and stillness of the dark was awesomely crystal clear.

Joshua had prepared Little George beforehand and practised many times on what to do when entering a position of reconnaissance. He was doing everything correct and Joshua was extremely proud of him. Joshua noted that Little George seemed to have a certain inner spirit of strength and knowing. Joshua needed to be on the other side of the road so facing the cross junction from the north east. He nodded to Little George and they moved on around until such time as they found the small break in the wood line then silently slipped into the forest. 'So far so good', Joshua thought.

They started to move back through the woods closer towards the cross section, looking for a position about ten to fifteen feet inside the forests exterior to suffice. Once Joshua could see the cross roads section through the trees they stopped and got on their knees to rummage around and find the ideal observation spot for him to lie. Somewhere where not too much work was required and the natural habitat would camouflage.

Once found, they started scrapping and digging. When the scrape hole was completed, they unloaded the equipment and put things in place. Joshua would be here for three nights so it needed to be as comfortable as possible as he would not, if all goes well, be standing up again for the next seventy-two hours.

Thoughts of the Army way back on the Continent fighting the Spanish started to come into his brain. However, that was then and this is now but he needed to be diligent, careful and use that experience well.

He laid down many times trying to get his position right. Once he felt comfortable and happy he fixed the small telescope and sighted it on the cross roads. He then checked both pistol and musket once again and put them in position. He checked his food and water supply. The last thing was the warm weather gear which he put on, including a very warm woolly hat and then lastly the over-blankets. Laying down and putting the thumbs up, Little George pulled over the ground sheet completely covering Joshua and his position with the earth line. He then put stones to hold it down using only the natural habitat as camouflage. Little George's last job was to go all around Joshua's position and check all angles of the hide and also, to cover any tracks or things they may have mistakenly been left.

Joshua was in and so Little George took hold of Harry and walked both he and Suzy back up out of the forest the way they had come in. Once out, he jumped on Suzy and with Harry tied to her saddle, rode off to Rebecca and the warmth of the cottage.

It only took a few minutes before silence and eeriness came through the woods. Joshua was totally alone now and he knew, through experience, that from now on time took its own pace. Patience was needed.

The morning came quite quickly and soon enough the first light of day appeared. Joshua was happy that the extra clothing and cover was sufficient in keeping him relatively warm. Joshua wasn't hungry or thirsty, it seemed even his body clock was being toned down in tune with nature in that, things happen and grow when needed.

Noon saw his lovely horse Harry pulling the gig with Rebecca and the children coming up from the Newlyn road to turn right heading to Helston. They stopped briefly at the cross section when he focused his scope on Rebecca's face, as previously discussed. She then got out her handkerchief and rubbed her nose, a sign that all is well. That put a smile on Joshua's face. She waited a few more seconds then flicked the reins for Harry to lead on.

The night came again as with the chill but with his warm weather gear on he was able to keep the cold at bay and, nibbling the food, prepared at the cottage, at regular intervals kept his hunger at bay. Throughout the day both people and horses were coming to and fro but nothing for Joshua to be anxious about.

In fact, he started to think about what he was exactly looking for and questioning himself but knew this was normal thoughts in fighting against the sanity of being in a hole, in the middle of nowhere. Funny thing was, when he was in the Marines he always fought on land but always got paid by the Navy. 'Never understood that,' he thought, but there you go, it is what it is. Perhaps it was because they travelled with the Navy. Anyway, that's the way his thoughts were drifting and as time went on they drifted to Rebecca, Christine, Little George and others in a gentle but very explorative way.

Joshua kept assuring himself that time wasn't an enemy. If you have a problem to solve in your daily lives it seems we have to have a solution as quickly as possible otherwise all else will fail.

Joshua knew that being in a hole, unable to move, with time of no importance, lets you analyse at a pace with the birds singing or the squirrels looking for food.

The next day Rebecca came again with the children in the gig at noon, the same time and the 'all is well sign' was given. Joshua felt relaxed and relieved for them but also for him. There was only one more full night and one full morning to go then, he would be home but, had he achieved anything, as at this moment he had not seen or heard anything out of the ordinary. 'He was doing well' he thought, 'it's a process Joshua.'

Late that night a group of riders came bustling down from the St Just road and headed quickly left at the cross junction towards Helston. Joshua got a good view of the leader and swore it was Bull. They didn't seem like a bunch going to a tea party, more perhaps they were going to sort out Rosevear and his cronies in Penzance. 'Give him one for me' Joshua thought.

Joshua's mind drifted again towards all sorts of scenarios but sleep and tiredness was getting the better of him. As with this type of situation he would cat nap throughout the day and try his best to leave his ears open for any unnatural sounds. That may work in the classroom but in the real world, when you sleep you sleep, albeit maybe a little lighter. The night passed easily and untoward and soon enough the sun rose to start a new day, as it does every day on this earth. How exceptional is that.

Rebecca passed a third time and signed in as 'all's well'. Joshua felt good that tonight was his last night, as at around two or three in the morning Little George will come to help him exit his position, as practised.

He started thinking about the gear and the food in which he had brought with him and felt what he had had was good enough, for he was weighing up when next he would do this, knowing that he would, but using different locations. He also thought if he could have bettered his performance, in which he suggested the answer to be no.

What he needed to do, was now done, albeit no clear information was gained to work with. But, information was the cherry on the cake and the hide itself had worked and the mechanics to get it set up worked as well, therefore, he was satisfied.

Again the night drew in and darkness prevailed. Midnight passed and it was time to start his exit strategy. He gently started to wiggle and squeeze himself up through the covering ground sheet like a slithering snake. What a feeling of relief his body felt when he started to move, stretch and stand up. All he wanted now was a lovely drink of brandy by the fire and a pipe to smoke; bliss he thought.

He calmly started to gather in his equipment in readiness for Little George to come with Harry so they could be away from this place with no delays. He packed everything away and filled in the hole where he had laid and put the foliage back as to once it was, leaving no traces. Once he was happy, he moved away from the hide closer to the small path in which they came in on and waited.

Joshua had hung one of his old scraggy hats on a branch which could be seen from the road. This was a visual message to Little George that all was well. If it wasn't there on his arrival at the said pickup point he was to gallop pass without looking back and go straight to Rebecca or Henry Hosking.

Joshua was lying at the forest end waiting and started again to reflect on the last three days. Although he saw nothing really untoward and gathered no useful information, he thought overall the hide went well and his mental state was good and still intact so with all said and done, it was a success and felt pleased.

Then on cue he heard horses and saw Little George sitting proud on Suzy with Harry in tow heading towards him. Little George stopped, looked over in Joshua's direction and noting the old hat on the branch, he remained still. Joshua moved quickly forward, picked up his things and ran towards them. Without saying a word Joshua quickly put his things over Harry, leapt on and both were off in seconds. It was only after they were well out of the way, in the middle of nowhere and about a mile from home, that they slowed to a stop and talked.

Joshua asked Little George if all was well at home and he confirmed that it was and they were awaiting his return. This was good news, so Joshua said his thanks for Little George being a good man and doing everything they had practised. Little George gave back a smile of pride. As the cottage was getting closer they decided they should get down off the horses and carefully walk the last hundred yards and keep their eyes and ears peeled.

Joshua told Little George that even after a busy schedule, no matter how tired he was, coming out and re-entering the home was to be classed as cautious as it was a time when many people let their guards down and more importantly, the enemy knew this. Little George listened intently to the advice as if he was learning a career.

Outside the back gate to the yard in the darkened lane they waited a few minutes. On creeping a little bit forward, they saw light coming from the back window and also saw the horseshoe on the window sill in the upright position. This was good as they had all made known that if there was a problem the horseshow would be turned upside down with the curve at the top. Feeling relieved Joshua patted Little George on the back and said "well done, let's go on in."

Joshua didn't expect anyone to be up as it was very early around five o'clock but he was wrong. Rebecca was up and dressed with a lovely hot cup of tea waiting. Joshua's smile was bigger than his mouth could make as he was so very pleased to see her. Rebecca was with smile too and although she was more dignified and reserved than her outward emotions showed, he felt she was pleased to see him which made Joshua feel warm inside.

On taking the tea, Rebecca also gave him his brandy bottle which he gratefully took and poured a large amount in to the tea. Taking a big gulp, he felt the brandy hit all the tubes in his body as it went deliciously down his throat. Sitting down at the table he noticed his pipe was readymade up for lighting.

"Don't think this will happen every time Joshua, but in truth I am glad you are safe. Now tell me all what happened and then I will tell mine." Just then Little George came in with the bags and said "the horses have been cared for and both are well can I have a cup of tea now?" "Of course you can Little George," Rebecca replied, "you have been very brave, now come and sit down with us and warm yourself by the fire." Little George quickly sat down with a big grin and said. "As I have been brave like Joshua, can I have a brandy?" They both laughed with a lovingly but strict "No" coming from Rebecca.

Little George had his tea and was told to get to bed and rest and Rebecca will wake him up when ready. They then sat for quite a while discussing things when Joshua decided that sleep was needed. Rebecca also had been up most the night. So with things still to talk about they let the fire down and retired. Although they slept in the same big bed Joshua saw the divider was still there, bigger than ever. However, he was pleased to get into a soft clean bed and once undressed and in, he was gone.

Joshua woke up early afternoon and lying quietly thinking, decided to get up and have a good wash. Rebecca and the children were already up and by the fire talking. He said good afternoon to all. Rebecca suggested they all have a good scrub and she would warm some water for the bath tub. A lovely stew was on as well.

Scrubbing himself clean in the bath, he was thinking that Rebecca and he need to talk about their next moves and would broach the subject after dinner, without the children. Although it was important to inform them of what they do, he somehow felt they should be shielded as well. It was a continual dilemma for him to get the right balance. However, it was early days for them all in this new type of work and he had learnt that somehow, life has a way of letting these things develop in their own time.

Late evening approached and the children went off to bed so with pipe in hand Rebecca and Joshua were alone and so started picking up on where they left off this morning. He explained to her that he felt the hide and three-day static reconnaissance went well and that he should do the same again soon. Rebecca argued that no new information was gained or facts to work on. Joshua had to agree with her observation and argued that all hides produce different things, sometimes gaining knowledge which can be worked and sometimes not. It was a cat and mouse game, or hide and you shall seek.

They eventually agreed that the hides were really the only way to gather information of movement but that the locations needed to be better chosen. Rebecca suggested they put a minimum information value on future sites. In other words, if that minimum value could not be reached then that hide doesn't go ahead. Joshua took his hat off to Rebecca as she sees things very analytical, where he see's things more as a challenge versus risk.

The knocking came early the next morning whilst all were in bed. Rebecca started rousing from sleep and on opening her eyes saw Joshua was already up and putting his protective vest and boots on. He put his index finger to his mouth, messaging a silent hush, then grabbing his pistol went through to the front door.

Standing to the side he asked, "Who's there?" A soft but determined voice replied, "My name is Connor and I have a message for a Mr Pendragon or a Lady Rebecca from Mr Henry Hosking's." With the pistol locked for action and aimed, Joshua tentatively unlocked the door and slowly pulled it back.

It was a young boy about the same age as Little George and Joshua felt straightaway he had an inward ability to think above his age, and had courage. Joshua also noticed the horse tied to their front fence. "I 'am Mr Pendragon, what is the message?" With that Connor passed him the envelope. "I am to await a reply Mr Pendragon."

Precaution thoughts went into Joshua's head. "I understand," Joshua replied, "Just wait there a little while and I will return." He closed the door and went straight into Little George and Christine's room. Little George was awake and already getting dressed. Joshua quickly explained the situation and asked him to sneak out the back and quickly go around the outside and look for any other riders. He will go back to the messenger and talk with him further.

Little George did as he was asked and Joshua went back to the front door. Connor was sitting down but stood straight back up when he saw him. Joshua asked the name of his horse and where he had travelled from. The horse was called Madam and he had travelled from Helston. All this was stacking up but he wanted to hear the 'all clear' from Little George before he did anything. That even means not reading the message and therefore taking his thoughts away from the feeling of caution from a stranger, even a young one.

It wasn't long before he heard Little George coming up behind him. Joshua turned and looked at him when Little George said "all clear." He then stood by Joshua's side and together they looked at Connor. Straight away Connor said, "Little George, it's me Connor." And with that Little George left Joshua's side and greeted Connor as young adults do with slapping and laughs. "You two know each other I presume." "Yes we do," Little George said, "We were in the poor house together a long time ago." "I work for Mr Hosking's now," Connor said proudly.

With that Joshua let things calm down a little. Little George and Connor took Madam around the back yard to be fed. Rebecca was up and dressed. Joshua explained what had happened and showed her the envelope. She nodded and suggested he light the fire, whilst she makes the tea and they will read it together directly.

R & J

Hope you are both well.

No 4 Bridge Street – Mousehole - One person –Alien – Check.

Be Careful.

Respectfully yours

A Colleague

They went over it again, trying to make sense of what, who and how. However, they are quickly realising that the information they gain is not always straight forward. In fact, it is becoming more apparent that things that come their way are more merely snippets of information from loose talk, sights or hunches, in which they have to put together and make four.

They agreed a plan that Joshua will go today and ride quickly by the house in question and check the area out, then report his findings to Rebecca and go from there.

Joshua quickly got himself and Harry ready while Rebecca fed the children, including Christine, who was now talking non-stop to Connor and vice versa. It was agreed that Connor would stay in the house and await Joshua's return with a reply.

Harry was up for it and fresh as a daisy. Bridge Street wasn't far, just through the town on the South side off the Lamorna Road. The day was fresh and chilly and not a lot of people were about. Getting closer to the target he eased Harry up, dismounted and started walking so he could take everything in. All was quiet, with Joshua noticing that the street in question was quite narrow, with normal type cottages, all terraced in units of ten.

Number four was nothing out of the ordinary, in fact these were lowly cottages directly opening onto the street. Probably fishermen's houses or something like that. The problem with this type of target is there is no room for manoeuvre or places to covertly observe as everything is too enclosed. With his passing done, Joshua remounted and spurred Harry on back home.

Connor was given his reply that the information will be acted upon by the end of the morrow. They said their farewells and Connor was on his way.

Looking at all angles, they couldn't devise a way to penetrate this No 4 without being noticed one way or the other. They also knew that it is one person. Therefore, the idea they kicked around which sounded really plausible, was to act as Parish Council officials, without the Councils knowledge of course, checking subsidiary rolls throughout the street starting at No 1. Whatever they found at No 4 they could leave, overcome or take prisoner. Joshua liked the plan for its simplicity. Rebecca would dress as a man with the clothing they already had, with additions of their protective vests and armed. Little George and Christine were to wait at the bottom of the road on the Lamorna Cross roads with Harry & Lilly should anything go wrong and a quick exit is required.

They fully explained things to Little George & Christine and the rolls which they were to play. Rebecca insisted they must wear protective mailing vests such as theirs and she would make them today out of the spare material they had. These must be worn by all without fail before the plan is put into action. Giving them pistols for their protection was out of the question, for now. All in agreement they rested and prepared. They would all get an early night and move out tomorrow middle afternoon around four o'clock.

Upon nearing the allotted time, Rebecca did a twirl looking quite naturally like a man. The children showed they were wearing their vests. Being happy with the preparation, false identifications and job roles, they were off.

Reaching the crossroads at the bottom of the street, Rebecca and Joshua dismounted then set off on foot to do their duty. Little George & Christine both stayed there sitting on Suzy while holding Harry and Lilly. If they were not back by latest six o'clock they were to go straight to Henry Hosking's at the Blue Anchor in Helston. On nearing the target area, a couple of people passed them by but didn't take any notice, which Joshua found encouraging.

Joshua nodded to Rebecca when they were at the door of No 1. "Ready?" "Yes," she said. So he knocked. A lady came to the door and asked what they wanted. Joshua explained they were Council Inspectors from the Parish Council and wanted to know who lived here for the annual subsidy rolls.

Reluctantly, she agreed and gave some information in which he wrote down spending only a few minutes of her time. With information obtained, the lady firmly shut the door on them. However, based on this first call they were encouraged their plan had in fact, plausibility and credibility. No 2 and No 3 went pretty much the same as number one.

Now it was No 4. Squaring up to the door as before Joshua knocked loudly and immediately felt he had knocked harder than he had with the previous. He was getting tense. Then he heard the faint but familiar click of a double pistol locking mechanism and a loud frightened voice shouted behind the door, "You Bastards!!" And then, the loud back blast noise of a heavy double pistol fire off. Joshua immediately threw his full weight into Rebecca to get her out of the way and shouted "get down."

The person had fired through the door and Rebecca was hit. Joshua couldn't believe it. He was going to fire back but nothing was there. They were both on the floor and needed to get away quickly. What a bloody mess.

Joshua, keeping on the floor, dragged Rebecca's unconscious body away from the doors entrance. Nobody came out of the houses, nobody would, not yet; it was all so quiet. Once out of direct range of the house and into the cobbled street, Joshua got up and with all his strength picked Rebecca up and through her over his shoulder. Little George was quick, he would give him that, as he was already coming up with Harry while Christine held Lilly. Joshua threw Rebecca over Harry like a rag doll and quickly got up himself into the saddle and rode off at a gallop.

Little George and Christine followed as they went quickly out of town and around the long way. Joshua couldn't afford, even then, to let people see which direction they were heading. When completely out of sight from everyone Joshua doubled backed around and headed into the backfields, eventually reaching their backyard to the cottage. What a bloody nightmare.

Chapter 13

Jacques now in France was enjoying himself, he felt confident. He was back on his mainland albeit Calais a long way from Morlaix but all the same it felt good. He didn't like England but the Cornish were even worse. Bloody pastie eating savages he thought. While a horse was being made ready he engaged in a few cognacs in the town's local. Sitting by the window in the corner seat, he was thinking what he would say to Bouchier when they meet at the Chateau.

He thought of the job in hand and what is needed to finish it. Time was the main factor but nobody seemed to care. They just think a job is a job so get it done. Being in the front line is so different than being at a desk, organising missions with no bloody experience, although they think they have.

He thought about Zoe and Pascal and how she would finish him. This was not his responsibility so why should he think like this? He knew it was the time dragging in completing the task. He also knew the English were not stupid although they do play it that way sometimes. His experience told him that their spies were good, which he reluctantly took his hat off too.

Weighing things up with more cognac, the more he realised he needed more men to finish the tunnel, place the liquid germ and get out. This is what he would demand from Bouchier. More men and a quicker time scale to end the job. One other thing he must know and that it what is the exit strategy.

The stable lad came in and informed Jacques his horse was ready. He weighed things up and decided he needed a good drink. He deserved it and one more day wouldn't make any difference. So he ordered a room and told the lad to take his kit up and he would pick the horse and all up at first light tomorrow. With that he ordered another bottle and eased through the next few hours with cognac and thoughts.

Next morning came all too soon. He had slept like a log and the drinking session was a good one. He breakfasted then went to the stables. He paid over the odds for a good horse and wasn't disappointed. He was a big bay with good lines and strong in stature. The lad seemed proud on what he had achieved and Jacques gave him a good tip.

Riding out of Calais gave him a sense of pleasure. He had over a hundred miles to ride and would do it in five stages, possibly four, dependant on the trail and how he felt. He wasn't going to bust a gut especially for someone like Bouchier but something was niggling him that time should not be messed with, or taken for granted.

After a long first day in the saddle he was nearing Caen and decided to stop for the night. He feasted and drunk his beloved Cognac and slept well. Few more pushes like today and he would be near or thereabouts. One thing about Jacques which he was proud of, is when he wanted to do something, he had the determination to do it and not just say it.

The next couple of days were the same but he was getting tired. He knew he needed all his wits about him when he meets his boss Bouchier. With a good night's rest tonight and a little of his favourite poured down his neck and a good meal, he would wake early and calmly go the last few miles.

Entering the grounds of Chateau Morlaix the next morning brought home the fact that Jacques employers were rich and powerful. He was tasked at the main courtyard and ordered to wait. Being subsequently cleared to enter, an escort appeared asking Jacques to get down of his horse. The horse was taken care of and Jacques was asked to follow the courtier round the back.

Jacques started thinking about his own mortality and how vulnerable he felt in this vast palace and its opulence. He was led into a quiet plain looking room and told to wait.

Behind the room in the library sat Bouchier and Philip Albret. "Against tough competition," Philip Albret said, "I convinced the Prince that my plan was the best to achieve their aim in softening the enemy. He accepted and kissed my cheek, so tell me Pierre, why has this fellow of yours come back to speak with you, before the objective is completed?"

Pierre gathered his thoughts and knew he was on dodgy ground if, he gave a fumbling type answer. "One of our softer agents in the Cornish town of Penzance known as Rosevear has been taken away by the authorities but, not before having a terrible beating by some local thugs." "So, what of it?" Albret interrupted. "We were going to use him for ferrying the germ and had already paid him some money. So we are going to use Ward the farmer instead at Sennon." "Bouchier, I am not interested in local goings on, what I am interested in is this plan working and working on time as I pledged to the Prince. My name and reputation is of the upmost importance so let me ask you again, what is this man doing here?"

Bouchier realised his boss Albret was not one to take to fiddling answers, and so knew he had to just tell it as it is. "He is here to ask for more men to reduce the time scale of the job." "That's better Pierre, and what are you going to tell him?" "That I agree and that we have men already earmarked and briefed to fulfil his needs."

"So Pierre, what you are telling me, is that the plan is on course and the timescale is correct or shorter as the case may be, is that the case?" "Yes Philip it is." "Good, then let us have our sherry and then you can leave through that side door."

Jacques got up when Bouchier entered through an opening in the wall and not the main door. They shook hands and got the niceties out of the way. Jacques didn't like Bouchier and Bouchier didn't like Jacques, but apart from that, this was business. Jacques got his views across and Bouchier listened.

They discussed the plan ahead that two extra frontline men were sufficient to quicken the pace. They agreed on four men to deliver the germ to Mr Ward's farm, hopefully within seven to ten days. Once delivered, two men will remain and the other two will come back to France. Bouchier mentioned that they had already chosen men to help Jacques.

The exit strategy was also discussed. The liquid germ would be poured into the ground and during the time it takes before the first victims are infected, a boat will have arrived off shore at Sennon to extract the five of them. Bouchier lied, he really had no intentions at all of doing this but, he let Jacques keep thinking he was. Jacques was going to mention to Pierre that it would probably be four persons returning, not five, as Zoe was going to kill Pascal but as he would probably be already dead, decided not to, as the less he knew the better.

Once the discussions were coming to a close Jacques felt happier as he had achieved his aim. He was advised to get lodging in the town and await further instructions. This he did by exiting out from the side door of the Chateau and walked across to the stables and fetched his borrowed horse. He missed Arc and the knowledge they both instinctively shared.

He acknowledged the stable boy's and once saddled, was off to the local town of Morlaix to the Inn, in the hope they had a spare room for as long as it took for Bouchier to give word.

With Jacques gone, Bouchier felt heavy. He felt Jacques was passing his best and wondered whether he should replace him but time wasn't on his side. So weighing it all up he sent word to the Inn at Brest where the four selected young men were waiting and request they come to the Chateau for briefing first thing in the morning. He needed the day and night to himself to get this right.

Jacques was in luck, a room was free and was welcomed, as over the years of service he had frequented this place many times and very much enjoyed the brandy. The owners knew he liked his drink and more importantly knew he paid well.

Jacques was in a contemplative mood so once his horse was settled and his key to the room was in his pocket he sat at the furthest table away from the bar and settled himself in. The Cognac was beautiful and it feathered his throat delightfully. He sat back and relaxed and anticipated that it would be one or two days before Bouchier called.

He stretched his legs out and felt his mind and body give way from the emotions and tenseness of the situation he was in, regarding the Cornish assault. This is when he felt he could think and, think he would. He chuckled to himself when he thought back to the time when one Cornish drinker in Penzance told him how they should seriously go to war with Devon, as those savages put jam on top of the cream with their scones and not cream on top of the jam.

He thought about the dagger hanging from inside his belt and the flint lock pistol tucked hidden away at his side and how heavy they feel. He also felt a slight unease that the mission was not going right and that something was niggling away but he couldn't for the life of him pinpoint what this niggling feeling of unease was saying. He realised his eyes were closed, as they usually do when he thinks, and on opening them he surveyed the Inn and the people in it.

As normal practice he started weighing up who was who and trying to guess what each did for a way of life. He also knew he was eyeing for any trouble, should it come. This was his way of life and felt himself get tense again. He knew he was becoming paranoid and that everyone else was just enjoying themselves or were they. He poured himself another large one and drank it slowly and smoothly back in one.

However, unbeknown to Jacques, sitting in the wings of the Inn was a middle aged non-descript male of average height, build and looks. He had been living and working in the area for many years and sold fruit and vegetables in the town. He owned a small cottage and had a wife. He never caused any trouble and lived his life simply.

He immediately spotted Jacques enter the Inn with his hard looking body, weathered good looks, black hair and those blue eyes of intelligence. 'So, he was back in the area,' he thought to himself. That means something is up. Jacques is, as with many others, bookmarked as, 'of interest,' and therefore he would get a bonus this month from a grateful Kernow, once he got word to London through the safe channels they worked.

Bouchier's messenger got to the Inn in Brest late and gave word to the four new young team members to report to Bouchier first thing in the morning. This they gave cheer and carried on drinking.

The morning came quickly and the four young men with somewhat slight headaches from the previous evening drinking session gave quick ride to the Chateau Morlaix. There they met Bouchier who was having breakfast and asked them to join him. He had already made his mind up which two would stay the full course in England and which ones would come straight back after the liquid was transported to Ward the farmer at Sennon.

He would like to think his decision process was based on talent to get the job done. However, these guys would have to stay in the same house as Zoe and therefore he would bring back the best looking ones so Zoe would not be tempted by their young zest and dare. He convinced himself that the two remainers were capable. He also threw into the mix that Jacques would have to manage them. Overall, the decision, somewhat tainted by emotion, was an average to good one and with that he felt comfortable.

Once all seated, the four tucked into a hearty meal and listened to the orders given by Bouchier. He mentioned Philip Albret many times and the fact that our very own Prince believed in Phillip. He felt this necessary to instil in the four men the importance of the task and how secret it is, that should they mess up in any way, their families will be shamed. He seemed to get the message across.

Once fully briefed he then asked for any questions. After answering, he advised all four they would report to the man Jacques and were to go back to Brest and await further orders.

On reflection of the briefing, Bouchier noted their youth and to send young men on a sleeper type mission seemed irresponsible. But Jacques insisted he needed the extra help to achieve success and their main assistance would be limited to only hard digging and carrying non covert working.

Bouchier now only needed to know the up to date situation of the Chemical Germ fluid for the next phase to start and for this he had to travel. With that he told the stable grooms to prepare his horse.

The four young men went as they were told straight back to Brest. They discussed the situation and the two remaining ones felt very confident that their skills were better than the other two who were coming back to France, once the germ was delivered. The ones coming back couldn't quite make out, or make sense, on why they were not picked, as their credentials were far better than the two who would stay. If only they knew.

However, now all accepting and knowing what was expected, they decided to drink and be merry and let the day and evening pass with wine, women and song.

Two days later Pierre Bouchier eventually returned to the Chateau from the alchemists at the Abbey of Landerneau and was livid with those bloody nerds, not understanding the utter importance of timeframes. Every time he challenged them they had an answer in that mixing the chemicals together to achieve the results was akin to making good wine, and that the process couldn't be rushed. The distilling process was crucial and then mentioned, like it wasn't important, that the final combination fluid would be combustible and should be carried with care.

He started to raise his voice to them but they wouldn't be moved. However, they did relent in that they would fill and plug the false bottomed kegs on his behalf, but after that it was up to Bouchier to move them out and away. Bouchier reluctantly accepted a finished time line of ten days for pick up. He wasn't too concerned about the possible combustion, after all it wasn't he who going to pick up and move them, was it.

Both the four men at Brest and Jacques at Morlaix were informed to be at the Chateau for breakfast the next morning. Jacques was relieved as although he liked the drinking side, he was getting agitated about Zoe and the state he left things with her and Pascal. However, the four young men were quietly disappointed as they had all the girls they wanted with the money paid in advance from Bouchier and for lots more drinks.

Next morning all the young men were once again seated for breakfast with Bouchier at the head. They were introduced to Jacques who quizzed each of them on where they were from, age, family and experience. Bouchier looked on saying nothing. When finished and things lay quiet Bouchier took over.

He briefed them in full, detailing when and where the Abbey of Landerneau is for picking up of the fluid and where the ship would be waiting to set sail and carry them to the waters off Sennon. In ten days' time it would be Friday week, which would mean that you must get the fluid on board and ready to sail by dusk. With average to good sail, you should reach the destination at midnight or before dawn the next morning being Saturday.

Jacques, a ship is waiting for you at Brest, sailing tomorrow, and docking at Plymouth. Please prepare the Wards at Sennon and get the cottage prepared for the extra two men. This was a lie but he wanted the four young men to believe they and they alone would sail to England. However, he couldn't afford them to go alone due to their immaturity but he liked deceit as it puts people off guard. Bouchier then instructed the four young men to go back to Brest, keep their heads down, behave themselves and get back here very early Friday morning in ten days to pick up the carriage and be at the Abbey in Landerneau mid-morning.

Bouchier felt good the project was back on with time scales to match. Jacques was pleased he was going back into what he did best after his somewhat bold dash out of Mousehole which, broke the sleeper's rule of silence, but had achieved the results he required. As for the four young men you couldn't take the smiles of their faces.

As the four young men left, Bouchier pulled Jacques back in to talk with him alone. "Jacques, I lied about you going back to Mousehole tomorrow. I'm sorry but I just cannot trust those four young idiots to pick up the barrels and get to Sennon without supervision. I have already discussed this with Albret and we have already sent a dispatch to the Wards in preparation of your arrival early Saturday morning. Jacques, Philip Albret has awarded you for your work a handsome sum of fifty pounds to spend on some time off and has also paid your lodgings at the Inn for the next ten days. So enjoy yourself and have a relaxing break but be back here Thursday evening for final briefing." Jacques hopes of seeing Zoe and looking after her were dashed but with a straight face and no outward sign of sadness and frustration he accepted Bouchier's orders; he had no choice.

Chapter 14

Little George arrived at the Blue Anchor in Helston sweating and out of breath, as was Suzy his horse. He must find Mr Hosking's and tell him what has happened. He knows where to go and quickly dashes in and goes to the back of the Inn where his master's room is. Knocking loudly and leaning forward he speaks to the door "Mr Hosking, Mr Hosking." He waits and hears movement within.

Mr Hosking opened the door and saw Little George in a very agitated state and asked, "what is it Little George?" He explained what went on and how Rebecca is poorly and bleeding from being shot.

Henry thinks quickly and asks Little George to stay here, he will be back shortly. Henry goes off out of the Inn and Little George sits anxiously in a seat in Henry's room waiting.

It wasn't long before Henry and another man enters and startles Little George into an upright position. Henry introduces the other man as a friend and Physician and asks that he take him quickly to Rebecca and do not spare the horses. As they both start to exit Henry takes Little George's shoulder and says in a calm voice, "Well done boy."

The front door to the cottage opened with the cold air rushing in and Little George enters with the doctor. It has taken a few tense hours but the sense of secrecy was paramount to their safety. Joshua knew it would take longer for medical aid rather than use the local Physician but telling a locum Doctor a woman has been shot would be around Mousehole and Newlyn as quick as wild fire. No, he had to be wise and secretive. Getting Little George to Henry Hosking for help was, the only way.

The Physician introduced himself and informs Joshua that he has been sent on the orders of Henry Hosking and without a pause, but with a sense of urgency, continued by asking where the patient lays.

Joshua showed him to the bedroom where Christine was so very gently bathing Rebecca's head with cold water. Rebecca lay on the bed still fully clothed with a blanket over her. Joshua had tried to inspect the wound but the clothing had interfered and meshed around in it.

To try and stop the bleeding Joshua applied padding and pressure, as best and as close to the wound as he could. He really didn't know what else to do but had done this several times whilst in service with his mates who had been hit.

The Physician went straight to her side and started doing the basics in which doctors do. He asked for hot water and towelling. Joshua had thought of this and had prepared accordingly. Rebecca was still unconscious but breathing steady.

The Physician started cutting the material away around the area of the wound which was over the right side of her right breast. The Physician looked back over his shoulder and saw three pairs of eyes looking intently at what he was doing. He politely asked them all to leave and wait outside and will call if he needs assistance.

Joshua, Little George and Christine reluctantly withdrew to the front room where the fire was roaring and closed the door behind them. Joshua wanted a drink but knew this was not the time as he had to have all his wits about him. He took the hot water from the fire and made all of them a cup of tea. He decided to have a pipe instead to steady his thoughts.

All were quiet until Little George got up and said he would go and tend to Suzy and put her down for the night and would also check on the Physician's horse and make her comfy. Christine stayed close to Joshua and held his hand. Joshua started reflecting on what went wrong. The ruse about being Parish officials seemed to be a good one but he was not prepared or even thought about a shot being fired from inside out through an unopened door. 'Why?' he kept asking himself. 'How could he have seen this coming?' Experience in the field is one thing but, what it did show or highlight, was his or both of their inexperience in this type of urban conflict. He knew he was beating himself up but also knew he was analysing for the prevention of future incidents. He was learning, but at what cost.

It was getting late so Joshua advised a very sleepy Christine to go to her room and sleep and he would call her if anything occurred. When Little George had finished he advised the same. Joshua would stay up and would attend to the Physician if needed.

The cottage seemed very quiet with only the fire roaring its heat and crackle. Joshua dozed off and felt a hand on his shoulder shaking him. It was the Physician and once he acknowledged him that he was awake and alert the Physician started to explain in a quiet voice that Rebecca was asleep and comfortable. The ball it seems had indeed penetrated her at the far upper right side of her body slicing some of the breast but, due to the protective garment she was wearing, it didn't penetrate deep to cut any main vessels causing a probable life threatening wound. However, infection is a major concern, as is the trauma.

The ball and splinter had been removed and the hole cleaned and stitched with the blood clotting well as he could see. He would stay with her till morning and change the dressings accordingly. Joshua offered him his sincere thanks and made tea for two with pipes to match.

The Physician took both tea and pipe in hand and sat down saying, "It is not for me to judge your doings as I have worked with Henry for some years, but what I will say it is thanks to the Lord you both were wearing your protective vests." He then asked if Joshua was injured in any way which he answered I don't think so. He quickly checked him over and then accepting he was unhurt went into check on Christine and Little George. Once completed and satisfied he went back to Rebecca and left the door ajar.

The cottage started to come awake early around seven thirty. The fire was on and Little George and Christine started cooking some bacon for all to breakfast.

The Physician came out and said they could go in and see Rebecca if they wanted as she is conscious but weak. Joshua mentioned to him that we do not know your name. The Physician gently replied smiling, "You can call me Doctor Smith." With that everyone smiled and went into see Rebecca.

Rebecca was now fully in bed and her clothes put on the floor by the window. Christine was first by her side and held her hand. Joshua and Little George went in turn and kissed her cheek with warmth and love. Rebecca was smiling and a tear left her eye and slid down over her cheek. The doctor then suggested that Christine stay with her and wipe her forehead with cool water but as for Joshua and Little George you should leave Rebecca in peace for a while.

Once back in the front room the doctor advised how and when to change the bandages and soup should be permitted with water on a regular basis. He said if Little George would accompany him back to Helston he would make up some medicine to give to Rebecca and some extra dressings to be applied every morning for a week. He would then come back and see the patient but if anything seems wrong in the interim, to get word to Henry.

On seeing both Gorge and the Physician off, Joshua closed the front door and sat down by the fire. He was feeling at a loss on what to do and so decided to go back to basics and start washing everyone's clothes and cleaning their weapons and importantly, take a look and mend the protective vest that Rebecca was wearing. This kept him occupied physically but mentally he was arranging things on how to move forward and who shot Rebecca and how could he get this information and, once he got it, what to do with it.

One thing he did know is all of them were safe for now and that Rebecca would live, which pleased him but whoever is out there and what they intended doing were still out there and it was down to him to find them. He needed to get a grip and grow up and take responsibility.

The cottage was once again calm and peaceful with everything cleaned and tidied up. Christine was with Rebecca and Joshua was resting in the front room, fire roaring with a lovely brew of tea and a pipe. He needed to speak with Henry and find out what if any news he may have.

Late that afternoon Little George came back with the medical supplies the so called 'Doctor Smith' had promised, also a note from Henry suggesting the need to meet early tomorrow morning at the Blue Anchor.

Rebecca was still a little brain dozy but she was getting to understand what was going on around her to the point that she now started suggesting things. It must be a woman thing, Joshua thought. He made them all some broth and tea and they ate quietly with Rebecca in the bedroom and Christine feeding the patient. Whilst they ate they talked. Rebecca mostly listened but whispering her thoughts and suggestions when needed. Although George Kernow mentioned the danger of this task at the beginning they didn't realise the level of which this meant but, they certainly do now. So all in agreement they wanted to carry on but from now on their safety and reducing risk levels must be a priority.

The night was closing in and so Joshua set his bed up in the front room for an early night ready for a fresh start in morning. Christine was staying with Rebecca and was adamant that she would nurse her accordingly and change the dressings when required. Doctor Smith had showed her what to do and with a little nod and smile from Rebecca it was agreed. For a young lady she certainly had tenacity and Joshua respected that.

The morning came with a new freshness and once Joshua had saddled Harry he was ready to go. The ride took just over an hour and reached the Blue Anchor just after seven thirty. Even at this early hour the Inn was moving with the early risers and the people running it. Young Connor was waiting and took Harry to the side stables. Joshua went in and met Henry having an early breakfast in the front parlour by the fire. "Good morning Joshua, please take a seat."

They exchanged pleasantries and sat down together to share the food and discuss. Henry asked Joshua to explain in fine detail everything that had went on. One thing Joshua has learnt when he is asked for fine detail, he means fine detail, as though he himself is visualising the moments in question. They got onto the subject of the house at No 4 and the subsequent disaster which followed and their indirect round about withdrawal to the cottage.

Henry listened intently adding nods and hmmm's along the way and stopping Joshua to elaborate on certain things. Henry liked debriefs to be methodical and of slow to medium speed so he can take all the information in. Joshua also found that this slowness in speed helped him be more aware of what exactly happened or was happening when looking back at each event.

Once his brief was finished, Henry took two pipes and offered Joshua one then reaching into the fire for a glow stick to light them. Both smoking and Henry thinking things over in his head he leaned forward and said, "Well done Joshua and well done to Rebecca, Little George and Christine."

"Now let me tell you what's been happening behind the scene regarding south west Cornwall whilst you and Rebecca have been in the front line, so to speak." Henry went on to discuss all the information he had to tell of which one Mr Rosevear the Landlord at the Turks Head in Penzance. Joshua had been thinking about him also. Rosevear has been taken in for questioning on the orders of Henry with the help of his support team, Bull and gang from St Just, covering it up with a fight that got out of hand.

It had worked and Mr Rosevear is now on route to London for a discussion with George Kernow.

Henry then explained that the person who shot Rebecca through the door of No 4 was in fact a sailor who had absconded from ship and was lying low as the authorities want him for murdering two ship mates and taking their money. He has now been caught while trying to run from the house, after the shooting incident, and got as far as Mousehole Harbour.

He thought you were the authorities of the Royal Navy and had nothing to lose and knew if caught he will hang and, hang he will. Thank God Rebecca survived through your quick actions. "The protective vests did that," Joshua replied. "Yes, they are good aren't they? Which reminds me" he said, "now that you are running with four I have here two new small lady pocket flint pistols which I suggest you give to Little George and Christine for their own protection and have had made two extra protective vests with extra material for these two youngens as well." "Yes," Joshua replied, "it seems that we are four and thank you Henry."

Henry continued but more quietly, "now there is some information being fed down from London which arrived late last night that a certain person we know as 'Jack' has been seen in a place in France, close to certain people known not to me but to George Kernow. This has raised suspicion and escalated things especially when this guy was presumably seen in Penzance not so long ago. This sighting prompted, among other things, why that traitor Rosevear of the Turks Head is now going into custody in London and not Bodmin. "What does this mean Henry?" "It means Joshua that something is coming or is being implemented." "What does this guy look like?" Joshua asked"

"A little like you Joshua but older, tanned, weathered, well-structured face, six foot plus, jet black hair and very knowing blue eyes, almost piercing with intelligence and calmness. In fact, we had an artist impression made of him." Henry then delved into his pocket and produced a small piece of paper with a sketched face of this man called Jacques and handed it to Joshua.

Whilst Henry was carrying on describing him, Joshua was looking at the sketch in hand and, his mind immediately flicked back to the Fisherman's Inn in Penzance the night he took young Christine from Rosevear's clutches and where Little George broke the window to help their escape. He recalled that when he was surveying the Inn on his entrance he saw this guy in the corner and thought then that of all the people in the Inn he would be the most problematic but, somehow knew this man would not interfere. It was the strength in his manner and the calmness in the eyes.

"I have seen this man," Joshua said, "once in the Fisherman's Inn when I took Christine away from Rosevear." Henry nodded then said, "so it is confirmed then, you must double your efforts Joshua and move quickly, if this guy has been seen in France in an area of interest to ourselves, we would surmise that he has taken further orders."

Joshua asked, "do you know anything more of this man Henry and please tell me all you know." Henry said what he could and nearing the end he mentioned "this man Jack or Jacques had one vice or possible weak link and that my friend is drink, specifically French Brandy, but Joshua do not under estimate him even if he is or hasn't been drinking. He is very experienced."

The meeting finished and both said their farewells. Joshua left the building with his mind bubbling with activity. He needed to think and get this right. Simply knocking on doors like a simpleton Council worker produced nothing but overt attention and life threatening outcomes.

Joshua walked to the stables, picked up Harry and strode out into the open. Gunwalloe he thought, that's where he needed to go. So with that thought in mind Joshua and Harry were off at a gallop.

Whilst on route he diverted Harry to Cury village and picked up Queenie and Cecil at Mrs Stephens place. They were pleased to see him and couldn't stop wagging their tails. He thanked Mrs Stephens for her kindness and offered some money but she would have none of it. So with both dogs on his lap upon Harry, who accepted these little mites lovingly, they headed for his cottage.

The cottage was dusty and felt lonely without him but seemed to wake up when he kindled the fire. The afternoon was mild and fresh and sitting in front of the hearth, fire roaring and windows open with a cup of tea and fresh milk which Mrs Stephens had supplied, Joshua lit a pipe and sat back looking at the ceiling. Both Queenie and Cecil lay with him snuggled up.

It wasn't long before Joshua decided to head to the beach. Leaving both dogs by the fire he walked gently down the slope to the rocks. Apart from a couple of people, the beach was empty it was late afternoon early evening. He got to his usual place and thought.

After an hour of pure freshness and being alone his brain got it. He decided discipline and planning in a step by step approach was the way. Planning long term stuff didn't work, sounded good but doesn't work on the ground. He needed intelligence and knowledge. He also needed to know his strengths and weaknesses of which there was many and use the strengths to his advantage.

So he thought we have two young adults both girl and boy who are extremely loyal and tenacious and can be trusted no matter what. One experienced lady of the world who again had brains and loyalty. And himself, experienced in life, not in love, he chuckled, but determined and again loyal. He would take steps on a daily basis having briefings every evening and be flexible to switch arrangements and movements accordingly to those briefings.

He would use the instruments given to him such as pistols, vests, optical and garments to the best they could bring. He also knew, if needed, he had heavy back up from Bull and his gang at St Just, again very capable but as for loyalty he couldn't reason.

With all this going through his mind and a determination to succeed he knew that the overall word which kept coming back over and over, was patience. However, he knew that good planning was a form of patience and he felt happy with that.

It was getting late and he wanted to get back to west Newlyn to be with Rebecca and the two youngens before the night was out. With no one on the beach Joshua inquisitiveness made him decide to use the tunnel in the cave, the one Rebecca took, to get back to his cottage. He was intrigued to use it just so he knew it was there and that he could orientate himself through it.

Entering the cave, he went to the back marker and pushed, as Rebecca had told him, the door moved. Joshua really couldn't believe that after all these years he never actually believed these things existed and now he was using one but, it seemed just normal in the field he was playing.

As briefed the tunnel route was straight and ended in his back field, covered by gorse. Unbelievably simple but very effective, he thought. Going back into the cottage the fire had gone out. He closed everything up, got Queenie and Cecil and with Harry in good stead, moved onto Newlyn at a good pace. Joshua started feeling more confident and felt he was getting somewhere and anticipating his new more structured approach, would produce better results.

It was nearing midnight before Joshua eventually arrived at their cottage. The light was dim as he entered and the fire, although alight was almost out. Little George was asleep on the soft chair but started rousing on the noise of the door closing. Joshua suggested he go to bed and would discuss things bright and early in the morning.

Joshua went in to Rebecca who was asleep as was Christine lying next to her. He quietly left the room with the door ajar. He tended to his horse Harry and went back in to cottage to make up his bed in the front room where he would sleep soundly. As though understanding the situation on being quiet, both dogs, after sniffing around like rats, lay with him.

The morning came all too quickly and Joshua rose with a new vigour to get the job done with the new structure he had devised. Joshua with the help of Little George and Christine got the cottage alive and warm with breakfast being made ready. Queenie and Cecil couldn't believe their luck with all the attention they were getting and running around the new place like demons.

Rebecca was awake and for the first time since the incident, aided by little Christine, was holding on to the wall for support, said "good morning." Joshua along with Little George got up and helped her to the soft chair in front of the fire. Queenie and

Cecil raced around her as they wanted in on the act. A smile came over Rebecca which brightened them all.

"So Joshua, tell me what has happened and what are your plans?" With everyone now in attendance Joshua explained in full what Henry and he had discussed. He went into all details and specifically focused on this person called Jacques or Jack. He passed the sketch around so all were familiar. Everyone listened carefully with no questions.

Joshua also handed out the new small lady pistols to Little George and Christine saying that this afternoon they will go back to his cottage at Gunwalloe and practice as he did with Rebecca. He was expecting Rebecca to stop him there and protest at bringing the children into this web further but she did not, only to nod her approval. It seemed that for the first time they had all together now understood that they are in this together no matter what.

Joshua outlined as from tomorrow the new structure would start. Little George and Christine as brother and sister enter Newlyn and Mousehole during the day and mingle and play. However, while doing this they must keep their ears and eyes open and note particular things outside the norm. They must remember everything from names, places and people's actions. However, they must never ever be alone from each other.

They must also report back to Rebecca every day. They were in complete acceptance and Rebecca stressed the importance that they must stay together at all times and in no circumstance will you separate, in which they both understood.

With the non-existence of any new information, Joshua was working out their next moves. Apart from Little George and Christine working the streets at day he would work the pubs at night. He had also identified and earmarked three full night observation sites which, if no information is gathered beforehand, would start next Thursday. One is the Mousehole Harbour, the second being the main cross roads again and thirdly, Sennon Woods. He explained his reasoning on the three targets and Rebecca nodded.

Mousehole Harbour he felt could only be safely completed at sea looking inwards watching the close activity in the harbour. Sennon was the place where a landing at sea was extremely attractive and the shortest distance overland to Mousehole. These places were briefly mentioned by Henry and George Kernow in the same breaths as the likes of the traitor Rosevear and so his assumptions were, they needed attention.

Rebecca asked what her role would be. Joshua delicately advised that due to her injuries and convalescence she would need to hold the fort and feed, nurture and give them a constant warm place to come back to. He repeated that they hold a meeting every night for all to input their thoughts. Queenie and Cecil will stay with Rebecca for company and support.

With that Rebecca asked Christine to fetch their new protective vests and her sewing gear as she would adjust them now. Joshua made another pot of tea for all and suggested he tend to the horses and get them ready for the trip to Gunwalloe for Christine's and Little George's firearms training. Christine looked at Rebecca with excitement and Rebecca nodded that she could use her horse Lily.

Joshua went into the outhouse to prepare all the firearms and holsters for each of them and to clean and prepare his optical instruments for the day and nights ahead.

Whilst Christine was being fitted, Rebecca went over again the importance that she must act mature beyond her young age. Christine was adamant that she was nearly thirteen and understood what she was doing and she was proud to be part of the 'family,' as she called it. Rebecca gave her a big hug and carried on the fitting process.

Once Christine was done it was Little George's turn. Christine, with her under protective vest on, felt very grown up and turned her attention in making the tea for all. When Little George was done and tea finished, they all went into the outhouse to understand the use of a pistol.

As the new pistols were the new lady type they were small enough to fit into a pocket but Rebecca wanted them strapped to their bodies under their outer garments without the least possibility of them falling out and also, could only be used should either want to. So straps and holsters were made to fit them both and once both comfortable carried on with what a pistol is made up from, stripped them down and put them back together several times. Joshua then went over the ball and shot cartridges so they understood what happened when the flint ignites the powder.

They were as near to the end of their training when Rebecca hailed them all in to the front room by the fire for an early lunch before their afternoon live firing training session.

With the horses fresh and everything stashed in the side bags they said farewell to Rebecca who asked that on their way back could they check in on her cottage at Marazion. With Queenie and Cecil by her side she waved them off.

The journey was carried out at a canter with no rush, keeping Christine in between Joshua and Little George. She was a little natural and Lilly liked her ease of gentle control. Once they were at Joshua's cottage they dismounted and got things ready for the firing. Joshua's land to the back was full of trees and shrubbery and the cottage being isolated was a great place to practise without any prying eyes.

They set up the targets and Joshua asked they get ready but not to load then went over once again the importance of what they were doing and that safety with these deadly pieces of arms was paramount. Once all the safety checks were done he showed them how to load and watch him fire first. His aim was true and the ball entered centre.

Joshua asked them both to aim and fire when ready. Looking at them both he felt so very proud that these young people were doing all this with pride and with a sense of feeling of helping Rebecca and him. Little George's pistol went off first followed quickly by Christine, they both missed. They went over the reload and they aimed again. This time they waited for his order to fire which he did, they both missed.

On organising them closer to the target Joshua got behind Little George to see what he was seeing and how he was aiming. On slight readjustments of both arm and sight he pulled the trigger and made a hit. Now he could adjust future shot with eye and sight. He did the same with Christine however; he noticed her right hand seemed to continually shake and when she pulled the trigger she again missed.

Christine was getting a little upset as she was trying her very hardest and the target wasn't exactly that far off. For some reason Joshua instinctively suggested she change her holding hand to the left and use her right to steady underneath. She reloaded, steadied and fired, it just hit the top of the marker.

Nevertheless, it was a hit and she threw a thrill delight. "My dear," Joshua said, "you are left handed, just like Rebecca." And with that she threw another thrill and reloaded.

They carried on for another hour with constant changes and adjustments being done but the lesson was being learnt. They were becoming familiar with the weapon and the fear of having or using them, now leaving them with being comfortable.

With a good run of hits Joshua decided that was enough and should dismantle, clean and put them back in their holster straps. With all pistols fully stripped and put back together correctly they practised taking them out and putting them back. This particular process had to be smooth and familiar and to their credit they practised and practised until it was.

Asked if they felt happy with their vests and the pistols and then, stating that for their protection, they must be worn at all times even going to the loo. They both laughed and Christine went a little red in the face but said yes they understood their importance and would wear them at all times.

With that Joshua was happy that the day had been a success and suggested they do this, every month. They then went back to the cottage to give it a little check over and then went on their way to Rebecca's cottage in Marazion.

Time was moving on and when they arrived at Rebecca's cottage the light was fading. Joshua asked Little George and Christine to stay back while he went in alone. They were getting the message, that caution no matter how clear and easy things look, was a priority.

Joshua peeped through the window and seeing nothing unusual went to the door and unlocked it. On entering things felt damp and cold but all seemed to be in place and nothing out of the ordinary. He called Little George and Christine. He suggested to Christine that she get some extra clothing for Rebecca while he went into the cellar in the scrub area to replenish extra ammunition and anything that could be useful. Little George tendered the horses.

Looking around the place and feeling happy they had everything they needed, Joshua locked up and they went on their way.

Joshua felt good in getting home to their cottage in Newlyn with Little George and Christine. On entering, they smelt a lovely rabbit stew. Rebecca was up and the fire was aglow. What a lovely feeling. Rebecca asked how things had gone and he explained it all and how successful it had been.

Christine quickly and proudly said "I am left handed just like you Rebecca." "That means you are both special," Joshua said. Rebecca gave him a roll of the eyes and gave Christine a hug and again mentioned that pistols are very dangerous and must be used very wisely. "Yes I know Rebecca," she replied.

When Little George came in after tending the horses, the stew was ready and they all sat by the fire with a hearty meal to eat and they were starving. They chatted further into the early evening and Rebecca allowed Joshua to look at her wound.

The Doctor had done a good job. The aggression had gone and the tissue was pink and healthy.

With that Rebecca wanted to retire and asked Christine if she would change her dressing. Little George completed the plates and cutlery washing and so Joshua decided to drag Queenie and Cecil away from Rebecca and take them for a little refreshing walk which, he couldn't work out, whether that pleased them being with him and not Rebecca.

Chapter 15

Pascal was in the tunnel and totally jarred off. He was meant to be digging but found himself sitting with his back against the wall and legs pulled up to his chest with his arms wrapped round. He was a scientist or alchemist as some like to think, not a bloody miner. His hands and arms hurt and his back was no better. What was he doing here?

He thought back to the time in the laboratory near Morlaix where he was a budding scholar nearing his finishing with a lovely master of the arts who trained him daily. He was seen as something special and was introduced to the Count of Morlaix, a Mr Philip Albret.

It was when his studies had finished that he was invited to the Chateau and from then on his life had changed from being a young person with intelligence and no money to whatever he wanted and money no problem. He had fun and women whenever he wanted and lived in a lovely house in Morlaix free of charge.

It was quite a few months ago he was asked to help out with a project he was told so secret that the invitation had come direct from the King to protect our beautiful France from the bullies of England. The rewards and prestige of a successful mission would allow a very privileged life style thereafter. Being young and seeing the advantages of such a life was the inspiration he needed in saying yes. His Mother and Father had fell on bad times and weren't seen as anything important so if he could do this mission and get the money and the house with small holding in which Albret and Bouchier had promised, how good would that be. He started feeling better but his job was mine direction and chemical agent supervisor using his brain, not a bloody shovel and pick.

Pascal drew the candle nearer and took out his instruments and started measuring angles and distances. Scratching pencil marks here and there on his parchment and doing his calculations, he concluded the tunnel was on course and that he was only seventy-seven feet from the X zone but the tunnel direction needed change and marked a different angle of the lineage. He took the chalk and marked the new elevation accordingly on the tunnel walling as he had done previously.

Once they were directly over the X zone they would dig a holding area of around three meters wide and one-metre-deep to pour the germ in and then let the natural earth and its elements take over. If correct the earth will drink the liquid at such an angle and volume and carry it naturally to the upper towns drinking well through the water bed below.

Once he had finished his new conclusions and was happy he then made up his mind that he would have it out with Jacques on his return and get this sorted out one way or the other. He wasn't a shoveller, he was an intellect and should be shown respect. However, one thing he did know, was that Zoe wanted him, he was sure. She had changed and her warmer affections towards him were clear ever since that bully Jacques wasn't around. With that he took the candle and went back up the tunnel to the cottage.

Zoe was at the table with a brandy in hand. She also liked a pipe. She was thinking of the situation and trying to come up with logical reasoning and conclusions. Pascal was in the tunnel supposedly digging, 'bloody idiot' she thought. Then there was Jacques. Jacques, 'what about him she thought?' She loved someone else and it wasn't Jacques or bloody Bouchier. But she knew also that she had to be very careful.

These men don't just lie down and say I understand my love, that's quite alright my dear, they have vengeance and she cannot afford for them to use any of that once this task is finished. They will find her and destroy her, unless of course she could get to them first.

She knew the man she really loved and he had pledged his love to her forever and was hopefully still waiting for her. He wasn't a man of stature but this didn't matter anymore, he was her childhood sweetheart from the sticks of south western France in a small village of Cognac. He was a farmer's boy working in a small vineyard owned by his Father. She started thinking of the beautiful days they were together and the sun and warmth of their love. How she got into this position was beyond her and how now she wished she had never met Philip Albret and the promises he gave her parents which all came to nothing.

She needed to think clearly and work this position to her advantage one way or the other. Jacques had been away now just over a week and should be heading back in the next couple days or thereabouts. What news would he bring?

Zoe started going over the plan, as explained in detail by Bouchier, and the point that this particular task at Mousehole was a prelude to the main mission designated for Penzance with a larger populace of destruction, prior to a navy invasion set for the summer or latest early autumn. He wanted her for both missions and, she also knew he wanted her for his wife once the Penzance mission was done.

He also went over very discretely about the poison he had given her and that the other persons being used for this initial mission were not necessarily earmarked for the main one. She should use it before the task was ended and if no one came back other than herself, nothing would be said and anything that she had done would be washed under the carpet, so to speak.

She would be safe. She went over this again and again and came to the same conclusion that Bouchier only wanted her back alive. The others would be killed in some way either from her hands or by other means leaving no traces as to jeopardise in anyway shape or form the next mission.

With her mind deep in thought and the pipe being smoked lavishly through slow long inhales she heard Pascal come out of the tunnel. She took a gulp of the brandy and quickly refilled her glass. What was she to do with this one? Jacques suggested she kill him before he got back but she hadn't got any further with the coordinates or how to decipher his writing. She knew he liked her and she had made every effort to forge an allusion that she fancied him. She actually hated people like Pascal who thought the world owed them a living due to their knowledge or position.

Maybe it was her upbringing of the lower middle class system that gave her this way of thinking. Whatever it was, she didn't like these types of people which included Bouchier and Albret. Jacques, she thought, was different in this as he was from working class like her. Funny that she thought that's the first time she had separated her thought process isolating Jacques away from the others.

Pascal came and sat down next to Zoe and rubbed her shoulder while taking the seat. "How are you?" He asked. "Very well thank you Pascal, how are you?" "Am tired and worn out, I have completed my latest calculations and chalked the tunnel with directions and angles for the next push." "How far to go?" "Around seventy-seven feet," he replied. Zoe made him a cup tea in a way that wives do for their husbands as if it is of no consequence.

"You're very clever Pascal, well done and you keep all this in your head, you must be very intelligent." Pascal patted his breast pocket and said, "I have to work things out and sometimes need pencil and parchment to scribble to get the sum right, if people could see my workings they wouldn't have a clue as I was advised very early on that I have to code everything effectively for me to understand, but for a foreigner not too. I also have my little instruments given to me by my master which help a great deal in giving me measurements of accuracy to complete my calculations." "Wow and I'm just a farmer's daughter."

Leaning back in the chair Pascal responded "Don't beat yourself up Zoe, it takes all kinds to fill the world." Zoe smiled nicely and thought you are so far up your own arse. Then said lovingly, "more tea Pascal?" He nodded his acceptance by pushing his cup towards her. Whilst filling his cup she looked at him with a smile and thinking, what a prat and felt like poisoning him there and then.

Zoe suggested he go upstairs and lie down as he has worked very hard. This he accepted and with tea in hand he got up and pecked her on the cheek. She again smiled and said, "Sleep well, you deserve it."

When Pascal was gone she pushed herself back into the chair, took a deep breath and blew out a long sigh and took a gulp of the brandy. It had never occurred to her that his calculations were coded. Bloody coded! How lucky she had been that she didn't kill him that very first night as suggested by Jacques. If she had she would have been worthless. In fact, the mission would have had to been abandoned or delayed until a replacement found. She realised she was a lucky girl and that the decision to kill him she would now handover to Jacques on his return whenever that be. In the meantime, she would play the blushing girl who fancies him.

She then had one last thought of going up to Pascal and having sex with him and with her guidance and coercion, gain the code to decode the calculations once and for all. However, could she be certain they would be correct or true and lasting? She weighed things up and taking another long breath she accepted the realisation that they would not. Therefore, she had to talk with Jacques. You are a very lucky girl Zoe; she thought to herself and then changed her mind about carrying on playing the blushing bride to that tosser upstairs. She needed to look after her own self and find a way out from here safely but knew she was in deep and therefore would need to use all her patience and guile.

Zoe drank the last of the brandy and headed upstairs to bed. Once in her room she bolted the door from the inside which she hadn't done since Jacques had gone to France.

Chapter 16

The two masted light Galleon with no insignia silently left the docks at London and sailed up the Thames heading east to a secret location, prepared earlier from the instructions of Kernow. It was dark and getting late. George Kernow had boarded only ten minutes before, as he trusted no one, and this meeting was important for the agenda on what he wanted for the plan to be a success.

The Captain was a capable man and gave George his quarters to do what he wanted. And what he wanted at the moment was a drink of Claret, which was duly given. On these types of rendezvous, he took only two escorts, whose sole job was to guard and protect him and stay out of sight.

The journey would take a couple of hours outbound and hopefully the same back once the meeting was finished. He hoped to be back in Whitehall by daybreak at the latest with the information to formulate his decisions.

George sat back drinking the Claret and started twisting one end of his moustache in thought about Hosking's and his resolute to be successful. He had many operatives but he liked the Cornish for some unknown reason, possibly their basic sense of humour, but that apart he knew they were a soft belly for a French landing as most of his armour and defence was in London and the French knew this. He also started analysing Rebecca and Joshua and the reports he had had so far impressed him. Mistakes had been made, he knew that, but he also knew this was their first mission and subject to the outcome he knew he could use their skills and aptitude later.

Hosking's he thought had been good in the field especially when working with Rebecca's Mother, Jeanne, and Joshua's Father, John. However, working in a more management type scenario behind the scenes, he was yet to be convinced. George was old enough and experienced to know that good people in the front line don't necessarily mean they would be good handlers. However, in the present situation Henry Hosking was an important part of the plan and given the limited and cropped information he has to work with, was doing a pretty good job.

Kernow closed his eyes and rested his thoughts. This was the way he worked information, wait, information, wait and then when he believes the timing to be right and with that information completely deciphered and analysed again and again, strike the plan into operation. This rendezvous was the last piece in the puzzle and activation had to be done by the morrow. The timing was tight but he had no choice, he needed to catch the mouse to get the cat.

The ship was making good steady speed as the Captain had promised and George wasn't minded at all with the sway and tilt. He was accustomed to this from his early career in the Navy until he was taken aside and advised to work undercover for his beloved Queen. With good service under his belt he then took over the reins from his mentor on his passing.

Always better with whom you know and not hearsay on what others may say or portray.

A knock on the cabin door and with a 'Come in,' the Captain entered reporting that the other ship is in sight, has displayed the correct torch code and will be aside in ten minutes. "Thank you Captain, please escort my friend to me on his boarding." They were in the middle of the sea ten miles off shore directly due east from Ghent. They hadn't and would not drop anchor but will hold firm together as best they could, just in case they need to separate and getaway fast. Cannons were at the ready.

Although the places have always been different, the procedure is the same until such time as Kernow orders otherwise. Kernow felt the ships bang together.

Kernow got himself ready and made a pipe for his friend as well as a nice drink of brandy. The door opened and in walked an average built man about fifty years of age, appearing like a vagabond dirty sailor sporting a red woollen hat with its end flapping down one side with a bobble on it touching his right ear. They immediately went to each other and boldly shook hands with total respect. "George," he said, "it's been a while, how goes you?" "Fine" George replied, "it's good to see you, old friend, take a seat, I have made you a pipe and drink as you like it." "Thank you George, I need it."

George was really pleased to see him and aching to get the information but knew he needed to give each of them time to explain to one another what they knew and what they don't know which, is just as important. The dirty sailor looking man did not say his name, nor did George say it either throughout their whole time together. However, this unassuming dirty scoundrel in George's presence was his equivalent in France and had been for years.

After discussing side issues such as weather, health and family, George was the first to take directional charge of topics which had to be discussed in depth and without error. Knowledge pure knowledge is what is wanted and this man would oblige without hesitation in a very clear and sometimes brutal manner of honesty.

"Is there an antidote?" "All the signs gathered since the time of Jeanne, John and Henry's French operation indicate that there is one," the sailor replied. "What makes you think that?" "The alchemists of the Abbey of Landerneau, as you know, were a subject that Jeanne had to gather information on."

The sailor continued, 'as you know Jeanne got close to a particular alchemist who beforehand we found had a weakness for the opposite sex and was a womaniser. We therefore allowed Jeanne to exploit that weakness even though he was a married man and getting on in years.'

'It appears that this man had been noticed on numerous occasions travelling to the Count of Morlaix to one Philip Albret and stopping over at the local inn. He hasn't been seen for a month, vanished. His wife has been seen in the town of Landerneau and hasn't stopped talking about her suspicions of him being killed by someone near to the King. It was also suggested after gaining her trust with low level chatting that her alchemist husband was a good man and had said to her once that whatever they ask me to do I will do but as a true alchemist I must also have the knowledge to undo. If it is in the nature of hurt, I must unhurt.'

'This language mirrors the information gently gathered from Jeanne, who had found out how and where, and as I thought this information critical, did not meet her but suggested she go directly to England and impart her information only to you. However, somehow they were caught in a trap and according to Henry Hosking's, dead, both her and John. Therefore, George, yes, I believe that adding this information constant from the alchemists bereaved wife, with that of Jeanne's, that there is an antidote and moreover, the only person who can give us this information is Jeanne.'

George listened intently and when the sailor fell silent leaned back and started slowly twisting the end of his moustache in contemplation. "And the rumours," he replied. "About whom?" "About Jeanne," George said. "They are true, she is alive." "My God man, tell me."

"Firstly let me say, that I have checked and double checked Henry Hosking's version of events on that fateful day and I believe them to be true. If I was where Henry was at that time, my briefing to you would be the same as his. To all intent and purposes she should be dead." George butted in and said, "I also have checked his version and monitored him more than others and probably more than I should and conclude his is good, but I always get suspicious when a party of three try to get away and only one makes it. Sorry, please continue."

"It appears that the Galleon carrying them away got away even with its damage from the French guns. Hence Hosking's close shave safe return. However, as with his story, Jeanne and John were blasted into the water. The Frenchie's retrieved the bodies that were still afloat. However, not just Jeanne but John survived as well. Being very poorly and near to death they were of no use to the French authorities. However, one Philip Albret who had watched the action had them taken, without notice to anyone, to the Chateaux living in the deepest dungeon in the hope they may survive with his trialling of new herbs and remedy methods and had nothing to lose. If they died they died but if they survived they could be valuable assets in some way or another.

"Unfortunately, John passed away, his injuries too severe. However, Jeanne started to improve and over a long period of time of being nursed she came out of being critical to surviving. It's ironic to think that maybe the very person treating her with these new herbs and remedies was the same alchemist she was told to befriend and who has himself now vanished, presumed dead.

We know all this as after two years of working, we have at last got a person on the inside, albeit at a very low level working in the kitchens so the information is extremely weak, sparse and made through gossip. However, what we do know is he had to deliver food to her jailer in the lowliest dirtiest part of the building and says he has seen her and his description confirms to us that it is Jeanne."

George understood very well that the information being supplied is through people putting their lives at risk and people like Albret and the other Counts to the King, do what he himself does in England and monitor's the monitors without them knowing. Information isn't straight forward and nothing can be presumed or assumed, only consideration and risk and counter risk planning from the information given. Both he and the sailor knew this.

George replenished the drinks and relit pipes. George then went over what he knew so far on the English side of things, especially the threat of a germ type warfare scenario, and that Jeanne & John's children namely Rebecca and Joshua, were working for him under Henry Hosking's in Cornwall. The sailor knew this already but didn't say anything and nodded approval. He had worked in the field as long as George, he in France and George in London.

George had one more directional question which, if true, would confirm the plan he would use. "Is it also true that Jeanne had an affair or romantic liaison with a person known as Jacques?" "Yes this is true, we encouraged it."

"And is it true that he fell in love with her." "I think George; they fell in love with each other. Jeanne was fully aware of what might happen and to her credit told us everything."

"Does Jacques know of her still being alive?" "I believe he does not. Jacques, we understand is the type of person who is determined and if he knew, we would have heard things. It's only through our suspicion and years of determination to find out for sure whether or not she was alive or dead, we have eventually found the truth of her being alive. Albret is very secretive in his actions and kill's people without any conscious. If we now know that she is alive then my boy in his service is probably also at risk as we talk."

The sailor moved forward and filled both his and George's drinks. George was thinking. The sailor then said, "Let me ask you a question, have you heard anyone mention a Spring Tide?" "No I haven't, why has this anything to do with this so called germ thing?" "I am not sure but when Jeanne was working the alchemist 'Spring Tide' was mentioned twice as I reported. However, Jacques also mentioned it once to her in whom she put in her report to me but I never put the two together until I went over the copies last week. It may be something or nothing." George got up from his chair and asked the guard outside the door to fetch the Captain.

On entering, George asked the Captain about spring tides. The Captain replied that reports have come in that an unusual spring or very high tide is due in the South, South West of England in two weeks. "Is this common knowledge?" George asked. "Yes, most people in the knowledge of ebbs and tides would be aware." "Thank you Captain, we will be finished here in a short while, please prepare for the off, we both need to get back."

"What do you make of it?" asked the sailor. "Not sure, but something inside has stirred and if this is something then we have only two weeks to find out."

"One thing my friend, do you know where Jacques is?" "No" the sailor replied. "Can you get a message to your man in the Chateaux?" "Yes, but he is not a man, he is a young fourteen-year-old boy and getting an opportunity to get a message to him without alarming anyone is probably once a week, when he visits the town market, which is every Thursday."

With that last piece, George instinctively knew what must be done. He needed his friends and their observations to discuss what he had in mind. It was audacious but feasible if, he could move the players accordingly in the time given.

Both knew their meeting was finished and that the information had flowed freely, both ways without hesitation to each, as both men liked. Both had to get back under the darkness and before daylight. They shook hands and said their farewells with respect for each other knowing the difficulties each face and the decisions soon to be made.

George knew he had been playing things defensively but with information he had had, he knew it was the right way but now the new information received has changed things and would act accordingly and that meant it was time to change the undercover passive approach to the attack.

With new orders given to the Captain the ship changed course to Falmouth, at best speed.

Chapter 17

Rebecca felt better each day and with that her sense of urgency with the task laid before them all. Joshua also started improving his activities in this new covert way of working. Little George and Christine were fitting in well and in general everyone was working together better as a team.

"Tomorrow we start our new three days' observation routine, are you happy with things especially Little George and Christine's involvement?" "I am happy Joshua and hope you keep them as safe as you possibly can, they are as eager as you to get on with it." Joshua responded, "Their safety gear and equipment has been done to the best of my ability and they have learnt well from both of us to keep themselves quiet and resourceful." With an approval nod of the head Rebecca got up to retire for the night. Christine was already in bed and at last Little George came in after tending Harry.

Joshua said good night and allowed Rebecca some time to get ready and into bed. Little George said his goodnights. Joshua finished off another brandy and as Rebecca was feeling much better from both wound and mind, Joshua was allowed back into the bedroom in the large comfy double bed, however, the large wooden divider was still there.

The new day arrived, and the first part of Joshua's plan was to start. Everybody was up and doing their usual things. Rebecca's was the food and clothing, Little George and Christine were the horses and Joshua's being the weapons and gear. The idea was to get into a kind of three-day routine, which he explained to both Kernow and Hosking's.

Although locations may change, the basic plan had been agreed. The last thing to do was pass the sketch of Jacques around so the image was clear in all minds and a reminder that their job was intelligence gathering, not to be seen, but to get that information back as quickly as possible.

When all things were ready, Joshua got on his horse Harry and rode off towards Penzance. His job was to scout, by joyful riding with occasional Inn stops throughout the surrounding area to include the cobbled towns of Mousehole, Newlyn and Penzance. Joshua and Harry were fresh and the morning air was bracing. He was to be back by two o'clock for food and drink and sleep until the late evening when he would go out to the first of his nominated observations posts.

Next were Little George and Christine. Their job was to mindfully play in all streets of Mousehole with special attention to the port and also the more blind alleys in the town. Again, they had to be back for two for food and drink and report any findings.

Once all gone from the cottage, Rebecca began to clean up and prepare things for their return. Although she was physically and mentally better from the shooting she knew she wasn't ready for the outside work and accepted her more echelon role.

The morning soon went by and all returned as suggested with no hints of anything untoward. All were safe and the reporting went well. Joshua was really proud of the young ones.

Once fed and refreshed from Rebecca's cooking, it was Christine's turn to tend any horses used through the day whilst Joshua and Little George went to their beds.

Around ten o'clock they were woken by Rebecca. It was a dark night and very cold so Joshua prepared his and Little George's equipment especially the warm weather clothing. Joshua went out and noted how clear the night was and the clear way he could see the stars. He repeated to himself that this was going to be cold one.

Their first post for night observations would be the main crossroads. Harry and Suzy were prepared by Christine before she turned in earlier that evening. They had already been around this area looking for good places, as with the other posts for the next two nights. They had prepared and discussed entry and exit.

As with all the posts they would completely circle the target and come in from the opposite direction. The position of the post location was just inside the forest overlooking the crossroads. Enough cover for not being seen and a good exit should they be. They would enter the post around the half hour past midnight.

They got to the post site on schedule and made cover in it by scrapping a shell scrape and Little George camouflaging the top before squeezing in underneath. Harry and Lilly were reined about one hundred yards back with good feed to keep them quiet. The silence was spooky as you became one with the woods and the night. They would stay there until four AM, until such time as Rebecca would ride by and if she saw a spark from Joshua's flint, she knew all was well and would gallop back to the cottage. If she did not see the flint, she would go directly to Hosking's and report.

The idea was for Joshua to use his scopes and lenses and for young Little George to hold the loaded pistols with flint in but not cocked.

Although the night being dark, Joshua's telescope and other new lenses could hone in on a face and give better evidence of identification other than just the eye. Not perfect but important. The hours passed quite quickly without a murmur, bar a few riders and a carriage of no importance. It was around the time for Rebecca to appear, in which riding Lilly she dutifully did and Joshua sparked the flint. With a gesture of her arm she acknowledged and turned about. Joshua and Little George decamped and went to find Harry and Suzy waiting for the return journey.

Hot tea for Little George and a brandy for Joshua were waiting for their return which was gratefully drunk. It had been an interesting day and night for all. It would all start again in a few hours' time which was now Thursday morning.

Time rushed by and the routine started again. The only difference this time was that Joshua and Little George would be undercover in a rowing boat on the sea tied to rocks outside and off to the left of the port. Although the location was different the routine stayed the same. Apart from the lights and sounds and occasional shouting from the town and movement of some drunken sailors going back to the anchored ships but again nothing unusual was happening. Rebecca came at four o'clock and the sign was given so Joshua gave the order to decamp when, looking at Little George, realised he had been sick and thrown up in the little boat. He hadn't said a word.

Again the tea and brandy were on hand after their safe return to the cottage. The only thing that was different from yesterday was a note from Henry delivered by young Connor.

R & J
Hope you are both well.
Closer Contact in Emergency
J. Trevenan – The Bull Inn - Newlyn.
A Colleague

Both Rebecca and Joshua understood and discussed with Little George and Christine that should anything happen someone must get to this person.

For some reason Joshua couldn't sleep well and was tossing and turning and in the end got up before everyone else.

Making a pot of tea, he made a pipe and after lighting from the made up fire, went outside. Again, it was chilly but the morning was coming alive with some birds singing. He looked inquisitively upwards into the clearing sky and then felt the hairs on his neck stand up. Strange, it was Friday morning.

Once all were up, Joshua spoke to Rebecca about Christine and suggested that she was looking tired and should stay indoors and help Rebecca today. Little George had got over his sea sickness very quickly and couldn't wait to get about the town and mingle. Joshua set off on Harry and whilst roaming decided to find the location of The Bull Inn in Newlyn, just in case.

Again, everything went to plan and it wasn't long before Joshua and Little George were getting ready for their night observation at Sennon. Again they had prepared the location previously. The only difference between this and the others was a little too way off and out of their comfort zone from around Mousehole. However, it had been agreed that they must cover all angles and directions as best they could with the resources they have. Nearing ten thirty they went to Harry and Suzy and once they were mounted, were off.

On entering the Sennon high woods from the opposite side they silently walked the horses close to the post site and tethered them quietly and left them ample fodder to enjoy. They crept forward to the edge of the wood and made their scrape as they have practised many times before. Joshua got in first and placed the scopes and lenses on the earth frontal ledge which needed minimum movement for him to use should he need to. He checked his vision range and started noting the main landmarks of interest. The farm was some way down in the valley, open pasture to the left and the right was the main inlet to the sea. He noted how dark and vast the sea was at this time of night and how threatening and all powerful it lay. All was quiet.

Little George was still about quietly covering the ground sheet lying above the scrape with all the leaves and twigs he could find so it mingled completely with the surrounding foliage. Once happy he then joined Joshua by lying on the ground and sliding his small body in under the sheet. Joshua gave him the pistols and with thumbs up between them they lay silent. It was Saturday morning.

Both Joshua and Little George had been still now for nearly two hours and the animals and birds had now accepted them as no threat and were now scuffling about their nightly movements as if they were not there. The night air was crisp and a clear night of stars and moon were above.

It was a faint noise from the farm area that first alerted Joshua and his ears pricked up and then a small light. Joshua immediately touched Little George's shoulder and, when their eyes met, Joshua put his right index finger to his lips and produced a very faint shhhhh.

Joshua, very, very gently, moved his head to the scope screwed onto the miniature tripod and already aligned on the farm. He started slowly to twist the scopes dial as well as massaging his right eye in the hope of getting a clearer visual of what and who was down there and what he or she were doing at this time in the morning. He identified the person as a man of good build holding a lantern looking outwards to the sea. Then he saw it, out on the sea a three masted galleon coming from left to right. What the…

Chapter 18

Jacques was bored stiff. He didn't like taking time off during a mission and time wasn't on his side. He knew it from past times working in his native France, let alone trying to move around like a bloody ghost in bloody Cornwall. However, it did give him time to enjoy his drink whenever he wished but he was a loner and that was just as well as he needed to be in his line of work so having and enjoying other people's company was out of the question.

Thursday week dragged closer and closer and he couldn't wait to be active again. True to his word, Albret the Count of Morlaix had paid for all his food and lodgings, which he appreciated on one hand but didn't on the other, as this guy was the richest and most powerful person around this place and was openly ruthless to the point, that no one dare to do anything against his wishes. A brute he thought to himself and Bouchier wasn't much better.

Jacques didn't drink this Thursday at all and made sure he ate well. He needed all his wits about him when he meets Bouchier this evening.

The ride to the Chateau didn't take that long. He missed riding Arc but he knew he would do that again in the next couple of days and looked forward to meeting his old and trusted friend. As always he had to use the tradesmen entrance and was told to wait in the anti-room while Bouchier was fetched.

Bouchier and Albret were in the next room drinking brandy whilst sitting in two comfy arm chairs opposite a glowing fire. The usher advised them that Jacques had arrived and Albret said "Thank you, we will get to him in a while". "Well Pierre, the time has come to implement the last phase of the mission. You have done well my friend, now tell me what you want and you shall have it". "I want Zoe, you know that," he replied. Albret started chuckling which riled Bouchier. "Oh yes Zoe, of course, the love of your life eh." Bouchier stayed quiet. Then Albret changed his all smiling face and leant forward with grimace. "You finish this with a resounding success and I promise you she is yours." "Thank you Philip", he replied. "However," Albret said, "I also want something." "What would that be my Prince?"

"Having the finished formula in our hands and the future success, we will have of it, I want all traces of this mission, including the people involved, to be wiped, as though it had never happened, completely and utterly without trace. This is what I want, and my liege King authorises so, is the need for utter secrecy." "What about Jacques?" Bouchier replied. "That means everyone, everyone except of course your young Zoe who, I will allow through the net for your loyalty to me and your pleasure to her but, only her." Bouchier got it, his own ruthlessness made him smirk with dishonesty and inner enjoyment of his own method of deceiving people. He understood.

Bouchier opened the ante room door and walked in saying boldly as he meant it but really couldn't give a hoot, "Hi Jacques, don't get up, how was your time off, relaxing I hope."

Bouchier poured each a drink, sat down opposite and started the briefing.

"Things have slightly changed Jacques, I want you and the four youngens to meet at the Abbey of Landerneau at midnight tonight. They have been informed. You are to collect the hundred barrels and supervise their loading on four large coaches pulled by four horses each. The coaches are already there with the stage drivers awaiting your arrival. Once loaded and you are satisfied, you are not to go to Brest but head due south from Landerneau to the secluded Daoulas Cove where a three masted galleon will be waiting for you as close to the shore as it can. The Captain has been briefed and knows what to do.

You will be heading around the Lizard Point and peninsular and hug the quiet inner waters of west south west Cornwall and anchor off Sennon. Once anchored you are to off load to the Wards and then it is over to you. Two of the four young men will then come back with the Galleon and two will remain in your charge. You know which ones I have chosen to stay and the ones which must come back and this cannot change.

You must be at Daoulas Cove by no later than break of day tomorrow, that gives you seven hours from the moment you get to the Abbcy at midnight tonight. The ship will sail directly once you have reloaded the barrels." Jacques got it and understood. He also knew Bouchier and the twists and turns he gives to put people off balance. "Understood," he replied.

"One other thing Jacques, when the germ has been laid you and Zoe are to report directly back here, is that clear." "Understood," Jacques replied, he knew this may happen. "What about the other two youngens and Pascal the budding Alchemist?" he asked Bouchier. "Unfortunately, for reasons and purposes above my control but for the Kings glory of future use of success you are to eliminate them." Bouchier waited for a response. Jacques had seen something like this coming as this germ type warfare wasn't exactly killing the enemy with chivalry as the French like to tell the world but he was older and wiser now to argue otherwise. He also had himself to think about and had a gut feeling that Bouchier had some other orders in which he wasn't telling him. "Absolutely understood," he responded with surety. However, Jacques didn't feel sure at all.

Jacques headed back to the Inn at Morlaix to pack his things as quickly as he could, have a last brandy and then set off for the Abbey. Lashing his horse in front of the Inn and jumping off, he dashed into the entrance and without looking properly, being preoccupied with time, he crashed straight into a little old lady coming out. With her begging hands filled with a few coppers she went flying into the wall and the money went all over the floor. Jacques couldn't have been more apologetic but as she looked up through her black netted veil into his eyes she hissed with a shrilling low hum like a snake, "Beware you, think you are strong than any other, the pup of its master will take you without you even knowing." Jacques went silent and took a step back while she went about picking up her pennies.

Jacques couldn't think of anything to respond except that he was sorry. She dismissed his claim of apology with a hiss and picking up her last coin shuffled away as quickly as she could. Jacques was stunned with her outburst of venom but couldn't get out of his head what she had said. 'The pup, the pup,' he kept thinking all the way to his room.

With everything packed and ready he reached the Abbey at Landerneau around half an hour early and, as mentioned by Bouchier, the horses, carriages and drivers were there waiting but not the four young men. He acquainted himself with the drivers and went off to see the main alchemist monk. All was ready, one hundred barrels. Then he heard them gallop up to the Abbey and watched them dismount laughing and full of young vigour.

He went to them directly and briefed them that twenty-five barrels a piece need to be put on each carriage with their belongings and to leave their horses with the Abbey. The barrels were not that big but were heavy enough that only one could be carried at a time.

He was supervising, so told them to get on with it and be quiet. Each one did as told and acted the feat as like a game in that, the first one to finish was the winner. Jacques felt the youth in them and shuddered at the thought that at least two, or maybe all, would not see the fruits of their labour and grow old to tell the story. Jacques laughed at himself for being soppy and realised that he himself was older now and that youth was a thing to be enjoyed. He tried again to laugh it off but it didn't work as it had in the past.

Jacques enjoyed a sip of brandy from his flask and when everything was loaded and everyone accounted for, jumped on his mount and led them from the front, due south to Daoulas Cove, as instructed.

It was a silent road with forest on the left and open plains on the right. The carriages were cumbersome and slow and Jacques had to rein his nag back into a slight trot being not much faster than a walk. This gave time for Jacques to think about what exactly is going on here and, how he was to manage this last phase.

However, it wasn't long, or though it seemed so, that Daoulas Cove was sighted and the descent of the carriages started. The place was perfect for such a mission. With the coaches at a halt, men from small boats already ashore, came to meet them with the Captain introducing himself. Jacques immediately got the understanding of what was about and started supervising the unloading, load and the reloading on board ship. The men from the ship also helped which made things easier for all and reduced the time it would have taken. Jacques was pleased that so far they were making good time.

When all was done Jacques too went to the Captain who didn't say much to anybody really. The sailors seem to know him well and just got on with things. However, what was asked was answered and Jacques was happy with that. A sailor showed them to their cabins and others helped with their belongings, which wasn't much.

Jacques wanted to stay on deck and so was given a seat at the stern. Once again, the Captain didn't say anything, just got on with his ship and crew and let Jacques be. Once away Jacques went down to see the four young bucks. He opened the cabin and they were nipping their brandy from their flasks and joking and laughing. Jacques didn't say anything except, "We should be on this ship till midnight tonight or at the very latest very early Saturday morning so I suggest you stop the drinking bit and get some sleep, you will be woken before we anchor."

With that he closed the cabin door behind him and went back up on deck. However, after closing the cabin door and just about to walk away he heard one of them inside start talking using a mother's mimicking type voice. He leant back and put his ear to the door and heard the one mimicking say, "Now all of you be good little boys and go to sleep or Mummy will be angry." They all laughed and Jacques couldn't help but laugh himself then carried on up the steps.

Back in his seat on deck and watching the men heave ho outbound, he started to relax a little and focus on what to do. He drew out his hip flask took a long slow gulp of the liquid inside and with a pulling together of the teeth combined with a facial squint and a closing of the eye's swallowed the stuff with inner satisfaction.

Jacques was enjoying the inner peace of being on board ship with nothing to do but wait. After an hour or so the Captain came across and mentioned that the wind was fair and they were making good progress and the timing set to reach drop off point should be alright. "However," he continued, "what we will find turning the cape of Lands' End, I do not know." Jacques liked this man's no nonsense approach in giving information. Jacques thanked him and with a tap of his hand to his forehead he went away.

The easy rhythmic movement of the ship and the ebb and flow of the sea allowed Jacques to relax and contemplate his position? He thought back to Bouchier's words of 'No trace of this mission.' Jacques knew he was getting on in years and that younger men were entering the field he had been in for twenty odd years. He also knew that Bouchier couldn't be trusted. He was himself physically able and felt good enough to carry on his work but mentally he was broken. He knew it, he craved peace, he reckoned he deserved some time in his life to enjoy the fruits of his labour without harm or injury to anyone.

Jacques stretched and looked up. He had been sitting there for hours as the sun turned itself in to the moon. The night stars were shining like little crystals against the black sky and the air was extremely clean. With his nipping of brandy and the fresh spray of water all around him, his personal thoughts were coming through.

Finish this mission and retire he thought, move away from the world. Buy a little farm stead from the money he had saved and get that inner peace he so craved. Move away from France to somewhere like Scotland and use a different name. Would Bouchier allow that? Why tell him he thought; he could just disappear.

If he was Bouchier would he just accept that he had disappeared without trace? With first-hand knowledge of his ruthless streak of treating humans like useless animals, he thought not. He would try and track me down. But why did Bouchier request, even order, that he and Zoe must personally report directly to him at the Chateau on completion. This never happened before. They knew where to find him if they wanted to talk. His reports were always on time, so why? The old lady sprung into his head, he started laughing to himself as a silly superstitious twit, but then stopped laughing and considered her words.

The deck door threw open and out ran one of the four young men spewing his guts as soon as he hit the railings. Luckily the wind and spray drew the vomit away from the ship. At least he got the right side correct, as Jacques chuckled to himself.

With that Jacques decided to get some sort of sleep and went down into his cabin located next to the other four young ones. He lay down with his arms behind his head and looked at the ceiling. He heard the young one come back into the cabin and overheard the other three taking the mickey out of him.

With his eyes closed his thoughts repeated on him and then he cried. The one thought he tried to always keep in the dark and locked away came forward. He would always love her, how he missed her and how so lonely his heart was without her.

It didn't seem that long before the knock on his cabin door woke him up. The Captain showed himself in and said, "We have turned the cape and the wind has dropped from us. I anticipate drop zone around two o'clock or thereabouts." "Thank you, Captain." With that Jacques started to get himself and his things ready.

Jacques went on deck to get his bearings and his thoughts together. He had been away from the Cornish mainland for a few weeks but it seemed ages ago. He decided to go back down and get the four up and ready for the task ahead. They were all asleep. He didn't pull his punches and told them with an authoritive voice to get up and ready and all to be on deck within fifteen minutes for briefing, no excuses. He slammed the door shut and chuckled.

Jacques waited on deck. Soon enough the young ones came to him. It was time to select who stays and who goes back with the ship once the unloading of the barrels at the Wards farm is completed. They all stood before him knowing what he was going to do. He thought about Bouchier choosing the weaker two and was tempted to change that decision, as was his right, and pick the other two who were more capable, more physical and more adapted for this type of mission.

However, he thought no, he would need to play the game. Something was wrong but he couldn't put his finger on it. He needed time to solve this problem nagging at him. He told them that the decision Pierre Bouchier had made back in France would remain in place and so prepare accordingly. The two stronger lads dipped their heads but again they couldn't work out why they hadn't got the mission over and above the other two scrawny and dim witted ones.

Maybe they were needed for a more dangerous mission in the future they thought, which preened their ego in acceptance of the decision. With that the Captain came across to give Jacques the news that they would anchor at the drop zone off Sennon Cove in one hour.

Things needed organising so Jacques set about managing things. Jacques soon realised that Galleons do not carry small boats but the Captain had made requirements for four small boats to be taken. The Captain also suggested that the two boats being dragged behind the ship, especially for this voyage, were available for his disposal to move the bulky kegs. The other two were roped down by the ships sides. He himself could use one of these for communication if he wanted. The last remaining boat would stay where it was for the crew, should things go wrong.

The whole crew and Jacques team became active and rushing about like flies. All the ships guns were being loaded and prepared; all hatches not important were closed. Jacques realised the small boats were not large enough to take fifty kegs each and so accepted that the landing of them had to be done in two journeys back and forth, the last would be manned by the two young ones going back to France with the ship.

All was in place and now the wait started. The ship was moving gently like a ghost across the water inching its way to the drop zone. Everyone was silent and in place. Jacques moved to where the Captain stood on the starboard side scanning his eyes across the Cornish headlands for the sign he was waiting for. Jacques too did the same. Jacques thought how rugged the Cornish coast was. Then out of nowhere it came, there it was, both the Captain and Jacques saw it at once.

The Captain started counting to himself. Out of the pure darkness came one ten seconds of flickering light, then darkness. Jacques looked at the Captain who spoke as quietly as he could in Jacques's ear, "We must wait five minutes, if the light shines the same as before, for the same length of time and in the same place, we anchor and set to."

Jacques could feel his heart beating faster and started to get that tense feeling before a battle, his senses were coming alert and he knew his body was getting ready for action. Then it came, the light mirroring the last signal. The Captain, moved his head to the sailor at the bow, who acknowledged then reached down into a covered box and picked up a lantern and with its light glowing swung it in both directions twice and then as quickly as before lowered it to be back in its cover case; complete darkness once more.

Jacques checked his pistols and moved in behind some crewmen, laddering themselves down to one of the side boats chosen to be the first to ashore.

The Captain manoeuvred the ship where he felt it best to lay anchor, as close as he could, considering the exit and safety rules of engagement and also turning the ship about before he did so. Happy with the ships final positioning he ordered the anchoring. The four young men came round Jacques who gave them orders to start preparing the first half of the kegs for offloading and do as the Captain orders but, await his signal before they cast off for the shoreline. They all nodded in complete acceptance.

The small boat with four oarsmen and Jacques pushed off and rowed strongly towards the shore.

All went well and once the small boat reached the beach Jacques jumped out and started looking around. He knew the farm and spotted it straight away so started walking towards it. Two of the crew followed armed with muskets. About twenty meters from the farms edge Ashley Ward came into view and approached them. "You are late Jacques." "We were doing well until we turned the cape and things slowed, is everything ready Mr Ward?" "Yes, we are ready." With that Jacques went with Mr Ward into the farm to see for himself what had been organised. The two sailors followed.

Jacques was acquainted with Mrs Ward and tea and cake was offered. Jacques took the cake but asked for a brandy. Mr

Ward started informing Jacques that only one medium two horse pulling trap was available for transporting whatever he was transporting.

Mr Ward emphasised the point that Mousehole was a village type town and anything larger like coaches would get noticed. Jacques accepted the argument which made sense. They may need to do more trips but safety and normal integration was needed. Mr Ward continued and explained that all things were quiet and nothing unusual has come across his eyes or ears since you were last here. Jacques let Mr Ward babble on as he wanted this time to adjust his thoughts and get a feel for things around him before he gave the signal.

Once Jacques was satisfied and feeling as comfortable as he could in that all was well and no compromise of the mission was apparent, he asked where the cargo was to be stored. "You have two options; you can have the secret underground cell within the walls of this farm cottage or it can go outside within the grounds in a locked barn close to the stables." Jacques asked to see both. The underground cell was large enough but a logistical nightmare and with the man power at hand he dismissed it. On seeing the barn and weighing up the ease in which to locate the kegs and the small timescale in which they will be here, nodded his approval. On passing by the stables walking back to the farm, Mr Ward suggested he look inside. With lanterns lighting the night Jacques immediately spotted his favourite Arc and went to him. Both horse and owner responded to each other. "Thank you Mr Ward." "Zoe organised it Jacques not me." "Then I shall pass on my appreciation to her."

Before entering the farm house and being constantly followed by the two sailors, he kindly ordered both of them back to their colleagues on the shore and confirmed that all was well and he will send the signal to the ship very shortly.

Sitting back down and feeling the time was now right he asked Mr Ward to signal the go ahead to the ship. Mr Ward acknowledged and said he would be back in ten minutes. Jacques sat back and waited.

The first two boats arrived on shore and Jacques was there to meet them. In each boat were two sailors and one young one of his team. He quickly gave orders to start carrying the goods to the barn where Mr Ward was waiting. Once completed the sailors rowed back to ship whilst the two young ones went in the farmhouse, introduced to Mrs Ward, given refreshments, non-alcoholic, and then told to wait.

Jacques waited on the beach ready for the last two boats. Watching the small boats leave then waiting for the crossover of the remaining two to arrive seemed like an eternity. He was also deeply in enemy territory which he did not take for granted and the sooner he was out of this exposed position the better. He felt vulnerable.

The two boats came into view and Jacques with the sailors and young ones repeated the exercise of carrying the remaining fifty kegs to the barn. Once completed Jacques went back to the boats and offered his thanks and goodwill. Jacques turned and made for the farmhouse.

However, before he went in he decided to wait and watch about a while. He sat away out of site and let the night take over him. His eyes were really nowhere but looking everywhere. The noise they had made during the unloading and loading wasn't much but now there was silence and Jacques needed to hear the night and what it had to say. He sat down and waited. Jacques watched the ship silently drift away right to left and then nothing but the sea, as if it had never actually been there. The Captain had done his job well, Jacques thought.

Jacques carried on his silent watch then after a further ten minutes took one last look across the sea, the fields and the forests above before settling on, all was well. He therefore got up and walked briskly back into the farmhouse and into the warmth of the fire and brandy drink.

With everyone now in the room together a sense of calm was taking over. Jacques was aware that dawn was approaching and needed to act and make decisions. He asked Mrs Ward if the two youngens can stay in the farmhouse until latest midnight tonight. They were to take guard of the kegs on four hour periods each. Jacques would return and lead them to the cottage but he really needed to get away now whilst it was still dark and prepare for the delivery. When all was agreed Jacques went off to saddle up Arc.

As he galloped away and feeling the wind through his face sitting on his old friend he felt a feeling of relief that the cargo was in Cornwall as planned. He went as fast as he could but remembering the Cornish lanes and the pitfalls they give horses he took things a little steadier. Getting to the cross lanes he turned right into Mousehole and then before entering the town stopped and got off. Taking the reins, he led Arc away from the cottage location and once satisfied with his little security diversion doubled back.

Leading himself through the yard he went to the back door. He waited a few minutes in silence then knocked the door rat a tat tat – pause – tat –pause, rat a tat tat. He waited, noting that dawn was coming. A couple of minutes went past when he heard movement inside and the bolts being moved back. Opening he saw Zoe and his smile was one of genuine thanks that she was alive and looking well. He went inside bolting the door behind him and turning towards her she hugged him with warmth and with relief that he was alive and now knew he would help her get through this. She needed to talk.

Chapter 19

Joshua was as still as the night and watched everything going on down on the farm land and beach area. Little George was getting a little anxious and Joshua calmed him down to be still and watch as he was doing. They lay silent like ghosts under the camouflage of their shallow trench type position in the woods waiting and observing.

While the galleon lay dark and still in the sea he noticed the small little rowing boat detaching itself and heading for the shore. Once landed, one man got out and walked directly to the first man Joshua had seen an hour ago. Joshua instinctively knew exactly who he was. Watching through his magnified lens he noticed the man's gait, shape and that inner confidence it gave off. Joshua was certain this was indeed the French man called Jacques.

Joshua wanted to dispatch Little George directly to Kernow or Hosking's to inform them on what was happening here but realised they would need more information to act in accordance with the threat. Was it a landing of battle, reconnaissance mission or what? He had to be patient and watch and gather that intelligence.

He watched it all, the unloading and storing of the kegs and the number of men involved. After an hour or so Joshua knew this was no battle front but a secretive meeting of landing of goods. He then watched the three masted Galleon silently leave as it had arrived. Now was the time to act.

Joshua gave instructions to Little George to go directly to the Bull Inn at Newlyn and contact a Mr Trevenan. "Tell him everything I have told you and await his instructions. I will carry on here observing, awaiting your return."

With all his stealth and acting like a fox Little George slid out the back of his cover and crawled along the ground towards the horses reined half a mile back in the woods. Suzy and Harry were waiting. Little George calmed them both with whispering and stroking. When both were calm Little George untied Suzy and walked her away with him. Getting to lane at the back of the woods Little George then mounted Suzy and rode as quickly as he could to the Bull Inn.

Little George got to the crossroads and headed straight on thinking he would have normally turned right to where Rebecca and his sister Christine were. Riding a few more miles he speared off slightly right with Newlyn two miles away. He wanted to stay quiet through the town but understood from Joshua the importance of relaying the information he had as quickly as he could, therefore he galloped on.

The Bull Inn was set away from the main hub of the town standing quietly at the edge. Little George got off Suzy and was surprised to find that the front door was open. He looked in through the windows and saw men still drinking and laughing. It must be three o'clock in the morning he thought.

Weighing things up, he decided to go around the back and find another way in. He was learning that the less people saw or knew the better. Seeing no one around and no other route in, he had no choice but to go in the front way and be bold. Ignoring everyone he noticed that everyone was ignoring him. He waited by the side of the bar until a man came and asked what he wanted. "I want to see Mr Trevenan." "And what is your name young man," the man asked. "My name is Little George."

Within a couple of minutes, a young lady escorted Little George through the back labyrinth of the Inn and knocking a door walked into a large room where she addressed a man by the name "Mr Trevenan Sir" and then introducing Little George. The young lady then left immediately. Little George noticed the man had been in bed asleep as he was dressed in his night clothes with a silky light robe wrapped over them. Little George also noticed that the man had a large sword dangling from his waist belt holding the robe together.

What he didn't understand was that he had seen this man before in the Blue Anchor in Helston many times with his once Master Henry Hosking and, he was definitely not, called Trevenan. Little George didn't say anything but turned around and saw another man sitting in a chair behind the once opened door fully dressed with pistol at his side. The man smiled.

Little George was offered some refreshment and asked to sit down. They both sat opposite each other when Mr Trevenan asked Little George to tell him everything. Little George did what he was told.

Trevenan paced the room after hearing what Little George had said. Little George drank more of his drink and was silent. Trevenan was silent also and continued walking backwards and forwards finishing up at the window looking through to the night sky. Slowly leaning forward on the sill and bringing his face ever closer to the glass pane he knew decisions had to be made. It was his decisions and his alone that would set the success or failure of what happens next. He wanted Jacques the Frenchman and he would use his skills to get him.

After thinking things through over and over the man slapped the window sill with both hands then turned around sharply and said, "You have done well Little George, now this is what I want you to do."

Little George was instructed to go to the cottage and inform Rebecca to prepare a visit this afternoon from himself and his men then go directly back to Joshua the same way you went in and tell him to stand firm and, if necessary, let the enemy come through his position. We need information. "You my dear boy are to be the go between and report back to me at the cottage when darkness comes or earlier if Joshua thinks it's otherwise too urgent."

With that the man calling himself Trevenan opened the door and shouted for the young lady. As she came in Little George was thanked and asked to get on his way with the orders given. On his way out Little George heard Trevenan start giving the young lady instructions.

Little George found Suzy tied at the front of the Inn where he had left her. Trevenan in the meantime was dressed and organising and writing letters to be dispatched forthwith with a haste of confidence and speed. The machine he thought was at last grinding into action.

Rebecca was just rising when Little George got to the cottage. Christine was fast asleep. Little George went over all what had happened and what Mr Trevenan wanted her to do. Rebecca knew what to do and started about the cottage in clearing things up and preparing food for many people. Christine was awoken and helped Rebecca. Little George knew that daylight would be approaching in an hour or so and needed to get back to Joshua. Rebecca filled a bag with food adding a small bottle of brandy, kissed his cheek and said, "Be careful Little George" before he and Suzy were on their way to the woods in Sennon.

Joshua was still watching when he saw Jacques come away from the house and settle in a small gully to watch and listen and see if the night talked. He felt a sense of admiration for him as that is exactly what he would have done. He then thought who was watching who. Joshua didn't move and carried on looking through the lens quiet as a mouse. After a while he saw Jacques get up and go back into the farm house.

Joshua then heard the rustling behind his position when Little George whispered "Joshua." Relaxing, Little George slithered back under the covered sheet into the scrape. Handing over the bag he again went over things. When Joshua heard that he must, if necessary, let the enemy walk through his position, felt a sense of dread and utter loneliness at basically being sacrificed and unable to defend himself should he be found by superior numbers. If he had any ego, it was now gone completely.

It wasn't long after Little George came back that Joshua saw Jacques go to a horse and ride away heading towards the main road. Joshua did nothing, he couldn't, he had to wait and be patient. He knew this was going to be a long day. He looked at Little George who looked dead on his feet and suggested he put the shawl over him and get some sleep.

Little George did as was told and Joshua went to the bag to eat something which Rebecca had made up and smiled when he saw the brandy and took a well-deserved mouthful. He would wake Little George up in a few hours and they would swap places so Joshua could also get some shut eye.

The hours passed without further drama and so Joshua woke Little George to replace his watch. He told him to focus on the barn where the consignment and the two men where housing and the house.

He showed him how to swivel the lens on the horizontal plane and the focus mechanism. It was broad daylight now and movement was now crucial to be as little as possible, if any. Joshua didn't stay awake long and went off to sleep. Little George felt good and excited at using the telescope as it made him see things that he had never imagined. Both muskets were loaded and ready as with their pistols.

The afternoon soon came and Rebecca was happy feeling the cottage was acceptable for a visit. What sort of visit, she didn't know? Christine had earlier gone into town to get groceries, meat and drink. All was ready. Around four o'clock three men appeared at the back yard entering the back gate. They had laid their horses out of site further behind in the field at the back of the lane which runs past the cottage back yard. From the front of the cottage people would have seen nothing untoward. The first person to enter the cottage was George Kernow alias Trevenan followed by his two life guards.

With introductions over and Kernow enquiring over her health after the shooting incident it soon became apparent that there were more people to arrive. Kernow thanked Rebecca for her pending hospitality and suggested that there may be one or two others coming here during their stay which may take between two and seven days, hopefully the lesser but we cannot rush this. This took Rebecca by surprise as she thought it was just for the afternoon and so had to start thinking about sleeping quarters and everything else to host the extra people.

The main room of the cottage was to be taken over by Kernow with his maps and writing materials as an operational type room and as suggested by Rebecca they could use her bedroom should they need sleep. This was agreed so she moved her things into Christine's room where she made an extra bed for herself and left Little George's bed vacant should he return.

Then as the day grew into night a familiar face entered the back door. It was Henry Hosking's who doffed his hat to Rebecca and asked after her health.

With refreshment given he then went straight into heavy discussion with Kernow. Kernow wanted exact confirmation on what Henry had organised and with Henry moving around the open map laid on the table, duly explained what he has done emphasising with his finger his men's positions and when they would be in place. Kernow nodded his approval then went on discussing different scenario's and assumptions and their responses should these things happen. His expectation, should things go to plan and with the latest information gained from Joshua, that either tonight or the days after they will have the desired answers to implement the trap.

With the fire stoked and lanterns lit, a steady rhythm of talk and silence fell upon the cottage main room.

With Joshua being asleep in the scrape it was Little George who noticed the extra movement of people at the barn and the horse and carriage being drawn up being filled with things. He decided to wake Joshua immediately. Joshua slid over and eyed into the scope. "Well done Little George, it would appear that they wish to move the consignment and not leave it here at the farm." Joshua considered things carefully, should he dispatch Little George or wait. It was nearing nine o'clock and night was in the younger part of darkness but the stars were out shining through its sheer blackness.

He decided to wait a further thirty minutes and watch. After watching through the extra time he was now sure that something was up and that this information was important. He told Little George of his considerations and to dispatch this to Trevenan. Little George once again went through the familiar procedure of exiting silently slithering out of the scrape, fetching Suzy and getting away. Once again he got to the cross junction but this time turned right to Mousehole.

Entering by the back yard, he went into the cottage. He wasn't expecting anybody to be up as it must now be nearing ten o'clock. However, he met Rebecca who gave him a kiss on the cheek and told him to go directly into the main room and speak to Mr Kernow and Mr Hosking's. Entering the room Henry smiled warmly at him like a Father would his son.

Kernow stood and instantly apologised for misleading his name as Trevenan. Little George understood why this man does things like this and then went on to inform them exactly what he and Joshua had seen with a clarity and preciseness he was taught by Joshua. They listened carefully and once Little George completed his story was told not to go back to Joshua tonight but to stay here and get a good night's rest and set off early tomorrow morning emphasising being in the woods before break of day.

The two men confirmed their agreement that what may happen tonight was just too dangerous for Little George to get involved either by accident or any other way and now armed with this new information they needed to slightly adjust the positions of

Hosking's men. Henry got the message and left to organise accordingly. Kernow poured himself a brandy and hoped he had got every angle covered, as best they could.

Chapter 20

Nearing eleven o'clock Jacques realised that the time had come for him to go back to the farm at Sennon and get the first consignment away and back here inside the cottage, with the two young men. They were now in the final preparation stages for when Pascal eventually gives the go ahead for it to be transferred up the tunnel for emptying. When not nodding off he and Zoe had talked most of the morning and during the day. It was blatantly apparent that she disliked Bouchier not only for his massive egotistical manner and his older age but for his total obsession towards her. Zoe and Jacques had now both decided that each would be as truthful as they could with each other. He in turn had expressed his feelings about not trusting Bouchier either and that maybe he felt threatened by him.

Although they shared the same bed it was different this time. For the first time they started asking each other about their loved ones and their hopes and dreams. Zoe explained how Philip Albret had bribed her away from her family and leaving her young love back on the vineyard. Jacques couldn't speak as openly, as his broken heart wouldn't let him but never the less tried his best. Altogether they both realised that something had changed between them and rather than playing games they started to understand that neither were comfortable with what was happening and both felt an underlying feeling of dread and being thrown to wolves. Jacques also mentioned the old lady he had bumped into and what she said and how she had said it with hiss and venom.

They both agreed, for their own futures, that they would carry on and talk plainly and openly as they could and keep each other informed. Zoe, realising the position she was in decided to completely open up and told Jacques that even though he had once said for her to kill Pascal for his incompetence before he left for France the fact was that Bouchier had earlier given her the poison to kill him anyway. Jacques responded by telling her that Bouchier had ordered him to kill the two young men and Pascal in order to leave no traces once the liquid germ was dispatched into the ground.

He also pointed out it was very odd that Bouchier had ordered him and Zoe together to be at the Chateau directly after the mission was done. When the book states; that once a mission is completed it is best for agents to disappear somewhere of their choice until things have calmed down and then only contacted by a courier by the agreed route.

"Jacques I really don't feel good about any of this, what are we to do?" "I feel the same Zoe and I really don't know what to do but I will find a way."

Jacques got Arc ready and when midnight struck he was off to fetch the first of the consignment. He told Zoe he would get back before dawn.

Joshua saw the horse and rider enter the farm and go straight to the barn where the man dismounted and started a discussion with the two other men. It was Jacques.

He saw him check the carriage and then disappear into the farm house. The two young men got on the carriage, clicked the horses forward steering to the front of the house where they halted. A few minutes later Jacques reappeared and getting on his horse went by the carriage seemingly giving the two men more instructions. With that Jacques led his horse steadily away from the farm and the carriage followed.

Joshua observing everything realised that what went into the barn and the length and man power it took to put it there the night before, only a small part was on the departing carriage. Meaning that in all probability they would return sooner or later.

Jacques took things steady as the carriage loaded with twenty-five barrels was moving a little too slowly for his liking. Jacques had to keep checking Arc's pace in order to keep carriage and horses together.

At the cross junction they turned right and getting close to the town Jacques realised he couldn't do his doubling back routine to confuse anyone looking. Instead he chose to slow down to a halt in a dark place by the trees and wait ten minutes. Happy with the silence of the night Jacques dismounted and walked the carriage forward heading towards the rear of the cottage and its back yard. He didn't like it at all the carriage had been too noisy and cumbersome. However, he had no choice in the matter how else could he get the kegs transported from the farm. With the back door of the cottage opened by Zoe, they all helped, apart from Pascal who was asleep upstairs, to man handle the kegs inside. When finished the two young men were introduced to Zoe who politely exchanged her happiness in meeting them and offering them a brandy, in which both accepted.

Jacques instructed them that they should now get a couple of hours sleep before being introduced to Pascal on his waking, who would then take over instruction on them helping in the digging of the tunnel. He also went on to say that when they return at midnight tonight to pick the next twenty-five kegs, he would not accompany them and they would be on their own. There was no reason to compromise himself any further and they would now be handling and moving on their own initiatives. This they were happy to do and both felt an inner self confidence of getting the job done faster without an oldie getting in the way.

Jacques talked with Zoe who advised him that she had prepared beds for the two young men in the third smaller upstairs bedroom which Jacques used to sleep in when not with Zoe. Jacques stayed for as long as he could but needed to get away and be on his own. His job there was done for the time being and he wanted now to get away to his isolated digs in Penzance where he felt safer away from everyone. He could then have a good drink and sleep soundly.

He lastly advised the two young men he would return before dawn tomorrow and reminded them of their courtesy towards a lady and their duty of work that the tunnel to be further on and the next batch of kegs to be here before sunrise.

As he said his goodbyes Zoe ran out after him. He turned towards her, "Jacques, you will not leave me will you?" He gave her a kiss on the cheek and said, "Zoe, I am a man of my word, I will find a way for us both to live as we each desire, trust me." With that Jacques turned, saddled Arc and headed off to Penzance. Zoe turned back into the cottage being left with three young men to cope and feed.

Chapter 21

Henry had done his job well. On receipt of his first orders from Kernow that very morning, he had acted decisively and with help of his right hand Bull, dispatched and deployed twenty trusted and experienced men in strategic positions from the main road cross junction through to Mousehole, Newlyn and Penzance. They were all paired up so communication runners can be sent immediately without losing the observations.

Kernow and Hosking's were in the cottage main room when the first of the observations came in around four o'clock the following morning. A carriage had been seen entering Mousehole moving to the North east of the town, location unknown as yet. There were two men on the carriage seats and one on a big bay horse leading them. The identification of rider is unknown but fits the description of the man known as Jacques.

And so throughout the morning the observations and reports steadily flowed in allowing Kernow and Hosking's to paint their picture of riposte. Every time the riders came and gave their information, they awaited further orders and every time they were given the same, which was, to do nothing but observe and report and let the targets carry on their mission without any interference whatsoever.

Rebecca was now up, cooking and working around the cottage. She was advised by Henry with the authority of Kernow that Little George should stay here until further notice and not at all to go to Joshua. Rebecca questioned Henry on how Joshua would be feeling about being out so long and isolated. Kernow sensing her empathy and logic nodded in agreement saying he would send a relief for Joshua so he could come back. Rebecca thanked him and carried on her duties.

By ten o'clock that morning reports had come in that the carriage had been spotted in the back yard of a cottage north east of the town at the top of Enys Road near the northern most water well. Also the man known as Jacques had been seen at approximately six this morning leaving that same cottage moving north out of Mousehole heading towards the cross junction.

With information being fluid Hosking's again went out to meet Bull, his man in command of the observations, to discuss and tweak his men's positions accordingly. Bull was also asked to pick two men for when night begins to fall, they were to relieve Joshua who himself was to make his way directly back here. However, they were to visit the cottage first and talk with George Kernow to understand exact location and entry directions. Happy with the new arrangements and Bull's suggestions to now widen the catch area, Hosking went back to the cottage.

Joshua was getting tired and kept nodding off. He knew Little George couldn't come back in daylight but was concerned for him anyway. Nothing was happening in front of him but alert he stayed as best he could. As day light began to fall for night he heard the familiar rustling behind his position and a voice he didn't recognise whispering his name. Pistol aimed at the ready Joshua poked his head through the back of the cover sheet to see two bearded ugly faces staring back. "Don't shoot Josh, we are to relieve you, orders from Hosking."

Joshua couldn't quite believe he was on the way back and being on Harry felt wonderfully free. Arriving at the cottage he quickly understood that Kernow had taken over. However, he went straight to Rebecca and asked after her and feeling a sense of warmth he hadn't felt for what seemed like ages. Little George and Christine followed in their happiness to see him. With a fresh pipe in hand and a glass of brandy in the other he went into the main room.

Kernow and Hosking stood up as he entered with Kernow first saying "Hello Joshua, very well done my lad, by the way you look terrible." "Thank you George," he replied. With pleasantries over they got down to business.

Without going through too much detail Kernow explained the up to date situation. "Why don't we take the cottage now and imprison them all?" Joshua asked. "That's not the way I work Joshua, that would simply stop an operation in motion, we'd have learnt nothing and have exposed ourselves, that is not clever.

No, we need more information and as I previously mentioned to you and Rebecca, we specifically want Jacques. In fact, to be more exact I want Jacques isolated without his accomplice's knowledge and I believe we need more time observing to achieve that goal." "Can I ask why Jacques is so more important than not stopping their dirty mission in its tracks?" "Yes you can ask, and you have, so let's leave it at that, for now."

Joshua looked at Hosking's for support to his question and Kernow's answer to it. However, he didn't get it, more a simple shrug of the shoulders to let things be. Joshua accepted this and felt that Kernow knew something he and Henry didn't.

Kernow was silent thinking, looking and waiting patiently for a pattern, if there was one, he would act with more definition and less risk, if there wasn't one, he would act more blindly with more risk. Joshua and Hosking were impatient but accepted George's experience and rank.

Early morning a report came in that two men were seen getting into the small carriage and heading north towards the cross junction. A woman was also seen but went back into the cottage. Kernow, Hosking's and Joshua were now taking turns to sleep or rather cat nap where they were sitting or, drifted into the large bedroom for a lie down.

Then the report came in that Kernow was waiting for. It was now eight o'clock the next morning. The man Jacques had been seen coming from Penzance through the cross junction to the cottage at Mousehole at four o'clock this morning and seen again leaving the cottage at six o'clock, as yesterday, a repeat. It was time to act.

With the cottage and Sennon being covered, Joshua was asked to lead a team into Penzance, find him and take Jacques captive. How he done this was up to his discretion. However, it had to be accomplished discreetly and he was not to hurt him in any way unless of course he resists. Once arrested he was to bring him directly to the Bull Inn at Newlyn, not here, not yet. A room was already prepared for his arrival and one of Kernow's men would be there.

Joshua accepted his new orders and was advised to take six men to include their leader Bull and set the trap. With that Joshua got himself ready and hugging Rebecca and the children goodbye he jumped on Harry and rode off to meet Bull and his five-man team.

Sitting at the edge of Penzance in the woods on the direct road out, Joshua was discussing things with Bull. Although he had seen this man on his travels with Hosking's he had always thought of him, a brute of a man, but now he was learning a different side, a more understanding with a diplomatic type inner manner.

This pleased Joshua and so started warming to him. They both knew the position they were in and the responsibilities they were under to make this successful.

If the pattern emerged correct then Jacques would be passing through around three to three thirty, the next morning. Then the cross junction to Mousehole a little later. Thereafter back through at around five thirty or thereabouts. However, something was bothering Joshua. If Jacques was startled or became aware of his pending capture as he rode, with unknown men before him and being fully armed, he would naturally fight or flee, that's what Joshua would do. Joshua pondered.

They decided to set the trap at a bend with a slight angled dip in the road just on the outskirts of Penzance town. The rider with any sense would have to slow up a little. They had ample time to prepare with two cut off positions in either direction from the centre stand point. Should he fight or flee they were to shoot the horse down immediately.

As evening fell, Joshua and Bull talked. Joshua had this hunch that he knew this man Jacques liked his drink and maybe, just maybe later in the evening, he would be at the Fisherman's Arms where he last saw him sitting in the corner quietly, alone and deep in thought. Bull and Joshua discussed the positives and negatives of this theory and realised they had nothing to lose in attempting to see if they were right. If he was there, so it was to be.

Leaving two of the men at the stand point, the other four and Joshua went off to the Fisherman's in search of their prey. The four men split up and surrounded both exits and entrance with their pistols locked back and ready. Joshua couldn't afford the risk for one or two of his men to go in first to check if he was in there as this man Jacques needed just the slightest feeling of indifference and he would instantly flee and if necessary with pistols blazing. So standing just outside the front doorway

Joshua and Bull turned to look at each other and with deep understanding they both took one last deep breath and with a quick nod of approval to each other they calmly but boldly walked in. He was there in the same place on his own with his brandy in hand. His body and staring eyes didn't flinch at all when Joshua went straight up to him, sat himself down opposite and firmly said, "Good evening Jack or is it Jacques?"

"Good evening Mr Pendragon," he responded calmly. Joshua couldn't believe that Jacques knew him and that took him by surprise and asked, "How do you know my name Sir?" "I have a good mind for people and names and I especially remember you when you came in here around a month ago and took on that Mr Rosevear and his bullies to relieve a very young lady of her duties to him, you done well Mr Pendragon." Jacques carried on, "I presume all exits are covered and that other man at the bar you came in with, with his pistol in hand looking this way is with you." "You are correct." Jacques mind was thinking fast yet he had to remain calm.

"How did you know I was here?" Joshua, being calm and mature replied, "we didn't but looking at patterns and habits it was a chance worth taking." "Hmmmm, so you have been watching me Mr Pendragon?" "I didn't say that Jacques and it isn't for me to answer such questions."

"So what do you want with me Mr Pendragon?" Joshua was quickly realising that this man was experienced and his manner was one of calm yet precise as though working on a mathematical sum. "We would like to have a chat with you that is all and I promise, as a Cornishman and gentleman, no harm will be done to you while you are in my care." Jacques was going to make a quip about Cornishmen but hesitated and decided that respectful silence was best.

Jacques was weighing the situation up and looking at all angles. What do they know? What don't they know, how long have they been watching? Eventually no matter how he looked at it and of his own mistakes he accepted and understood the seriousness of this situation and, if he made one false move he knew he would be shot immediately. Jacques looked at Joshua and Joshua looked at Jacques. Silence reigned between them until Jacques relented, took a deep breath of acceptance and surrendered his pistol and knives quietly on the table. "Thank you Jacques," Joshua answered.

"Shall we go?" Jacques nodded, slung back the last of his brandy and went with them. Walking between both Joshua and Bull and before they got outside the building Joshua turned around and handcuffed him and Bull frisked him for more weapons. Jacques accepted it all and knew that his fate rested with this man called Pendragon.

While one of the men went to find Jacques's horse, another was dispatched to the Bull Inn at Newlyn and there to Mousehole should Kernow not be there and inform him that the man called Jacques was in their possession.

When all were mounted Arc was lashed to Bull's horse and away they went picking up the remaining men at the previous trap point. The route to Newlyn and the Bull Inn was pretty straight forward and now early evening pretty much deserted and at a steady walk and trot took around an hour.

With Bull and his men guarding Jacques, Joshua went in to find the room of Mr Trevenan. He was directed to the back of the Inn by a young lady. Outside the door stood one of Kernow's life guards and was advised to wait while he went in. Kernow was in fact here. The guard came back out and suggested to Joshua that the prisoner be brought straight up and all the rest of you to wait in the bar and feed and refresh yourselves on Mr Kernow's thanks.

Joshua did what he was told and handed Jacques over to the guard who immediately opened the door so they could all go in. Kernow wasn't there but the other life guard was. "Thank you Joshua" the other guard said, "we will come back to you downstairs in a little while." Alone with the two guards Jacques was ordered to strip off. Jacques knew these guys were another level and didn't hesitate. Once they had gone through and searched every little hem, curl and buckle of his complete attire and were happy that nothing could harm their master they allowed Jacques to redress himself. They were polite but firm.

Although there was no window, the room itself was deliciously sweet and delicate with drapes, lanterns, pretty ornaments and a lovely fire which was roaring warmth. At the centre of the room was a square table with two upright chairs opposite each other. On the table was another cute and pretty lantern, one bottle of brandy, two glasses and clay pipes. Asking Jacques to sit in one of the chairs the two guards then left. He wasn't bound, gagged or blind folded. He was free to move, look around, stretch or anything. He looked at the brandy and was tempted.

The seconds turned into minutes allowing Jacques to consider his position and let him think. Jacques did exactly this trying to fully understand his position and sort things in his head. Why they hadn't killed him was really playing with his mind. His was in deep trouble and he had to remain calm. The past started coming through his thoughts from early childhood to particular events that he was grateful for. He looked at the ring on his finger next to the little one on his left hand with its unusual shape of the letter 'J'. He smiled and was content.

Jacques heard the key twist in the door and in walked a man of crisp appearance with an experienced face of seemingly kindness. The man sat down carefully and with precision opposite. The man quietly looked around the room while twisting his groomed moustache in thought. "Absolutely lovely," the man said without looking at Jacques.

Then the man looked Jacques straight in the eye and with a calm polite manner said, "Good evening Jacques, my name is George Trevenan, have you killed any Cornishman or Englishman whilst on this mission of yours?" Jacques looked at him to try and work him out but the question was one of absolute brutal truthfulness with a beautiful delivery of quiet strength and Jacques knew this man, whoever he was, was good and held authority. "No, I have not Mr Trevenan." "That's good Jacques."

George continued, "and yet from your cottage in Mousehole and in collusion with the treacherous Mr Ward at Sennon your operation is to ultimately kill people of this land?" Jacques thought carefully about his response and knew only the truth would keep him alive. "Yes." Trevenan again replied calmly, "I understand."

Trevenan continued his calm clarity of questioning "and may I ask how you are supposed to do that Jacques?" Jacques answered clinically, "by poisoning the Mousehole's northern drinking well through the natural gravity of its water feed."

"And by what means do you intend to poison the water?" "By dispensing a chemical germ into its feed line about twenty meters from the well allowing two to three days for soaking and the help of the pending spring tide to fully carry it to its destination being its underground northern water pool of source." "The spring tide you talk about, is it the one due this Saturday?" "Correct." "Hmmmm, very ingenious," Trevenan replied. Then he was silent allowing the quietness and mental strain to increase. After what must have seemed an eternity of silence between them and feeling the time was right he said it, "By the way Jacques, before I forget, Jeanne is alive."

Jacques was stunned, his mouth dropped and his heart pounded with utter fear of loss and found. His heart and mind were in total confusion. His heart had been totally destroyed the day he heard she had drowned. Every night and day since, he has struggled to get through without his lost love. He had somehow managed, through the very depth of despair, to slowly sew his heart piece by little piece back together. Now this person says she is alive; he sunk in his chair unable to fight.

Trevenan let this news of Jeanne sink in and waited in silence, not moving a muscle. "Where is she, is she safe?" "She is in the deepest dungeon at the Chateau Morlaix under the Count Philip de Albret and no, she is not safe." Jacques was in turmoil; he didn't know where any of this was going. "What do you want of me Mr Trevenan?"

"I want you Jacques to carry on what you are doing and not endanger yourself. I want you not to kill any of my people and I want you to get Jeanne and bring her back home, that's what I want." "What about my compatriots in the cottage?" "That is up to you Jacques, what I will say is that if we can cooperate and agree a way forward then no harm will come to them, now I will leave you in peace to consider things."

Trevenan got up and was half way to the door when Jacques spoke, "and what if I get Jeanne freed and back here, what of me then Mr Trevenan?" He turned around and said in a clear voice so there was no misunderstanding, "If you and I can achieve what I want then you and Jeanne are free to live the rest of your lives together, now I will leave you in peace."

As Trevenan left the room and the door relocked Jacques had time to think. 'Jeanne his beautiful love is alive' he wanted to shout. That bastard Albret and what of Bouchier he thought, he knows everything Albret is up to, he is the pup of Albret. He said it; he couldn't quite believe he had just said the word pup but knew he should have said the dangerous pup. He kept thinking about Jeanne, Jeanne is alive, how wonderful, how beautiful, how life is so joyous with love in its midst. He will save her, he will fight for her and he will love her again.

Kernow left his life guards outside the room and went on down to the bar area where he met his men drinking ale and eating their hearts out, at his expense. Kernow's plan was taking shape however, the next move was a risk he had weighed up and down over the last weeks and could see no other alternative to keep the control he needed to finish the job successfully. He located Joshua and took him to the side and asked how he was. With Joshua replying, "very well Mr Kernow, very well." "Good," Kernow replied, "we need to talk, please take a seat while I talk with Bull."

Bull was to take himself and his men back to Hosking's at the cottage in Mousehole and inform Henry of what had gone on and that the guard and observation team be continued but directed and redeployed to only the small cottage identified as the sleeper's headquarters and the farm at Sennon, with, the emphasises on doing nothing but observe. With Bull and his men gone it was now only Kernow and Joshua.

With both men seated, it was down to Kernow to start. "Joshua, since we met a few months ago I have been watching you and I must say that I am really pleased with the way you handle yourself and the tasks you have been given. You are a credit to your Father. How is your relationship with Rebecca, I mean is it one of intimacy?"

"My relationship with Rebecca, Mr Kernow, is one of friendship and trust and no we are not intimate." "And the future?" Kernow asked. Before Joshua had time to answer, Kernow continued. "Joshua, please believe me that we are at a critical stage in this mission to save hundreds of our fellow people and I would not ask these questions if they were not necessary."

Joshua understood Kernow's position and replied truthfully, "Although it may not be Rebecca's intentions I do hope that one day Rebecca and I may get closer and that I would ask her hand for marriage." Joshua thought to himself that he had never said anything like this to anyone, especially after his first wife passed to the Lord and whom he loved dearly and thought he would never love again. "Thank you Joshua for your honesty, this game we play isn't easy at times."

Joshua listened intently as Kernow now knowing that intimacy had not taken place felt more confident and continued. "What I am about to disclose to you now will give me satisfaction that it will remain between us both and no other shall hear." Joshua thought a while and gave his assurance of secrecy which Kernow responded by saying, "So be it."

"Joshua, as you now know by our earlier conversations that your Father John, Henry Hosking's and Rebecca's Mother

Jeanne were on a mission a few years ago in France and that it
didn't bode well in that your good Father and Rebecca's
Mother lost their lives. It has come to our attention and belief
that Jeanne, Rebecca's mother is alive, and I want you, with the
help of Jacques who hopefully has considered his options well,
to prepare for France and get her back safely to us." "And what
of my Father?" Joshua asked. "The reports that came in at the
time of your Fathers drowning have never been contradicted or
contested and therefore we must presume that in fact he did
drown."

"Does Henry Hosking know of this." "No he does not, as I
said, no one knows except Jacques upstairs and he was
informed for good reason." "Why was Jacques informed Mr
Kernow?" "Because Joshua, they were lovers and I used this
most upper of all emotions as the fulcrum or pivot towards him
to cooperate with us."

Joshua, although intrigued, was feeling inwardly excited about
being given this type of secret information and was
understanding the wonderful world in which Kernow moved
and that although grand and powerful, it must be a very lonely
life and, knew that he was being drawn into it deeper and
deeper, which he wanted.

After a small silence Kernow asked, "would you like me to
continue Joshua?" "Sorry, I was thinking and trying to analyse
the information you are telling me, please do." Kernow then
went over a few things of clarification and asked that when in
the next ten to fifteen minutes he goes back to Jacques, that

Joshua accompany him and listen in to all what is said between them.

Kernow also suggested that once they have finished with Jacques, that he not hurry off back to Rebecca but a debrief between the two of them must take place to thoroughly discuss, confirm, agree with full clarity of responsibilities on what happens next and this may take hours. "Are you happy with this Joshua?" 'Yes I am ready." "Good then let us have a drink and let Jacques stew for a little while longer. Patience and correct use of time are important tools to get want we want to achieve Joshua." He was learning.

Kernow held Joshua at the door and suggested that he wait outside until he's asked in. He explained that he didn't want Jacques to be diverted in any way shape or form with another person in the room until such time as he himself and alone has voluntarily accepted that he will cooperate. If he does, then good, we can then invite you in to divulge our plans together. Kernow, Joshua thought was a wise thinker.

Jacques heard the door unlock and swing open and Trevenan walked in, in a calm yet thoughtful manner. Jacques indeed had had the time to consider. He was not in a position to barter, he knew that, but knew he may get some concessions or at least promises that will ease his conscience.

"Well Jacques, have you come to a decision?" "I believe I have Mr Trevenan but before I answer, I would like to ask two or three questions if that is permitted?" "Of course," Trevenan replied. "Do you intend to kill any of my party here in Cornwall?" 'No." "Do you want any secret information that I may have or not have as the case may be on and above this mission I and my team are on?" "No." "Do you want me to betray my nation?" 'No." "One last question if I may, if we succeed in getting Jeanne to safety to these shores and she doesn't want me, what of me?" "Then Jacques, we have concluded our business and you are free to go but rest assured we would want you to retire and if we find you again messing in the lives of our good people of our good Queen Anne, we will kill you."

Jacques fell silent and let the answers flow into him to mitigate his judgement. "Then Mr Trevenan I believe and conclude that in the best interest of my party's safety and my own, and that of my love for Jeanne, with the knowledge that I will not betraying my nation outside of this mission, I will cooperate; what are your suggestions?" "Thank you Jacques, I believe you have made the right choice for all concerned."

"As for suggestion's I would like to bring in Joshua Pendragon who I believe you already know and, maybe now, we can all have a drink and relax a little. Help yourself Jacques, it's the best French brandy one can buy." Jacques cooperated.

With the three of them now around the table they set themselves into discussion. They all agreed that the main emphasis was to let the mission run naturally, it had to, as seen from the outside world. It was down to the intricacies of managing it that was needed to be agreed between them.

Being open and as honest as one could there was no room for delicacies. Many points were discussed and either agreed, classed as unimportant or couldn't be agreed and would need further thought. One point Jacques raised was the order he had been given by Bouchier to kill the three young men once the chemical had been dispensed into the ground. "How do feel about that Jacques," Trevenan asked. "I do not feel good about it all Mr Trevenan especially on the orders of one Pierre Bouchier as though life was a trivial thing and he could wave his hand and have authority over God."

Trevenan responded to his observations that he also didn't agree with Bouchier's orders but, somehow understood the need for this brutal action as this mission of yours is dirty and extremely unchivalrous. It would look seriously bad on the French in their bid to promote their good King Louis with neighbouring Countries as he is trying to do.

However, Jacques went on, "If he did not kill the three men, Albret and Bouchier would be suspicious and activate a search team." They carried on the discussion to agree a plan to save the lives of the young three. While talking, Trevenan sent for the young lady to fetch food and further refreshment. The other main area of concern was Zoe. This was again discussed at length with an agreement that it was up to Jacques to sort this out and turn her support by promising a life without Bouchier. Whatever he decides an armband of yellow and black would be shown on him when he exits the cottage tomorrow morning as a sign that all is well and the plan is proceeding as agreed.

The only other factor was that the cottage was loaded with explosives and all doors and windows were filled with gunpowder and booby trapped in case of an attack. With one flick of a flint in the right place, it could bring the cottage to dust and all within her.

Tomorrow was Monday and the kegs liquid germ had to be emptied into the ground by no later than Thursday to achieve its run and soak for Saturday into the pool below the water well where that particular well feeds. That means that Jacques and Zoe were expected in front of Bouchier no later than that weekend. No exit route had been planned for them, as flexibility to escape their own path back was seen as crucial. However, what it did mean was that the three young men would need to be killed or seemed to be killed and breathe their last this Wednesday or Thursday at the latest.

With time pushing on the meeting started coming to a close. Jacques needed some sleep, as did they all, and be at the cottage before daylight. They got up, shook hands and all went to the door. The young lady was there and asked she escort Jacques to his horse, Arc, and then report back. They would get a message to Jacques tomorrow night at the Fisherman's Inn on where next to meet.

They had done well. Trevenan was working on emotional trust to achieve his goal. Jacques really had no option and was trying to minimise the plots failure and save his life. Joshua was in the middle and thinking that maybe hostages would be needed to acquire its success.

Joshua and Kernow now relieved from Jacques, started to prepare themselves and make their way back to Rebecca at the cottage in Mousehole, as what needed to be here was done. It was getting late and they needed some sleep. However, Kernow needed updating from Hosking's before he thought about sleeping. Fetching their horses Joshua rode with Kernow and his bodyguards.

Getting to the fields behind the cottage Kernow and his men dismounted and allowed Joshua to carry on to its back yard as normal procedure, they would follow on foot shortly afterwards. Joshua was pleased to see all were up and went to Rebecca and pecked her on the cheek and asked after her and the children who also came round to him. The atmosphere was one that Joshua relished and had missed for so long. He then went into the main room where Hosking's was busy around the map table and soon afterwards Kernow entered with bodyguard's being left outside to guard.

Chapter 22

Whilst seemingly free to ride back to his lodgings, in the midst of Penzance, Jacques was confused, bewildered but somehow alive. He did not see this coming, bloody English. How was he to get out of this he thought. He could simply flee and leave them all to it but what of Jeanne and Zoe. He was in a bloody tight fix. However, where there is darkness there must be light somewhere and just maybe this might be a blessing in disguise. He must find that light. Reaching his place of refuge, he silently entered his room, reached for the brandy and lay back on the bed. All these years in control he thought with all the accolades it brought him and now, in the gutter struggling for survival, he must think very clear and straight for his very own existence. He felt eighty years old and was tired of this continual fighting.

The early hours soon came and Jacques was on Arc in the freezing darkness riding to Zoe at the cottage. He knew he was being watched and whoever they were are acting discreet and professional which funnily enough impressed him. Trevenan was keeping his promise which gave him some comfort.

Zoe was waiting and as he entered she hugged him and said, "Jacques I can't take much more." "Zoe, we need to talk, where is Pascal?" "Asleep upstairs" she replied. "Did the two young men leave on time for Sennon?" "Yes, they have worked hard and slept little, while Pascal has worked little and slept hard. They were going to beat him up for being so idle and rude to me so I had to step in and quiet things down."

Jacques took Zoe into her bedroom and as he did she started to undress. "Zoe put your clothes back on, we need to talk." Zoe reluctantly but then again pleased, did as she was told but knew something was instantly wrong and asked, "Jacques, what is it, you have somehow changed I can feel it." "I think we have been compromised Zoe." "How do mean Jacques and please speak clearly so I can understand." "We are being watched, all of us, even now the two young men are being observed." "How do know?" she asked. "I have seen them and I also know who they work for." Jacques continued in a fearful brief tone. "Zoe, we are in trouble." Jacques expected tears and crying but instead got a silent resourcefulness and a "So what are we going to do about it?"

"Zoe, please tell me exactly and truthfully what you want to do with your life, assuming we get out of this alive?" "I want to go home and start my life again with the love I left behind." Jacques considered the position and asked. "Zoe, I believe I could make a deal with these people but I need your total support." "Jacques if you can give me the chance to meet my lost love again and let me live a life, you have my full support, now do what you have to do and keep us alive."

With timing just about right the two young ones appeared with further kegs. Jacques started warming to their zest in getting the job done.

Jacques enquired after the tunnel and was surprised in what they had done. Pascal was asked to come down and explain exactly where they were with this tunnelling and when will it be finished. Pascal, calmly acknowledged the request and said, "the tunnel and liquid trench will be ready with the pace of these young men in probably two more days, that would make it late Wednesday night."

"That's good Pascal," Jacques replied, "then all you three men be ready to leave before midnight Wednesday or at the latest one o'clock Thursday morning, no excuses, be ready or be left behind." "Where are we going?" Pascal asked. "Back to France where else."

Jacques then thought back about the order from Bouchier, to eliminate them and not let them leave breathing. This was there lucky day, only they didn't know it.

Zoe made them all breakfast and started tidying the place up as best she could in and around the piles of dirt and rubble brought up from the tunnel excavations. After reassuring Zoe, he would be back same time tomorrow, and satisfied that the tunnel was again being dug with young gusto, Jacques went for the door.

However, once outside immediately felt in his pocket for the yellow and black armband and put it on. He was sure that Trevenan's men would relay this message immediately. Back on Arc he rode fast to Penzance.

That evening while he was at the Fisherman's Inn a message was given to Jacques requesting he be at the Harbour front at nine o'clock. On arrival at said time, Trevenan's men took him into the shadows and searched him. Once happy they escorted him on board a small but well gunned schooner where again Trevenan and Joshua were there already.

Trevenan had indeed got the message of cooperation and handed Jacques another armband for Zoe, on her departure from the cottage. They were counted as acknowledgement of cooperation to any of our men and for them not to approach. "Well Jacques," Trevenan said, "Have you the time when this plan will start its operation?" "We will be ready to leave midnight Wednesday or one hour past in to the early Thursday morning." "Good and what of Zoe?" "Zoe is ready to leave as well and indeed she has pledged she will trust me." "Very well Jacques and you will diffuse the booby traps and the gunpowder bombs on your leave, we don't want any accidents, do we?"

The geographical areas were once again discussed as with timings and when all three were in agreement Trevenan went over the plan again. Jacques looked at Trevenan and although he was on the other side, so to speak, respected his thoroughness and methodology.

Once Jacques had left, Kernow called one of his most trusted runners with urgent messages to be dispatched forthwith without any delay. With the seed laid, now the plan of execution could take hold.

Chapter 23

The moon was full and the night dark and clear with stars glittering in its background when Jacques entered the cottage around ten o'clock Wednesday. The young lads had indeed worked well and were covered in dirt but full of laughs and zest as they boasted to Jacques that they had delivered the tunnel with time to spare for a brandy. Jacques congratulated them and let them have their drinks. His mind was on Pascal and Zoe and getting them all out of here.

"Where are the kegs Pascal?" "Where we said we would put them," he replied cockily. "Good, then get yourself ready as you three are to leave in one hour." "And what of Zoe?" he asked. "Zoe and I will clean up the mess, pour the chemical into the ground and set the fuses and meet you in two to three hours." "Where are we to meet?" Jacques was tired of this young man's bravado and continual asking questions upon questions. "Pascal, get yourself ready and once all three of you are, then and only then will you be given instructions on the rendezvous point for getting back to our glorious homeland, understood?"

With carriage and horses ready they all clambered round the map with lamps glowing. The point in which Jacques jabbed his finger was Gunwalloe Cove also known as Church Cove. They noticed it was quite a run for the horses but Jacques convinced them it was the best place as being far enough away from Mousehole and the closest and safest place for extraction of three young men after a successful dangerous mission. They nodded their agreement.

They were to go into the Church and wait there for pick up around an hour before sunrise. Do not let yourselves been seen and keep the horses away from the Cove out of site. You will be going aboard a ship and there is no room for them, just yourselves and your belongings.

When the three men had left, Zoe and Jacques sat down opposite each other and both leaning forward held each other's hands. "Jacques, are we in trouble?" "Zoe I cannot tell you everything but I can assure you we are safe for now, now let's get things sorted here and get ourselves away from this place."

Jacques did as he promised. With the gunpowder defused he went into the tunnel. Counting the kegs to one hundred he was satisfied that all was in order. Whilst Zoe was sorting out her last things Jacques went outside and got his beloved Arc. He also got Zoe's horse ready with her gear. Going back in and taking one final look around both upstairs and downstairs he was ready to go from this place. Zoe was also ready. Standing together inside the doorway Jacques put the armband around her arm and said, "This is for good luck to us both," and then he put his on as well. They both rode to Newlyn to wait at the Bull Inn where they would be met by a young lady.

Bull and his small team saw them leave and stayed low in the shadows. Waiting half an hour he ordered one man to go forward and enter the cottage building through the main door

Jacques, Zoe and the three men had come out of. This was a brave thing to do and Bull knew it but the man he picked he trusted and would reward him well.

After a few long minutes of waiting the man came back out of the cottage with lantern lit and a hand waving them in. Bull broke his cover and moved forward leaving his other two men to cover him. Bull was amazed at the wreckage to the inside of this small cottage and the mountain of earth that filled it but he went on and done his duty. Finding the tunnels entry point he scampered down and crawled his way through. He found the kegs as described and counted them as one hundred and checked the seals for tampering as best his could. The seals were perfect and untouched and the liquid had not been emptied. Taking one keg with him he scrambled back out.

With the information gained he and his man exited the cottage, went to their horses and rode the short distance to Mousehole harbour to meet Kernow.

Kernow and Joshua, on board the ship, received the information and the one keg and informed Bull and his men to go back to Hosking's at Rebecca's cottage as he has further orders for them. Kernow then ordered the Captain to weigh off and head for Newlyn. Joshua had the keg on the table and started breaking the seal. Kernow gave him six small metal cylinders which Joshua started to fill. Each time one was filled Joshua handed it back to Kernow who screwed a cap on tight. Once all six were filled Kernow handed four back to Joshua and kept two.

When Bull and his men reached Rebecca's cottage they were all given refreshment. Once again Henry Hosking rearranged his men and the tasks they were to do. Two men were immediately dispatched back to the cottage and guard it from the inside until relieved. They could, eat, drink and sleep but not light a fire or smoke inside due to the gunpowder being unknown. Also to stay alert as the people who will take over will be coming from London, probably in two to three days' time.

Kernow and Joshua sitting in the Captain's cabin relaxed a little in that the plan had started well and so rewarded themselves with a small brandy.

The ship left Mousehole heading the small way to Newlyn. Entering Newlyn Harbour Kernow dispatched two men to go to the Bull Inn and bring back Jacques and Zoe and must show them courtesy and respect. When Jacques and Zoe entered the Bull Inn the young lady was waiting for them and escorted both to the main fire place and waited upon their needs of refreshments. The conversation between Jacques and Zoe was mostly of silence with an air of nervousness.

However, eating what they could and drinking neat brandy eased their tensions a little. After a while the young lady politely informed them that they were both wanted outside in the back yard where their horses were stabled. Zoe looked at Jacques with dread. "Be strong Zoe, be strong, trust me," Jacques said.

Two men were waiting and politely asked Jacques for his weapons. Jacques responded accordingly but Zoe looked frightened at what was happening. Jacques saw this and quickly reassured her that everything was fine and do not worry. The men looked at Jacques and nodded towards Zoe to do the same. Zoe did as was told but the two men, not knowing her, asked the young lady of the tavern, who worked for Kernow, to frisk her, which she did and found nothing untoward. "Thank you my lady," one of the men said, "and now please may we escort you to the ship." This kindness and courtesy had an effect on Zoe and calmed her a little.

Asked to leave the horses they walked on board the ship being greeted by the Captain who escorted them and their belongings to separate cabins closest to the Captains. Brandy, pipes and flints were in the cabins on the table with lamp and bed with blankets for their comfort. The Captain suggested they get comfortable and someone will be along shortly.

Thirty minutes later they were asked to join their hosts in the Captain's Cabin. Trevenan couldn't have been more courteous towards Zoe and even offering her a chair and both Trevenan and Joshua not sitting until she had. Once all were seated Trevenan started "Thank you for coming Jacques and thank you also Ms Zoe, my name is Mr Trevenan and this gentleman is Joshua Pendragon."

Zoe was totally confused, these were pure Englishmen, what had Jacques done, oh my God, what has he done? Trevenan saw the fear and bewilderment in her eyes and was prepared if this happened. "Ms Zoe, I don't know what Jacques has said or not said but would you like me to explain?" Zoe saw the brandy and replied, "If I may have a brandy then I think that would be good Mr Trevenan."

With the first brandy drank and glass refilled Trevenan asked Jacques if he would allow him to explain to Zoe what has happened and what had been agreed. Jacques was quiet but gave the nod, so Trevenan explained and Zoe listened intently. He mentioned Jeanne being captive under Philip De Albret for his own use, which made Jacques feel sorrow and pain and his puppet Pierre Bouchier, which made Zoe shudder. He also mentioned that Jeanne was Rebecca's mother who Joshua Pendragon was deeply in love with and is asking for her hand in marriage. This made Joshua go red with embarrassment and made Jacques sit up a little as this was unknown to him.

He also mentioned that he didn't wish anything from them except their help in getting their beloved and dear Jeanne back to England and in exchange for that help they would release them both and the young men to their own freedom and liberty. He again, gave the opposite angle in the same calm tone as before. That should she not agree to help and cooperate then she would be held in her cabin under arrest until they achieve their goal.

Then, as agreed with Jacques, she would be freed on French soil unhurt and at her own liberty to do what she pleases. However, if she was found in England again working against our gracious Queen Anne, she would be killed. Zoe understood the explanation and was agreeing to much of it but the last item startled her into a realisation that this was her life or death. Now she quickly realised why Jacques had done this.

Trevenan suggested she may have many questions and that it would be a good idea for all to go back to our cabins to relax and consider things carefully before any decisions are made. They would be weighing off to Gunwalloe any minute now to pick up the three young men and maybe we should all meet back up in an hour or so. With everyone getting up, Zoe and Jacques left for their cabins to do exactly what Trevenan suggested, escorted by two men.

When both had gone Kernow looked at Joshua for his thoughts. Joshua wasn't convinced that Zoe was on board. Kernow agreed. This may have been a mistake but they had thought it through and thought it best to try and get her on side.

Zoe was lying on the bed when a light knock on the door came. It was Joshua and asked if he could come in and talk. Joshua suggested she hadn't heard the entire story and asks he be permitted to tell. He explained in detail how his father had been killed with Jeanne on their escape whilst working in France and how it had come about the hearing two years later that Jeanne was indeed alive and could, with careful planning be rescued, we ask for nothing more. Zoe listened patiently. He then went to explore and delve into her future plans on what she would do when set free. He also, under guidance from Kernow, was to mention Pierre Bouchier.

Zoe started to calm herself down and talk more openly to this man. It was now Joshua's turn to listen patiently. He thanked her for her allowing him to talk and would now let her be so she could consider her decisions. As he was leaving, Zoe said "thank you Joshua, I believe your honesty."

Zoe went out of her cabin and crept into Jacques to question him and also thank him, for now she understood he could have just escaped and left them all to their death, at least now she had a fighting chance. She found him laid on the bed and so quietly lay down by his side both silently looking up at the ceiling. With minutes passing and no words spoken Zoe asked quietly, "Jacques do you know this lady Jeanne?" "Yes," came the reply. "And is this the women you have talked about in your heart?" "Yes."

"How did she take it?" Kernow asked. "I found her to be more encouraging than before and believe she may well make her decision to be a positive one." "Well done Joshua, however, either way we will push forward, maybe we should have used her as a hostage as you suggested."

The three young men were getting anxious and nervy about when and who was picking them up. Pascal didn't seem bothered and showed off to be braver than the other two. He had also stopped off at the Halzephron Inn a mile or so before the cove and although it was late and closing he made them give him a drink and take away a large bottle of brandy. He offered it to the other two who refused.

It wasn't until four to four thirty that the Church house door swung open with Bull and his seven men entering. The three men immediately stood up. Bull spoke politely saying the ship was ready to take them back to France and to please follow him. As each one went through the Church door they were asked if they were carrying any weapons and if they were, the Captain asks they be given to us now and handed back to you when leaving. There is a no weapon policy on board, it's a sailor thing.

Looking at each other for support they were taken by surprise at this order but none the less they accepted it as it made sense and they had really no reason not to, they were going home.

Getting into the rowing boat they were oared out to the ship. Jacques and the Captain were there to greet them and three of the ships men and Jacques showed them and their belongings to a large cabin for them to sleep. Once inside Jacques asked if they were in good health and looking forward to getting back to France. Pascal couldn't help himself and blurted out that this ship is English and crewed by bloody Englishmen. Jacques looked at him and said, "My young friend, all is not what it seems; the game we play is never straight forward. All will be well and we shall all feel the soft earth of our beautiful France under our feet tonight. Now relax, stay in the cabin, have a drink and congratulate yourselves on doing a fine thing for your Country. Food and drink will be sent to you throughout the day and I will be back later this evening."

With two bunk beds either side of the cabin the two young men raced for both top beds. Pascal skulked to one of the bottom ones and started mumbling about Englishmen and how inferior to the French they are, calling them bloody savages while gulping the brandy from the bottle.

The more Pascal thought the more anxious he became. He wasn't happy, things didn't stack up and that made him annoyed. If two plus two doesn't make four, then there is a problem. He rationed that he could play their game acting stupid like the other two here or be bold. The ship also could be no more than a good swim back which was an option, and, being still dark was a plus sign to that option. The only other was to wait but then he would be in the middle of the sea and he would have no way of escape. The English could simply kill him and throw his body overboard. 'Never trust the English' Bouchier had said.

He went into his belongings and found the little pistol he had not handed over. He had to do it, it was logical to an educated and intelligent Frenchman, yes he would get away. The other two heard his movements and asked of his well-being. When hearing what he was planning they tried to reason with him that Jacques could be trusted. Pascal would have none of it, his mind was made up. "If you two young idiots believe that then you cannot be proud Frenchman or, have no brains like the English." The two looked at each other across the cabin and knew they would stay with Jacques.

With one last gulp of brandy Pascal slowly opened the cabin door and left. Moving along the gangway with pistol at the ready he made his way to the steps leading to the upper deck. With no one insight he quietly went up. Opening the upper deck door into the fresh air he found himself alone. Looking around he saw the headland behind him and as calculated was a long but doable swim back. He could then regroup and find his own way back. Bending down he went to the side rails and slowly started to climb over when he heard a loud shout, "Oi! you stop where you are." Pascal turned his pistol, fired and then jumped.

The two quick reaction marines on board heard the commotion and quickly rallied to the point of confusion. The sailor had been shot but was shouting "Get him; he has jumped overboard, shoot him." With muskets loaded they leaned over, aimed and fired. The man was still swimming away. They reloaded, aimed and fired. This time the man stopped and floated still on the sea. The Captain quickly ordered for a small boat to be launched and a small crew to fetch the body back.

The four of them were in the Captain's cabin talking and discussing when they heard the noise and commotion. Kernow's life guards were quick to react and protect them. The Captain soon came down to brief Kernow on what had happened. Kernow asked him to speak openly to all present. "Very well," said the Captain "we believe the man to be known as Pascal," and then went on to explain in a no nonsense matter of fact method.

"What of the other two young men?" Jacques asked. "I have no idea Sir, I thought it best to report the initial action and then be advised by good selves." "Thank you, Captain," said Trevenan, "please carry on with our voyage we will deal with the other two." Trevenan looked at Jacques and Jacques got the message and left the cabin.

Jacques slammed open the cabin door to see the two young men looking in fear. "What the bloody hell is going on?" Jacques demanded. The two tried to explain what had happened. Jacques listened and decided to calm them down and inform them the reality of what was really meant to happen to them on orders from Pierre Bouchier. Jacques had had enough of pondering around these young men and they needed to hear the truth and he was going to give it to them clearly so they bloody understood the seriousness of what is happening around them.

While Jacques was gone Kernow felt it was the right opportunity to inform Zoe that she doesn't have to go along with the plan if she didn't want to, it was her choice. "Mr Trevenan, I have weighed things up, discussed matters with Jacques and listened to your good colleague Joshua and feel, if you wish nothing more of me and that I am free to pursue my life thereafter, then I believe it is a reasonable answer to say that I will cooperate." "Thank you, Ms Zoe, we promise we wish nothing more and, I am sorry about Pascal." "Thank you and no need to be sorry Mr Trevenan." Joshua listened to them speaking and tried to weigh her up thinking one minute she is hard as a man and the next she is soft as velvet and then Rebecca sprang to mind which, made him smile.

Jacques re-joined Zoe, Trevenan and Joshua. Trevenan suggested all that could be done for now is done and we all retire and try and get some rest. We will be on this ship until tomorrow night when at the hour of eight we begin our approach.

Later that day and away over in the lovely town of Morlaix the middle aged non-descript man was behind his stall selling his fruit and vegetables as he always did. The young man from the Chateau Morlaix was doing his weekly Thursday shop for stores for the Philip Albret's household as he also always did. Walking up to the middle aged man and looking at the fresh produce on display and ordering what the head chef had written down, the man quietly asked, "How are you my son?" "I am well Father, thank you." "Friday tomorrow night at midnight, leave the lower back scullery door unlocked and only speak to the one named Joshua." "I Understand Father." "Be careful my son and I will see you in England." With groceries ordered and loaded on the cart the young man of fourteen was gone.

Chapter 24

Going over the plan and the last minute details Trevenan wished them good luck and the three of them went down the ladder into the boat. It was eight o'clock Friday night and the sky was moody dark and rainy with hardly a star to be seen and only a small moon. They would need to back here in ten hours' maximum or left behind. Once all safely sitting down, the boat pushed off from the ship rowed by two strong sailors and two armed marines heading for the French mainland, to the small cove of Plougasnou about ten miles due north from Morlaix. Once away clear the Captain gave the order to swing the ship about and as it did the sails pushed out and away she went.

The sailors rowed hard against the swell and delivered them safely to the tiny out of the way inlet. The two sailors remained behind and got everything under cover to await their return. As planned the horses were there waiting, reined and silent with one spare in which Joshua took control. Once all saddled up Joshua and Jacques nodded to each other and with Zoe and the two armed marines galloped off at pace.

On the outskirts of Morlaix they came to a halt, dismounted and went over the plan once again. Joshua particularly asked Zoe if she was good and has she any last questions if so to ask them now. She shook her head and said, "I am ready Joshua." "Have you the letter?" Joshua asked. "Yes," she replied. Joshua accepted her answers but like Kernow he had doubts she may not go through with things hence the cover of the two marines who had been briefed to take over should she not complete the task only she could do. With that they split up, Zoe and the two marines headed for the Inn at Morlaix and Joshua and Jacques headed for the Chateau.

Zoe and the marines entered the stable of the Inn and once handing over their horses they were welcomed and shown to their rooms at the back away from any noise. The rooms were spacious with a large double bed in each and adjoining door. The marines stayed with Zoe and never let her out of their sight on the orders of Kernow, not even to the toilet. Zoe accepted this as a precaution as she was old enough and wise enough that she would indeed do the same if the roles were reversed. They all stayed in Zoe's room and waited for the appointed time.

Joshua and Jacques saw the Chateau and detoured completely around it to get to the desired spot. They reined the three horses a little further back in the cover of the trees and slowly and quietly edged their way forward to the centre left back of the Chateau. They were in sight of the scullery side walk with steps down to the door but also, able to see the front of the large drive way to the front of the house. Joshua noticed that to get to the scullery door they would have to walk twenty yards on gravel and that created noise, they needed to be careful. Quietly they discussed this and nodded in agreement. They now laid down under a large tree with sweeping low branches that gave excellent cover and got themselves as comfortable as possible then silently waited and watched.

The hour passed with nothing. Sitting in acres and acres of land the Chateau itself seemed ghostly quiet with its silence. Then Joshua heard the hooves of a horse galloping towards the front door. Tapping Jacques on the shoulder he responded by giving the thumbs up sign.

Joshua drew the telescope and zeroed in on the now dismounted rider. It was one of the two marines who spoke fluent French. Rapping the front door, the rider with a letter in one hand and holding his horse's reins in the other waited anxiously. Nothing, so he rapped again. This time a flicker of light could be seen getting closer to the inside of the doorway. The grand door opened and the marine confidently and quickly handed the man the letter and said in French, "Mr Pierre Bouchier, urgent." The man took the letter as a matter of business from an urchin and closed the door shut. The marine jumped back on his horse and rode out quickly.

Pierre Bouchier and Philip Albret were in the parlour playing dominoes and drinking wine when the door was knocked. Albret turned his head while still stroking the young maid's hair that was kneeling like a lap dog by his side and said with a relaxed and couldn't be bothered attitude, "Enter." The butler came in and apologised for disturbing them at this time of night but he had a letter for Mr Pierre Bouchier delivered just a while ago saying it was urgent. The butler handed it to Philip Albret himself as it would have been rude and bad mannered if he gave it directly to Bouchier. "Thank you, now please leave us in peace, I'm getting a headache with all these interruptions," Albret said.

"So Pierre what have we here, a sealed letter for your attention, I wonder who it is from, shall I open it for you?" Bouchier knew that Albret could seem to be joking but underneath this man may be deadly serious and if he said no, could turn in an instant, he would play his game. "Please do my Lord Philip; I have nothing to hide as a servant to the Count of Morlaix." "Then I will," he said, but before he did he slapped the young maid on the head and ordered her to pour more wine for both Pierre and himself and then quickly lay back down by his side so he could stroke her. This she did instantly without murmur or hesitation.

Philip broke the seal and opened the letter.

My Love Pierre,

I write in favour that the mission has been a success and praise yours and Count Morlaix planning.

I am in wait at the Inn at Morlaix with my passion being aroused for you and your strong hands touching me.

You may find this letter a little naughty but please come quickly and release me from these chains of wait.

Zoe. Xxx

"Yippee!" Albret shouted, "Yippee" he said again, "it's been a success, they are back. Excellent news my Pierre, excellent news, more wine, more wine," he ordered to the young girl.

With that he passed the letter to Bouchier who sat back and read it. "Indeed my dear Count, excellent news and what would you have me do with the rest of the letter?" "What are you Pierre, are you not a Frenchman, can you not see the woman for the woman, go and tell her that Count Philip De Albret will reward her himself. Now go and let me alone," as he said this he put one hand down the front of the young girl's bodice and gulped another large glass of sherry with the other. "As you wish Philip, thank you, we will see you tomorrow." "Yes, yes, now leave us and mention to the butler that we are retiring to bed and wish not to be disturbed." Philip Albret was elated not only was the mission a success, but he would be promoted up the line before his good King Louis.

Bouchier was also elated and now he would get his reward, she will love him and want him more after he had finished with her tonight, he was convinced, his pride, position and ego knew no bounds especially now that his master Philip Albret would probably be knighted. He quickly ordered the stable boy to get his horse ready and went to the butler and told him that the count has retired and not to be disturbed, he himself would be back tomorrow.

Joshua and Jacques saw the horse being led around the front of the Chateau by a young boy. He then saw a man come out of the main front door, jump up in the saddle and whip the horse forward into a straight gallop. Jacques leaned into Joshua and whispered into his left ear one word, 'Bouchier.'

It was nearing eleven thirty but Joshua decided to wait further and be patient, it was feeling a little too early to move forward, he decided to wait a further hour that would take them to twelve thirty, one o'clock. Joshua leaned over to Jacques and whispered, "one hour." Jacques nodded without any objection and laid his head back down watching. Joshua was impressed.

The two marines now lay in wait in the adjoining room with the door between them locked with them having the key. Zoe was lying on the bed feeling nervous and very anxious. She had to do it, she had to, she kept thinking to herself. Then she would hesitate and reconsider, what if she didn't, what if she didn't. She went to the brandy bottle and poured herself a drink.

Lying back down, she knew this was only going to go one way. The consequences of her actions tonight would seal her fate for her life time. 'Oh Zoe,' she thought what of the consequences. 'Oh Zoe, what are you to do.' She decided to have another drink.

It was midnight before she heard the knock on the door. The time had come for her to get up and face life. She got up and slowly went to the door and on unlocking it she saw him. Bouchier boldly pushed the door wide open and strutted in with such confidence that he went straight to her, pulled her roughly towards him taking her very breath away. He then kissed her passionately with his tongue going deep down her throat and his hand going up her skirt straight between her thighs. She felt physically sick and repulsed, but she had to think, think girl, think.

She pulled away and in a heartfelt dizzy manner said, "Oh Pierre, Pierre my saviour, thank you I couldn't have lasted another minute, let us bed together and be entwined as one." With that he starting throwing off his clothes laughing and saying, "Zoe, you will have no other after tonight, you are mine forever." Zoe let him strip off as she went to the cabinet and poured the brandy, one for each of them. With her hands shaking she slowly reached for the small cylinder and poured the contents into his glass. Turning around, she saw he was nearly undressed apart from his pants and how aroused he was.

"Pierre, I am nervous on how I will manage your passion towards me this night, please let me have a small drink to help calm me, here I have also made one for you so I am not alone," she then offered the glass. Bouchier took the drink like a man of no consequence and said, "of course my little sweet I can understand you being nervous, here's to our life together' and chinked his glass with hers then swallowed it all, Zoe did the same.

Bouchier took his pants off went towards her and picked her straight up off the floor and took her to the bed. "I will undress you in here," he said boldly and started unlacing her bodice. Zoe was paralysed with fear, she had to play for time but how much time she didn't know. "Pierre can we just kiss and hug for a while and let my body get ready for you." "No way," he said, "when I am ready, I am ready, you will learn my ways my little sweet, do not worry you will love it."

Zoe laid back and could do nothing. His hands were all over her yet when she pulled them away he got more aggressive. So she went limp in body, looked up to the ceiling as if in a trance of surrender then, with nothing else to be done, took a deep breath and screamed at the top of her voice.

Hearing the scream from the other room the marines quickly unlocked the adjoining door and came rushing in. They immediately went for Bouchier and wrestled him to the ground then tied him up like a rag doll with a gag in its mouth. Bouchier didn't see it coming and was absolutely taken by surprise, he then started to cough.

They took him next door into their room. One of the marines came back and asked how she was. Zoe was shaking, she had never ever done anything like this before. The marine asked in which glass she poured the chemical as they were side by side on the cabinet. She said, she couldn't remember. "No matter," came the reply and quickly gathered up both and smashed them on the ground. "Where is the cylinder?" Zoe pointed and the marine pocketed it. "Zoe, listen to me, you have done nothing wrong, get yourself calm, we must leave within the hour, is there anything you want?" "Yes she said, I want out of this bloody room and I want a bloody drink."

Bouchier was on the floor wrapped over completely on the other side of the marine's bed out of Zoe's sight. His convulsions had steadied and his body lay limp but life was still in it as they could hear his coarse breathing getting lighter and shorter as the minutes ticked by. Although Zoe was in the marine's room and had taken a few shots of brandy she was still coming to terms on what she had done but she was getting there as the marines kept up their talking to her.

The hour had moved on and Joshua knew it was now or never so giving Jacques a nudge they checked their weapons and went direct to the scullery steps leading down to the door at the side of the Chateau. The gravel seemed loud under their feet but the air was fresh and the night silent which made it seem louder than it was.

Going straight for the latch, found with relief, it unlocked and with a slight push the door opened. Joshua then waited a minute with Jacques behind him. Jacques was now beginning to understand the way Joshua's brain worked, wait then move, wait then move. With everything silent they both quietly stepped inside. Again waiting a minute, they heard a young voice break the eerie silence, "Joshua," it said. Quietly Joshua whispered back, "Yes, I am he." With that the young man came forward away from the dark corner where he had been crouching and waiting. "I didn't think you were coming," the young boy said. "You are a very brave young man and yes we are a little late, we had to be sure the timing was right. Joshua talked with the young man for quite a while asking him question after question as he needed to gain knowledge of what was before them. Weighing things up he then asked the young man to lead them to the captive Jeanne.

Quietly they followed the boy around the Chateau and then down the deep steps which kept going and going. The young man was carrying a jug of water giving credible reason for him to be there should he be seen. Joshua and Jacques stayed back a distance. Joshua thought they must already be thirty feet below ground yet still the boy continued.

Then they heard him. "What do you want here boy at this time of night." "Sorry Sir I was ordered by my master to give water to the lady." "Well you have now leave it there and piss off." "But my master will punish me if I do not give it to her directly." "And my master will cut my head off if you do, now piss off before I whack your arse." Just as the young man was turning back up the steps he put one finger in the air meaning one guard. Joshua and Jacques rushed around him taking the guard by complete surprise and instantly knocking him out cold. He just didn't see it coming.

The keys were quickly taken and the cell door opened but with difficulty. It appeared that the door hadn't been opened in a while but the cats hatch at the bottom of the door seemed to be swinging easily. They took the guard's lantern and went in. Raising the light up, Jacques saw Jeanne first and immediately went to her.

She was not well and seemed to be emaciated with lice running all over her. Jacques bent down, put his hand ever so gently on the side of her face and whispered so lovingly and very tenderly her name "Jeanne." It was meant for Joshua to have been the first to get to her on specific orders from Kernow but somehow he felt that Jacques should be first, especially what he was now seeing, so remained at the door.

Jacques tried again and this time her eyes opened and she said quietly and tenderly, "Jacques, the love of my life, I knew you would come" and then her eyes closed. Jacques started to weep seeing his love in the state she was so he bent forward and kissed her gently on the forehead. He wrapped the worm eaten blanket round her and with his strong arms picked her up like a new born baby. Holding her safely in his arms he looked up and swore that Philip Albret will pay with his life for treating his beautiful lady like a dog.

Leaving the cell behind them Joshua dragged the unconscious guard inside and locked the door then threw the keys on the floor. With the young man leading they made their way back to the scullery. Joshua allowed Jacques to take Jeanne out to the horses and wait there for him.

Joshua asked the young man if he was ready who, responded with a confident, "yes." So they found two jugs and freshly filled one with wine and one with natural sourced spring water. Joshua then got out two cylinders and poured the chemical into both of them.

While Joshua was pouring the germ the young lad fetched two freshly washed small linen towels and once Joshua had finished laid them on top. These were a sign that both wine and water has been freshly replenished. Joshua said "be very careful, I will wait here for your return." The young man picked up the jugs and went swiftly to Philip Albret's bedroom door.

Directly outside the door in the vast corridor against the back wall was a beautiful mahogany bureau with fresh flowers, glasses and ornaments. Quietly replacing the two half empty jugs on the silver tray with the two freshly filled ones he quickly came back down.

Joshua was waiting for him and said, "well done young man, we have one more task to complete and then we are off so wait silently here in the scullery until I come back for you. I will be as quick as I can."

Joshua darted back to where the horses were reined. Jacques was there already in the saddle with Jeanne being held strongly in his front arms. Joshua said, "we must wait for the others Jacques, it is too early to go back." "Joshua, I have trusted you and understand your meaning but I am afraid Jeanne is very weak and if I don't make a start back to the rendezvous point now at a slow pace then the fast ride later will most probably kill her. Joshua I have trusted you with my life and so I ask that you trust me now." Joshua understood the logic and agreed it made sense. He would have to wait on his own.

It was nearly thirty minutes before he heard the rider coming up behind him. He crouched down and waited. Seeing it was one of the marines he stood up. "Where are the other two?" Joshua asked. The marine explained that the poisoning of Bouchier, pointing to a body lying across in front of his saddle, took its toll. Zoe didn't want to be near him or this place ever again and so is being guarded by the other marine and have gone straight to the rendezvous point. "Apologies, it took us quite a while to sort things out with both the lifeless Bouchier and Zoe."

They got Bouchier's body down off the horse and carried him back into the Scullery of the Chateau. The young lad led them the back way to Bouchier's bedroom where they entered, stripped him naked and put him to bed. "That's it," Joshua said, "now let us all get the bloody hell out of here while we are still alive." Being led back to the scullery the three of them dashed out to where the horses were tied. The extra horse was meant for Jeanne but now that Jacques had got her, the young lad can ride him. Time was nearing three o'clock, they had better get moving.

Chapter 25

George Kernow was in the Captain's chair thinking. Although the pickup point is at five o'clock in the morning at the small cove at Plougasnou he felt agitated. He had got this far by being tactful and unpredictable. He decided to wait a while to see if his feelings would change. He took the brandy and drew the pipe as the galleon rolled idly with the waves awaiting his decision.

He thought to himself that two years ago he was at the very same point in his mission when they were surprized by a French galleon and was lucky to get away with his life, Jeanne and John were not that lucky. How did they know, was it a coincidence? He had time to change. He waited and considered then reconsidered. He shouted for the life guard outside the cabin door. When the guard came in George said, "Please fetch me the Captain."

The Captain duly arrived and was asked to sit down and take a brandy. The Captain refused the drink but readily took the pipe. George went over his thoughts of agitation and asked the Captain for an alternative pick up. Both of them went to the table and leaning over assessed the large map. Although George was nervous the Captain also was dubious and vented his doubts on the ships safety going into another pick up point in another secluded cove in enemy territory. "So what would be your solution Captain?" Looking at the map even closer with fingers running up and down the Captain was silently giving further thought. After several minutes he then tapped the table map with his large forefinger at a place called Roc'h Loue't Point, one mile, North West of Plougasnou.

His suggestion to overcome both his and George's agitation would indeed require them to switch pick up point to a near and more open type peninsular of land where open sea was all round and no Galleon could sneak up within cannon distance unnoticed. This would also alleviate George's fears that if someone did indeed know about Plougasnou this would definitely counter act that danger.

George smiled, made himself and the Captain a pipe and drawing with deep breaths lifted his brandy glass and said, "Roc'h Loue't Point it is, make ready Captain and send messengers, we have little time."

George was taking no chances with this extraction. Last time it was catastrophic and covert. This time he would go overt both on land and sea in meaningful purpose. He ordered a full platoon of heavily armed marines to land and secure the new rendezvous in readiness to receive our fellow escapees and repulse any attack from the enemy should they come. The ship also would be at full alert with extra cannon at the ready. It was also agreed that once our people are in the boats the ship would dare to move closer to them so speed up this most dangerous and vulnerable part of the exit strategy.

The first to arrive at the initial rendezvous point at Plougasnou was Zoe and the marine. Zoe's hands were tied together as well as her horse being also tied to the marine's horse.

Although she was in fair spirits the soldier was not taking any chances with this lady. They were stopped by a small rear guard of marines who directed them to the new pick up point further up the coast.

The next was Jacques and Jeanne who was still holding her frail body close to his chest. Although being surprised by the marine's orders of the new pick up point he wasn't daunted as he knew this was a vital time in the operation and would probably had done the same himself. Asking for water he poured what he could into Jeanne's dry mouth and with his lips ever so gently kissed it closed. The soldiers looked at each other but Jacques didn't care.

Not long after came Joshua, the marine and small boy. Galloping at full speed without let up from the Chateaux they were getting exhausted. However, being explained the change in plan they quickly understood, said their thanks and pushed on again at full pace. With job done the rear guard marines quickly followed them in behind.

The marine commander satisfied that all people who should be there were, signalled the outlying ship to move closer. The two rowing boats pulled by a full crew of able seamen strained into the deeper waters while the ship turned into meet them and close the gap. The marines on land became ultra-alert waiting. They were to stay and defend the point until such time the boats had reached the ship and off loaded its precious cargo. Once this was achieved and signalled accordingly they were to withdraw and hide. Another vessel would return at midnight to make their escape. The marine commander accepted the plan as another day in a soldier's life but really knew that going back for his platoon on top of this important extraction would seriously and unnecessary expose the ship for too long a period.

On board Ship George Kernow being kept up to date suddenly felt the ship turn its heavy bows into land and in darkly silence waited, and waited.

What seemed like an eternity, a loud knocking came on the Captain's door which, made Kernow jump into life. "Come in," he responded sharply. It was the Captain who entered reporting that all persons are safely on board and the ship is now at full sail heading home. With a feeling of massive relief Kernow asked if all persons were well. "Everyone except for the lady named Jeanne, she is with the medical officer as we speak." "Thank you Captain, thank you, you and your crew have done well, please could you inform Joshua that I wish to see him."

When the Captain left the cabin George got his already made pipe and large brandy out, sat back and after taking deep gulps of both, let out a big sigh of relief.

Feeling exhausted but proud that the mission had been a reasonable success, Joshua sat opposite George Kernow explaining in every detail their actions upon leaving the ship. George was not one to be messed with and only precise and honest detail would do, good or bad.

"So you allowed Jacques to get to Jeanne first, even though you had strict instructions that you should be first." Joshua was unaware of the importance on why he needed to be first as Kernow never explained and, didn't ask. "This is true, I did allow it but the circumstances and the feeling inside him at the time allowed it to happen." Joshua then went on to explain the circumstances. "Did you hear Jeanne say anything?" "No, she was too weak and covered in lice and what I could see seemed to be dying." Kernow was silent; he needed to speak to her urgently.

Joshua carried on with his debrief with Kernow interrupting where he thought necessary. "You also allowed Jacques to ride with Jeanne alone?" Again Joshua defended his actions as a man of integrity. Kernow, although giving Joshua the third degree was inwardly impressed with the man in front of him thinking he was very much like his Father. "Joshua, I know you are tired and you have explained things well but I need to know from your own lips is Philip de Albret the Count of Morlaix dead?" "I cannot answer that question yes or no as we couldn't get to him directly. Other things took precedent in the time we had, such as Zoe's indifferent actions of Pierre Bouchier and Jeanne's extremely poor condition." Kernow knew these were tough questions. "So Joshua, would you say your mission was successful?" "I would George, we achieved ninety percent of the desired results with no casualties which in my book is good." "I agree however; you have forgotten the English troop of marines defending your rendezvous point still on French soil." Joshua didn't respond to that remark. "For the record Joshua, I believe you have done well and thank you for your excellent debriefing. I suggest you get some well-earned rest and we will meet here again later this evening. However, before you take to your bed, could you inform Jacques I want to see him."

Jacques was in the medical quarters next to Jeanne holding her hand when Joshua found him. He informed him that Mr Trevenan wanted to speak with him. The doctor on board realised as soon as he had taken Jeanne as a patient that this man would not leave her side and, hearing that Jacques was wanted elsewhere, came over and calmly reassured him that she would be in good safe hands until he returns. As Jacques gently kissed her forehead Jeanne slowly roused and moved her shaking weak hand to the left side of her lower neck line. Jacques watched in silence but didn't know what she meant.

She then started pointing and fumbling the top hem of her blouse. Jacques mirrored his hand to hers and felt something in the hem line. With both hands he started to unfold whatever was in there when finally, he pulled a ring out marked with a 'J'. "Oh Jeanne, you are the love of my life, I will love you forever," he whispered tenderly. He then took her shrivelled left hand and gently slipped the ring on her finger as he had done many years ago. However, her fingers were so bony it slipped off.

Ripping a small piece of linen from his shirt he delicately wrapped it around the ring and tried again, this time it stayed on. With her eyes closed Jacques noticed a loving tear drop slide down her cheek. Jeanne then fell back into unconsciousness.

"Thank you for coming Jacques," George said, "brandy?" Without hesitation Jacques responded with a "No thank you." George looked in utter amazement but said nothing.

George went on to thank him for his integrity and keeping his word. He also asked if Jeanne had said anything in which Jacques replied, "She had not, she is so very ill." "Yes I have heard and Jacques, we know you love her very much and like you we will keep our promises but I must ask you to leave the doctors and medical staff to do their job without hindrance and give her the best chance to pull through." "I understand," he replied, "I will do my best but I have one question." "Please speak Jacques." In a deadly and serious tone Jacques asked, "Is Philip de Albret dead or alive?" "When we left him he was alive as to whether he is now, we do not know." Jacques was a little confused by the answer but nodded in acceptance of it.

"Now Jacques, I want you to talk with Zoe and the two young men to find what their wishes are and we will do our best to accommodate. However, afterwards I suggest you get some sleep and we will all meet later this evening."

When Jacques closed the cabin door behind him George drunk a large glass of brandy, put his arms behind his head, stretched his head back and looked up at the ceiling. What was he to do? He had to make big decisions for the safety of his people but he also needed to play the long game. He could renege on his so called deal and kill Jacques and his compatriots and live with the belief that inner security was kept. Or not kill them and keep the integrity he had made for possible further incursions.

He was very tired and needed rest but wanted one more crucial piece of information before the meeting tonight. One of Kernow's bodyguards woke him at the requested time, it was early evening and he had the sleep he so urgently needed. Now, washed and refreshed he went to the cabin door.

On entering the medical room, he quickly looked around and spotted the gaunt face of a woman at the end bed. A young orderly stopped him and asked what he wanted but was told to be quiet. George Kernow carried on walking up to Jeanne's bed as the young orderly ran out. Sitting next to her he couldn't believe this was the beautiful Jeanne Pendarve he once knew. He touched her hair but she didn't move. He whispered her name but again she didn't respond.

He pulled back the blankets and was shocked at the sight of just skin and bone before him. My God he thought. Just then the head medical officer rushed in and told him to leave. Kernow turned around and told him like he told his orderly to be quiet. However, with the officer came the Captain and two armed marines who would have none of it. Kernow was asked politely once again to leave and leave now. Kernow realised he had pushed his authority too far and that the Captain held jurisdiction on ship.

Kernow did as he was told and sort of came out of whatever was driving him back into reality. Once outside he asked if he could talk with both Captain and Medical officer together in private.

"I apologise most sincerely gentlemen for my misgivings but I need most urgently to talk with Jeanne." "She will not answer you as she has been given sleep remedies." Both men could see Kernow's anxiety but said nothing. "Gentlemen, I will say this again I need to talk with her in the highest matter of the defence of our realm and our good Queen Anne and I need to do it now."

"It may kill her if you just startle her into wakefulness," the medical officer replied.

The Captain intervened, "Looking at this from both sides and the importance of it, how long do you need to talk to her for?" "I need only to ask one question for now, the rest can wait, if and when she pulls through." The Captain turned to the Officer, "can you help Mr Kernow achieve this?" The officer was quiet for a while then said, "Given time I can gently reverse the sedative solution but I can assure you her mind and body will not take any pressure questioning at all and we may lose her if you did." "I will ask her one question and one question only, I promise."

The three of them were quiet while Kernow and the Captain waited for the Officers response. "Very well, I will start the reversing process but on one proviso that I stay in the Medical room, close to you but not close enough to hear." Kernow agreed and was asked to come back in two hours at seven bells.

Back in the Captain's cabin Kernow tried to relax with pipe and brandy. However, he was so close now to the information he had wanted all along his nerves were becoming frayed.

Another brandy should do it he thought. As the minutes ticked by he had sent word he wanted to see Joshua and Jacques in his Cabin at eight o'clock sharp. Subject to the meeting with Jeanne before would determine their fates one way or the other. He closed his eyes and breathed slowly but it was no good he needed to move and decided to go up on deck and speak with the Captain.

"Are you alright?" the Captain asked. "Yes, fine thank you," Kernow replied, "I am just a little edgy after all what has gone on and I really do need to speak with Jeanne." "Well you won't have to wait much longer it will be seven bells shortly."

They then went on to discuss routes, destinations and time frames for the voyage back to England. If all went well Plymouth and not Falmouth would be their chosen port of call due to better medical facilities for the patient Jeanne. However, due to the French persons being on board and information needed in London they had to be flexible and this could change. The Captain didn't pry but understood Kernow's position and situation. The bells then tolled seven times. "It is time Captain for me to leave you, thank you for your time and understanding."

On entering the medical quarters, he was stopped by the Chief Medical Officer. Kernow asked how the patient was and if she was ready. "The patient is ready for you Mr Kernow but don't be fooled by her surprising and alert appearance. She has been given things to make her be this way but it will last only five to ten minutes, we will then put her to sleep again. She remains very seriously sick." "Thank you," he replied.

Walking over to her bed Jeanne was sitting up and turned her head towards him as he neared. As he sat down by her she smiled but didn't say a word.

Sitting down by her bedside and looking at her gaunt and deathly appearance Kernow was lost for words. Taking a deep breath and getting his pencil and notebook ready he looked directly at her and in a calm and precise manner asked, "Jeanne, thank God you are alive, where is the antidote?" Without any emotion Jeanne clearly and simply replied, "There isn't one." George thought she misunderstood him so asked again. "Sorry Jeanne, I missed that, where is the antidote?"

Jeanne looked at him in amusement. She had never done this before but time, deadly experiences and lost loves, had shown her what is important in life and playing Kernow's games wasn't part of that anymore. She would tell him the truth but she was finished, done.

"Mr Kernow, I tell you the truth. The alchemist I befriended was also the person who saved my life in the dungeon. If it wasn't for him, I would not be here. He confided in me as he hated Philip de Albret and what he stood for. The virus or germ he devised was too virulent and aggressive for the supposed antidote to work. Every time he tried to calm the germ down it then took too long to kill, in the time frame, Philip de Albret required. The germ also became volatile with combustible tendencies. More importantly though he wanted it to stay in the blood stream and for the life of him couldn't work out why it kept seeping into the wind pipe and lungs. This I tell you is the truth from the alchemists own lips". Kernow was dumbstruck; he couldn't quite believe what he had just heard. All his actions, experience and dedication have come to nothing. He looked at Jeanne in stunned silence taking in what she had just said. The way she said it needed no response. Nothing could be gained from more questioning. Jeanne was looking directly at him without a trace of emotion. It was then the Medical Officer came over and touched him on the shoulder.

Kernow realised he had somehow misjudged somewhere or someone along the line but realised his time was up . He got up, touched Jeanne on the hand and left the room. The medical Officer and his young team immediately got to work.

Jacques was in Zoe's cabin establishing her intentions now that things were completed as promised. She had taken the Bouchier death badly as it were an act of treason. Jacques didn't see it that way and tried to reason with her that it was a life and death situation and he and others would have done the same. No one has the right to bully and coerce others into a lifetime of imprisonment with someone you abhor. It is called slavery. "Zoe, please do not feel this way. It was your bravery that saved me and the others. We owe you immense gratitude for our lives ahead and I for one am very proud of you." "Thank you Jacques, that means a lot to me. Maybe given a little time I will come to see things your way." "You will Zoe and if you need help no matter what or when, I will be there." With that they hugged each other warmly.

Releasing each other, Zoe continued, "And how is the love of your life?" "The doctor on board is extremely worried for her, as am I, but he has put her to sleep to rest the body and mind and with good medical attention he is hopeful she will pull together and get better." "I am pleased for you both Jacques." "And what of your future Zoe, what do you wish." "I wish to go back home away from this life of deceit and be with my young true love and live together happily." "Then so be it Zoe, I will ask Trevenan and am sure it will be done." Again, they hugged each other and Jacques left to visit the two youngens.

Zoe laid down on her bed and inwardly felt much better after talking with Jacques whom she well trusted.

"So what do you want?" Kernow asked both of them. Joshua went first and said, "Now that the mission is finished he would like to go back home to his cottage at Gunwalloe to rest up a while and visit Rebecca." Jacques went next explaining the wishes of Zoe and the two young French men. "That's fine Jacques, but what of you?" "I wish as promised when we first met to be with Jeanne and I believe that be her wishes also." They waited in silence. Kernow took a drink of his brandy and scanned his mind over the mission; it's objectives versus the overall outcome. He had successfully saved Jeanne. He had found the sleepers, stopped massive civilian casualties and, they have the barrels of the chemical germ secured. What he didn't have was the categorical proof that Philip de Albret was dead or alive. This was disappointing but you can't have it all he thought. He also didn't have the antidote. However, he reasoned the alchemists in London will have to work a little harder and find it through reverse engineering. He smiled inwardly and chuckled. Joshua and Jacques saw this and looked at each other in bewilderment. Kernow then stopped, looked at both of them and in a serious confident tone said, "Agreed on all counts."

Earlier that morning about seven thirty the young girl felt Philip de Albret stirring awake. She quickly got out of the bed and ran around to the bottom end, knelt down and started gently massaging his feet. He liked this to be done every time while he awakens. If she did not, he would soundly thrash her and the bruises from last night were a reminder of how powerful he was. Her Mother and Father were poor and the little money he gave her allowed them to buy minimal food to live. She took what he dished out and said nothing back but 'thank you,' as he liked her to say. She thought and prayed, if given the chance and knowing where Philip de Albret kept his money, she would take it and immediately run away with her Mother and Father far away, never to be seen again and live a better life.

Then suddenly he kicked her and she went flying backwards on her bottom. "It's a beautiful morning" he said aloud. "Fetch me a fresh glass of my best wine and hurry up, I have a little headache." She got up immediately knowing what he was like if she didn't do things as he wanted. He then said, "Stop, before you get the wine go over to the cabinet and open the large jewellery box." This she did and when the box was opened he said, "what is in there?" "A crown my prince." "You are right my dear, now fetch it here then get the wine, quickly now." As he held the crown he smiled and said to himself, 'now I will be a prince.' He then sat up and gently placed the crown on his head acting like a king being coronated. The young girl came back in after filling the large glass full of red wine. On giving it to him she was told to kneel.

With wine in one hand, and a steadying hand on the crown with the other, he loftily shouted aloud, "to the new Prince of France." He then gulped the whole glass down in one. Arrogantly throwing the glass across the room he ordered the girl to kiss him and get back into bed. Again, she did as was told.

With his crown still on his head and the young terrified pauper girl lying beside him, Philip de Albret started to cough.

The End

Appreciation & Dedication

My sincere thanks to Roger Bolton for his knowledge and guidance, and love to my Mum & Dad